Wind in the East

MALIHA ANDERSON BOOK 4

By

Steve Turnbull

Wind in the East by Steve Turnbull. Second edition July 2016
Copyright © 2015, 2016 Tau Press Ltd. All rights reserved.

ISBN 978-1-910342-48-0

Published by Tau Press Ltd.
Cover by Jane Dixon-Smith (jdsmith-design.com).

To my parents.

CHAPTER 1

Johannesburg, South Africa, 1908

i

When she had been young and credulous, Riette had believed in her mother's fairy story where Riette's father was a heroic Boer farmer. She said his name was Pieter and that he had been murdered by British soldiers. She claimed he had been her lover, or in some versions of the story, her husband. As the years passed, Riette learned from the taunts of the older children that her father, whoever he was, would never have *loved* a black prostitute. That was not what a whore, or the daughter of one, was for.

Then there had been that day when a worker from the diamond mines, still grimy from his hours in the ground, had put his hand on Riette, and her mother had not stopped him. Instead she had glanced at her empty gin bottle and run her tongue across her lips.

Riette had escaped to the streets as soon as she could where she sifted garbage for the occasional trinket she could sell, by stealing, and, yes, sometimes when things were really bad, letting some miner have a look for sixpence, or maybe even a feel for a shilling. No more than that. She was not her mother.

That was another life now, Riette thought as she leaned against the tree that grew beside the cart bridge a mile out of the city. That was the life of a person she no longer inhabited. Marten would be along soon. This was where he'd told her to wait for him.

When the church bell struck two that morning, she had crawled out of her hole in the alley that ran down by Holy Trinity. She had wrapped herself in the pretty *kanga* Marten had bought for her—her only honest possession—and, for the last time, left the cramped gap in the stones that had been her home. The night was cold and she pulled the ragged, stolen scarf tighter round her shoulders. There was no moon and the sky was heavy with stars like polished diamonds.

Marten had said she mustn't tell anyone they were going. They were lucky to get this chance and they didn't want any trouble. Of course, she had told the other girls about Marten—she wanted them to be jealous and they were, when they believed her. She had to keep the *kanga* well hidden; there were those who would knife her for it.

Marten loved her. She loved him. Even though they came from different worlds. Riette wondered whether she should change her opinion of her mother. Maybe the man who had fathered her was a good man. Maybe he had loved her mother. No, she was just a prostitute who got with child by a man who had the money to pay. She liked to think maybe her father was better bred, but what gentleman would go with the likes of a black whore?

It had been strange walking out of Johannesburg. The city was a place of dangers for any street kid but she knew what those risks were. She knew how to avoid the gangs, the crushers, the slavers, and she had a sense for the men that were hurt in the head. But outside the city, even though it was just a short walk, were different dangers—ones she didn't know.

Marten wasn't a miner or a gentleman, he was a farmer. A good man but he had no prospects, he had three older brothers and the eldest would inherit the farm. The only future Marten could hope for was working for his brothers, little better than being a slave.

Meeting him had been a miracle for Riette, though it didn't start that way. She recognised him as a country bumpkin by his clothes, his bleached hair almost ginger, pale eyes always wrinkled against the sun and the way he looked at everything. He stared about him, in awe of the buildings that surrounded him on all sides to a height of three or four storeys.

And there was that bulge in his country-sewn jacket that attracted her. She had glanced around, and seen a couple of the others had spotted him too, but she was closest. If she didn't act now someone else would get it. She almost ran at him, and that was the mistake. She knew better but she thought she could get his money and be off before he realised he'd been robbed.

Later he told her he'd seen her coming out of the corner of his eye. She bumped him and slipped her hand inside his jacket just as she was coming out with the apology.

But his hand clamped round her wrist. Shocked at being suddenly trapped, she tried to yank herself away, and kicked him in the shin. He swung his leg away and grabbed her other wrist. People were looking now. She struggled to free her wrists but he lifted his arms and she was almost dangling.

"You're a girl," he said surprised.

She laughed at him and stopped struggling. "Want a feel then? Cost you half-a-crown."

Then a crusher had come, all ready to drag her off to the nick, but Marten had said it was just a misunderstanding and she was his guide. The copper wasn't pleased with that story but he didn't argue because Marten had money. So she knew he was a soft touch, and handsome-looking. She was thinking how she could get a shilling out of him, when he held out half-a-crown for her. She hadn't seen that much money in a month of Tuesdays, so she'd offered him a look and a feel. Then he'd been upset and angry with her.

It took a time for her to get used to him and his honesty. She met him whenever he came into the city and she always washed herself to be presentable, and he'd never asked for anything from her except to guide him and show him places he could get good deals.

Then one day he'd pulled her into an alley. And she realised the time had come for her to give herself and she didn't mind, she liked Marten a lot. But he didn't want her to give herself, he just wanted a kiss. Her mother never let the tricks kiss her, but Riette was not her mother. They kissed for a long time and, though Riette didn't believe her mother's stories, Riette knew this was the love her mother had talked about.

But Riette was a half-breed and Marten was Afrikaans. They didn't know any place in the world that would accept them. Until the day Marten had come into the city and told her about a place they could go. He'd met a man who told him about a new colony in Australia. They took anyone and wanted couples who would have families. And when Marten asked if she wanted to go, she did not even have to think about it.

So now she was leaning against a tree, in the strange and frightening countryside, in the middle of the night and eloping with the man she loved. Back in Johannesburg there were some would wonder where she'd gone, but street kids disappeared all the time. Nobody wondered for long.

ii

The big clock in the kitchen chimed once. Time to go.

Staying awake while his brothers drifted off had been hard, though it got easier once they started to snore. Marten sat up in the bed, waited until the whole house had settled, then climbed down from his bunk, careful to avoid his elder brother's outstretched arm and leg.

He collected the bag he'd prepared from its hiding place at the bottom of his clothes chest. He had filled it with necessities: a change of clothes, plus his needles and different types of thread for when they needed to repair. Once he was in the kitchen he lit a candle and glanced up at the image of Blessed Mary above the door, the wondrous Child on her knee. It always seemed they were looking right at him, and now they were accusing him. Running away from the family.

He never mentioned Riette to his father or anyone else in his family, of course. They never would have let him go back to the city if they had any idea he was meeting a *kaffir*. The fact she helped him get good deals and saved the family money would not have helped. The idea he might love her would be unacceptable—impossible because he was meant for Saskia Orman.

Her father was Herman Orman and though Saskia would inherit nothing from her father, being their twelfth child, to be linked to such a family through marriage would bring a lot of good to his father's farm.

But he did not love her. His mother said that love was overrated; she had not loved his father when they were married but they had grown together. Marten did not agree. He knew what love was, and the only thing he felt for Saskia was the proper respect any man should have for a woman.

He'd kissed her once or twice at the gatherings, when the sun had gone down and nobody really cared what the youngsters were doing. As long as it was just kissing. Least that's what they said, but having a new wife already with child proved she was fruitful, and that was important. He did not like the hypocrisy. His father said he read too many books. Marten did not think you could ever read too many books. He would teach Riette to read.

Once the clock had struck the half hour, he gathered up his things and put on his coat. He had a long walk ahead, and he would get hot in the leather, but he'd been told a coat would be a good thing to have with him in Australia.

He was not really sure where Australia was excepting it was a long way from the Transvaal, and his family would never find him. He and Riette could have a life together.

Marten had been making his way home in the cart when he met the wandering pirate on the road. The man had asked for a ride. Marten had been a little unsure because the man was swarthy with a lot of black hair. Marten had read Robinson Crusoe and the man reminded him of the Barbary pirates who enslaved the hero. But that excited him too. This was a man who had seen the world and, once up and seated, he entertained Marten with tales of travelling above the clouds, and visiting strange lands.

The pirate, he said his name was Roberts, explained he had been hired to find people to start a new colony on an island off the coast of Australia. From his description it was a paradise. Marten, with his imagination fired up, knew a farmer would be a much better colonist than the city dwellers the pirate had been recruiting. He said as much and Roberts had sounded surprised, as if he'd never thought of it, but agreed.

Roberts saw Marten's interest and had tried to dissuade him; he said he'd already got a full manifest. But Marten had made up his mind and insisted the man tell him where the ship would be leaving from and, reluctantly, he had. As the man said, there were always some people who did not arrive in time to take the trip.

Marten said he and his girl would be there. At the mention of Riette, the pirate had brightened up, saying couples were always welcome in colonies. Marten understood that; it was just like Noah and his Ark, you needed to make children. When Roberts asked if she was already with child, Marten almost blurted out they weren't even married, but managed to catch himself.

When he'd told Riette of his plan to get them away, she had been pleased. And she had not been upset when he said they'd have to pretend to be married—and where that thought led was something

Marten looked forward to. He was a farmer; he knew about breeding animals, and he understood the stirring in his loins when he touched Riette, just the same as it had been with Saskia.

They could always marry properly later.

He walked the couple of miles from the farm to the bridge. It was a moonless night. His heart pounded as he approached the place and could not see her. But then there she was, asleep curled in the roots of the tree. It was nearly three o'clock and the air was freezing cold. He woke her with a kiss. Her bare arm wrapped around his neck and pulled him in tight.

"You're warm," she said and her moist breath was like a butterfly against his cheek. He dared to do something he'd never attempted before. He let his hand touch her as they kissed once more. The thin fabric of the *kanga* hid nothing and he felt the moving shape of her body as he ran his hand down to her hip. His breath quickened. And she pressed her lips even harder against his.

He tore himself gently away from her. "We must not miss the flyer, beloved."

He leaned back and stood. She found his hand in the dark and pulled herself to her feet. He averted his gaze as he realised she had pulled open her *kanga*. He breathed again as she re-wrapped it tightly about her.

Together they walked south, holding hands and not speaking.

iii

They knew they were approaching the place when they met other people on the road. There were couples and single men. There was even a whole family—father, mother and six children—on a cart drawn by a plodding old horse that could barely manage the weight.

There was a crowd gathered around a gate opening on to a track. Six men with guns lounged and sat nearby, but if anyone paused, the guards lifted their guns and moved the slow ones on, towards a stand of trees. A flickering of firelight showed between the trunks.

Marten shuffled along with the other people and did not slow down. He let Riette walk on the side away from the guards and she pulled her scarf up over her head, as he had seen her do many times in the city. He did not understand why she did it. She was beautiful, and he thought it glorified God for her to be seen. But then these were rough men and perhaps it was best they did not see her beauty.

He'd been told the ship would take off just before dawn, whether they were there or not. Anyone late would be left behind. But they were not late, and he was glad for that because the alternatives had plagued his mind. Riette could return to the city, but what would he do? Suffer a beating from his father and be forced to lie in the face of difficult questions.

Once past the guards he could feel the excitement mounting. His own and also in the people around him. Riette put her arm around his waist as they walked. He could feel the warmth of her along his whole body. He laid his arm across her shoulders and pulled her in close.

They passed through the trees and stared in amazement at what was beyond: Lit by fires burned to embers was a great metal machine, some sort of flyer. So great was its length that its far end was hidden in the night. He had seen the Dutch and German airships that landed in Johannesburg, and the British flyers with their great steam-driven rotors, and sometimes the ones as fast as hawks with their long wings.

And he had seen the soldiers with their flying artillery and gunboats, that had exacted such a price from his people less than ten years before. He hated the British, and could recite the tally of farmers' lives that had been stolen by them.

But this machine, it resembled nothing he had seen before. It did not have gas bags like the Zeppelins, nor the British rotors. It did not have the smooth lines and grace of the hawk-like flyers, nor their wings. It reminded him only of a long and thin tin box, but one of such dimensions it could hold a church and have room to spare.

There were windows high up at the front of one end and, in the side, there was a hatch big enough to admit a barn, with a great ramp leading down. All was shadows outside but within there were lights burning with the constancy of electric.

Once again he was reminded of Noah: This was the Ark that would carry him and Riette to their new world, free of sin. *But we are the beasts*, he thought, *we are the ones to be corralled here until the time comes to be herded two-by-two into the pen. What happens in the pen?* The only thing he could think of was slaughter. He held tighter to Riette and guided her to a fire of bright embers, around which a few others had gathered.

No one spoke but an older woman offered him a mug of hot soup. It smelled good. He gave it to Riette. She clasped both hands around it, warming them. She breathed in its fumes and took a sip, then a longer drink. He looked over at the shadowy face of the woman, half-lit from the red glow, and smiled his thanks.

A gunshot split the night. There were shouts of fear, and a child's scream that died away. Marten jerked his head round towards the vessel. There was a man silhouetted against the interior light at the top of the ramp. He held a rifle pointed into the black of the sky.

"Time to go," he shouted.

All around people gathered up their belongings. Some, like Marten and Riette, only had a small bag each and were soon walking across the grassy space, before those with more had even begun to move.

There were shouts from behind. "Leave it, get moving." Then shouts of pain and anger.

Marten kept his face forward, not looking back, not wanting to see what he knew was happening. There may be a new world, but these were not good people. Better not to antagonise them. *We'd just get crushed the way the British crushed us.*

The ramp was also the door of the great opening, and it was a difficult step up onto it. Marten scooped up Riette, she was light as a new-born calf, and placed her on the metal. She in her turn helped him climb up. The surface was not flat, but was a pattern of criss-crossed beams of metal. They picked their way carefully across it. The crowd grew closer and more tightly packed as they approached the top. There were guards strung across the ridge, with a gap between them at the centre. No one wanted to be too close to the guns.

A teenage boy, only a little younger than Marten himself, tripped beside him but Marten did not help him up. He focussed on their destination, where the internal lights shone out.

They broached the top and looked down into the chamber. There were steps and the deck was filling up with people as they flowed down into it. At floor level there were no entrances but, at regular intervals, ladders ran up to a metal gallery. At that level, there were doors to the interior and men with guns at each.

Marten and Riette reached the bottom of the steps. Marten glanced back then moved forward quickly to make room for those coming down behind them. He led Riette across the deck into the far corner. He felt safer with two walls behind him and a view of the whole space. And sitting directly below the gallery, it would be less easy for one of the guards to shoot at them.

People still poured in. He had not realised there were so many out there in the dark. Were all these people in search of a new home? Some were unkempt and poorly dressed; they were the ones who were alone, and were all men. Some whose clothes were of good quality, usually the older ones. Marten wondered what could have happened to them that they needed to change their life.

The tide of people became a trickle and the last stragglers came over the top as an echoing metallic crash boomed through the hold, reverberating off the metal walls. The grinding of cogs and winches filled the air and he saw a cable, thicker than his arm, tighten between the hull of the vessel and the hatch. Effortlessly the huge door lifted upright and Marten's last view of the African sky was as it was just turning blue from the black of the night. Then the world he knew was lost to him.

Massive bolts slammed into position around the door and if they had had any doubts about their journey, there was no longer a choice.

All about him he could hear people whispering to one another, some were crying, one voice lifted in hysterical laughter that made him shiver. Then it happened. It felt as if he no longer had any weight, as if his whole body had become as light as a dove. People screamed about him; there were shouts from the men. The crying became louder.

He knew this was the science invented by the British that made things light so they could fly. It filled everything and emptied it of weight. It was the thing that had made the British victors across the world, and gave them the power in the Void beyond.

But he was a farmer. He lived on the ground and his life was in the earth itself. It was an abomination against God, and yet it would carry them to their new world. He looked down at Riette, she glanced up with wide eyes; she was scared but she had not cried out. So he smiled down at her and squeezed her closer.

iv

The hold smelled of sweat from the two hundred people spread out across the floor. Riette had dozed, on and off. She could not see the sun so there was no way to tell the passage of time, or whether they were even moving. Marten still held her but he too slept because there was nothing else to do.

He had not let go of her since they had reached the gate. She was grateful. She craved the comfort of his touch. He had reassured her when they became light. It was magic. Like being drunk. Like the Chinese dream smoke.

There was a couple sitting not far from them—who were not much older than Marten and Riette—their clothes had once been of good quality but were now threadbare. The man had a pocket watch and declared the time to be eight o'clock. Riette moved from the crook of Marten's arm. He twitched and held her tighter then loosened his grip. Riette unwound herself, looked in his bag and found some bread and cheese.

It was better food than she had seen in the week since she had last seen him, when he had bought her a pie from a street seller. She chewed on the bread and looked around. Others were eating here and there. One or two did not seem to have brought anything and stared with longing at those who had.

Marten had called the man who had told him about the vessel a pirate. She knew what pirates were. There were stories that went among the street people, places to stay away from, people to avoid. The docks could be rich pickings for street people because that was where crews from the bigger ships would spend their coin and sometimes give it away to those in need. Maybe they felt they needed a balance to ensure their entry into heaven. Even if they weren't giving it away, most were easy to fleece.

But there were the rougher parts of town, just a little further out from the docks, where the less savoury went. Those were the places the crushers did not patrol so frequently and the Excise men stayed away from. There were men who claimed to be pirates there. And her sense of who were the bad ones was triggered by every face.

Like the ones she'd seen as they were coming aboard. They were ones she would never offer a look or feel, because it would lead somewhere very bad. And she was not her mother.

Marten leaned up on his elbow. She passed him the rest of the bread; she realised she'd eaten half the loaf already. Perhaps he saw the worry pass through her, because he smiled. It always made her feel strong when he smiled: knowing there was someone who liked her for herself, not for what she could offer, whether it was her skill at stealing or her body.

Then he leaned over and brought his face close to hers. His breath was not fresh but she didn't mind. He pressed his lips against hers and, for a moment, she just felt the dreamy lightness and his closeness. Then she remembered they were in public and pulled back. She glanced nervously around. The couple near them were looking at them. The man was frowning, but the woman smiled.

Marten never opened his mouth when he kissed her. Now they were as good as married, she would be able to practise those skills she had been told about by the street girls on the game.

There had been no sight of any of the ship's crew since the great door had swung shut, hours before. As the time passed a murmuring built up in the human cargo. Finally a practical soul organised an area as a latrine on the far side of the deck from where she and Marten sat. They strung up a couple of blankets and acquired buckets from those who'd had the forethought to bring them.

There had been an argument close to them, as a bucket-owner was persuaded to let it be used by the community. Their argument about ownership was easily overridden by the suggestion of piss and shit seeping across the deck.

Riette had never had more than a hole in the ground, and many times just the street. But she knew people like Marten had little sheds in their yards. She had even heard that rich people had special rooms inside their houses, which was disgusting.

Nobody looked at you when you lived on the streets. It was like being invisible, unless it was the crushers because they were always looking. You could piss on the main street and no one would look. Not that she did that; she always used an alley, but there was no way to be alone. You did it when you had to and no one would look. Except the old man who paid to watch, but one day he wanted a feel when she did it. She avoided him after that.

But now she had to use the bucket. Others had already picked their way across to the blankets, and she'd seen how people watched, though they pretended not to. She was doing it herself.

Marten had already been. He'd given her arm a squeeze and stood up, nodding in the direction of the blankets. She sat back against the wall and pulled her knees up, wrapping her arms around her legs. She watched him as he went away from her, making her feel empty and alone in this space full of people.

She looked away when he disappeared behind the curtain. He did not take long and was soon heading back.

"You best go soon," he said as he sat down. "Be careful, it's hard to walk with no weight, and—" his voice trailed off as he tried to find the words, his face turning red "—water moves slow as well."

She frowned not understanding his words. He saw her confusion and worked up some spit in his mouth. He stuck out his tongue and let the spit roll off it. It was unreal the way it slithered down to the tip of his tongue and made a big droplet on the end eventually pulling itself free and descending slowly to the floor.

The realisation of what he was describing dawned on her, and explained some of the cries from folks who had gone behind the curtain earlier. She nodded. And climbed to her feet, and straightened her *kanga*. Every other woman was wearing Western clothes, but she was proud of Marten's gift.

She took small steps at the start as she got used to the way she bounced across the floor. It would not do to take a tumble: The *kanga* and scarf were the only clothes she possessed. She felt the eyes on her but she knew everyone who had braved the walk had suffered the same, even if they weren't her colour. It was because someone moving across the deck was the most interesting thing happening on the journey.

She managed the buckets easily enough—Marten was right they were nearly full—and the stink was terrible. It crossed her mind she probably had it easier than the other women; she did not have to fight her way through all those layers of skirts and petticoats.

The walk back did not seem to take as long and she was soon nestling into Marten's strong arm.

Time wore on. Someone sang hymns in Afrikaans, and many people joined in around the space. Riette did not know them, though she had heard hymns when she was in her hideaway below the church. They finished the last of Marten's food and water then dozed again. The day passed into night according to the man with the pocket watch but the electric light never changed.

Riette felt she might need to brave the buckets again when the vessel bumped as if it had bounced on something and, shortly after, their normal weight returned.

v

With metallic crashes that split the air, the bolts holding the great door shut slammed back. The grinding winches started up and Riette saw a crack of darkness appear around the edge of the door. It was blacker outside than it had been when it had been closed. They had departed at night, travelled through the day and arrived at night once more.

But the dark was nothing compared to what came next. The door had been lowered only a short distance when an icy wind ripped through. It cleared away the stench of human waste in seconds, but replaced it with air so cold and damp it sliced through Riette's *kanga.* It was worse than the coldest part of the night on the coldest night of the year, and mixed with a rain so fine it hung suspended in the air, soaking everything it touched.

Across the floor people rushed to put on the coats they had been told to bring, if they had one. Others, like Riette herself, had none and did the best they could. She pulled the scarf closer around her shoulders and over her head. Her body's reaction scared her; tiny bumps raised across her skin and she shook with shivers she had only experienced when she had been ill. Marten took off his coat and wrapped it about her.

It did not warm her, but kept the wind from her skin.

The door hit the ground outside with a boom that shook the whole vessel. The wind howled as it tore around and through the ship. It was as if they had arrived in the blackest pit of Hell.

Dressed in shiny stiff cloaks and hats that seemed to repel the elements, guards appeared from outside with their guns at the ready, and the exodus began. As they were the furthest from the exit, Marten and Riette were the last to climb the steep steps and face the full onslaught of the knife-sharp wind and freezing rain. Electric lamps shone down from sturdy gantries, lighting a path from the base of the ramp along a muddy path toward some shadowy buildings in the distance.

The metal of the ramp was cold and slick with rain. Riette slipped and cried out as her bare foot hit a sharp edge of metal. Marten reacted instantly and swept her off her feet, holding her tight to him. He stumbled down the rest of the ramp and bore her off along the trail following the rest. She buried her face in his shoulder, her face against his soaking shirt and shivering in the cold.

Trailing behind all the others, they arrived at a set of low brick buildings. Marten climbed the half-dozen steps and pushed inside through a wooden door. Riette felt the warmth of the interior flow across her dripping limbs.

"I don't like Australia," she said.

* * *

Riette woke and opened her eyes. Weak sunlight filtered through a window. She had slept indoors when she lived with her mother but there had been no glass in the windows of their shack. And that had been a very long time ago.

She rolled on to her back, the wooden slats of the bunk creaked and moved under the thin pallet under her. The ceiling consisted of neatly nailed wooden planks. She was more used to stone that was so close she could reach up and run her fingers across its rough surface. Those nights and mornings in her stone cave, she had wondered whether, if she rubbed it for long enough, the rough slabs would become as smooth and worn as the steps of the church.

She lifted her arm and reached for the ceiling. It was too far away.

"You're awake."

She turned again and found herself face-to-face with Marten. He leaned one arm against the bunk on which she lay. She reached across and stroked his cheek, rough and unshaven.

"How are you feeling?" he asked.

"Hungry."

He lifted his other arm and presented her with a hunk of bread. "It's not the best, but there's plenty."

She sat up and adjusted her *kanga*. She took the bread, and tore off a chunk with her teeth. She looked around as she chewed it. Luggage was piled in uneven clumps near each set of beds. But there was no sign of the occupants.

"Everyone's been called out to be registered," he said to her unspoken question. "I said you were not well and they let me sign for you." Marten glanced down and then back at her, with a slight look of concern on his face. "I said you were my wife."

She kissed him. "We'll be proper married soon enough. Let them think it true."

He handed her an apple. It was wrinkled but clean of mould. She took a bite, it wasn't too dry. "What does Australia look like?"

He smiled. "We're not there yet, this is a staging post. We travel on again later today. Not everyone goes to the same place so they split us up."

"They won't split us up?"

"No, of course not, they want couples."

The door at the far end of the dormitory banged open and some of their fellow travellers entered; they moved to their bunks. Some sat and others lay down. One of the older men stared at them with a grim dark face like a thundercloud.

Riette held his eye for a moment then looked away. She knew that look, the ones with so much hate for themselves it overflowed into despite for anyone different. Especially the blacks.

Over the next hour everyone returned and collected their belongings in readiness for the word to move. The younger children whined and cried; the ones that were a little older invented their own games and ran between the beds and the adults until they were shushed.

Food was brought, more bread and dried fruit, and Riette made sure Marten stocked up. He was not used to going hungry, and did not understand the need to keep a supply in reserve for those times when you couldn't steal what you needed.

For a while Riette stood by the window. She rubbed some of the dirt from it. Not far away was a wide grey expanse of water under the grey sky, always moving, with enormous waves crashing endlessly on

a stony beach. She had never seen the sea but she knew what it was.
Between the beach and the buildings was a whole rolling field of
grass and stubby bushes filled with birds—and not a gap between
them, so many of the creatures they could not be counted. And when
the inconstant wind changed direction the air became filled with their
raucous cries.

It was mid-afternoon when the doors at each end opened and
the men with guns entered. A voice from the other end commanded
them to board for the next part of their journey.

vi

Marten put on his coat and gathered up his gear, weighed down with
the food she'd insisted he keep. Riette watched him, her arms
wrapped around herself. She was scared again, as he was. But she was
the bravest person he knew. She had survived the city streets and,
despite the horrors around her, she had not lost the blessed goodness
God had given her.

He knew she wasn't pure in body, how could she be? She was
the daughter of a prostitute, but her heart was true, and what was
God's love if not forgiving?

He wondered if his father would ever forgive him. He'd left a
note on the kitchen table, explaining that he was eloping with Riette.
He did not say who Riette was, just that he had met her in the city,
that he loved her and they would make a life for themselves in
Australia. It was not that he was ashamed of Riette—he loved her
with all his heart—but his father's mind was closed. If he knew
Riette's nature he would see Marten's actions as sin, and would take it
as his own. A sin he would never be able to expurgate.

They found themselves once more at the back of the travellers
as they filed out into the unremitting wind. He wrapped Riette in his
coat as they descended the wooden flight of stairs on to the muddy

trail. At least it was no longer raining, though the clouds scudding across the sky looked as if they could provide more at the merest tempting of fate.

The wind changed direction and the air was once more filled with the dismal cries of the nesting birds. It was like a choir of mourners.

The line of travellers snaked along the track towards the landing field. They passed a gate where two armed guards lounged in their oiled coats and heavy woollen shirts. They barely glanced at the people trudging past. But as Marten passed by, holding Riette close to him, the one nearest looked at Riette's ankles and feet, then looked up at them both with a frown creasing his forehead.

The wantonness of Riette's bare legs had shocked Marten too when he first met her. In his world such a display of naked flesh in a woman was a sign of lasciviousness and sin, or so he was taught. Yet she was more like a child, and no one cared how much skin they put on show. And the rules were different for the blacks.

Marten dismissed the guard's glance as he rejected all those who thought her lewd. It was true she had offered herself to him in gratitude for rescuing her from the crusher, but she had been grateful when he had refused. When they were alone together in Australia, when they were in their own place, he would not refuse her offer.

It would not be so very long before they were off once more.

The track led uphill to a flat area. He had not seen them in the night but the whole field was fenced in metal netting a dozen feet high and there were six towers placed at intervals around the perimeter. He could see three men in the lookout post at the top of the nearest, placed just along from the gate.

The vessel on which they had arrived was gone, crushed rocks showed where it had lain. But another metal monster lay at the far side of the field. Where the first had been nothing more than a utilitarian riveted steel block, more appropriate for transporting non-living cargo, this new vessel had smooth lines like a bird. There were short stubby wings along its length and tube-like projections at what appeared to be the rear.

It did not have the width or breadth of the first ship, but its length must have been similar.

The front of the line of passengers had already reached the door in its side. Not the huge opening that had marked the first ship but something more appropriate to man, though still large enough for five to enter walking abreast.

The line came to a stop and then moved in fits and starts as people were allowed inside the ship one or two at a time. Marten could not guess the passage of time and the sun was not visible through the constant grey cloud that hung over this place.

Riette snuggled against him clinging tighter. She must be cold. He wished he had taken a blanket from the dormitory for her.

* * *

For Riette the afternoon passed in a haze of cold. She clung to Marten for the little warmth he could provide. Her hands and feet were numb. She prayed that Australia would be warm. She did not mind where they went, as long as she could feel her limbs again.

She wished they had not been at the end of the line. She wondered if perhaps Marten was embarrassed by her. Did he not care for her after all? Then his arm shifted and pulled her even tighter to him so she could feel his heart beating in his breast and the flexing of his muscles beneath his skin.

She knew in her heart he loved her, but there had been so many betrayals.

They queued for so long that the daylight had begun to fade but finally there was just one more group in front of them: a family of five dragging their bags across the muddy ground. The smooth body of the metal bird glistened. It was not raining but the air was filled with wind-driven moisture that covered everything.

Light spilled from the open doorway and the yellow light promised warmth. Not much longer now. At the door, holding a board and pen, was a thin man with skin so pale he has like a ghost. He checked off names and had one person from each group make their mark. Any baggage they could not carry was taken away. Though the process took a very long time, it was strangely comforting: the difference between a gang and the crushers.

The people ahead of them were let through. Riette had the sudden feeling the door would be slammed in their face, that they were too late. The pressure from Marten's arm carried her forward and they stood in the entrance.

The man looked down his list. "Names?"

Marten cleared his throat. "Marten and Riette Ouderkirk."

The man flipped through the papers clipped to his board. Marten had promised he would teach her to read and write. The man found the place. He passed the pencil to Marten and turned the board pointing at a space on it.

"Make your mark here."

"I can sign my name."

"As you please," he said. He sounded like a man who never smiled but Riette was sympathetic; he had been here in the cold with everyone else.

The man glanced at Riette then looked away. Then looked back. Marten was writing his name as the man snatched the board away and yanked the pencil from Marten's fingers.

"She can't go." He waved a hand and pointed at Riette. "She's a black. She'll have to go on the other ship when it gets in."

Riette felt her mind go as numb as her body. There was no thought in her at all. She watched with the same unreality as when her mother had let the men touch her, maul her, penetrate her.

Marten's face twisted into anger and fear. He pushed the small man who fell back hard against the metal bird. The man flailed for balance then collapsed. Marten grabbed her arm and pulled her towards the door, towards the light. A big man forced his way between them. Marten's grip tore at her flesh. An arm wrapped round her neck, crushing her windpipe, and yanked her back.

Marten would not let go. His fingers gouged into her flesh, the nails drawing blood. He shouted her name again and again. She saw his mouth opening and closing but the sounds barely registered. Then, all of a sudden, he released her. She saw him go down, the butt of a rifle stained with his blood jerking back up.

Arms pulled her away from the doorway, away from the light, through the darkening evening. She watched Marten's body being pulled into the vessel, the light shut off by the closing door. The heavens broke open releasing a deluge of rain. But she felt nothing.

Then she was in a room, long and low. There were many men, drinking, laughing and cursing. Touching her, feeling her. Her *kanga*, her only honest possession, the only remnant of Marten, was ripped away.

I am not my mother.

CHAPTER 2

Pondicherry, South-East India, 1909

i

Maliha pulled the scarf back over her head in a reflexive movement, not even noticing she did it. The habits of wearing a sari had returned to her as if she had not spent nearly eight years dressed in Western clothes, and the last couple of those constricted by a corset. It was not a feeling she thought she would ever miss, but while wearing a sari came back to her easily, the amount of skin she was revealing was not something she adjusted to so easily.

She sighed. The sun was high and strong, and all work on the building site had stopped. It would not restart until the heat of midday had passed. She chafed at the delays in the reconstruction of her parents' house—her house. And of the *ashram* she was having built as a part of it. She had not revealed the truth about the *ashram* to anyone. There would be trouble when she did.

Pondicherry was so backward. The French had not made any attempt to bring the local population up to at least a grasp of civilised behaviour. They were happy just to own this tiny part of coastal India and rub it in the nose of the British. If the British had wanted it they could have just taken it at any time in the last one hundred years. They had burned it to the ground once.

But that was a long way off. It was more of the British-ness that had rubbed off on her in her years at school that made her so impatient at the slow progress of the work. The workers lounged in the shade of the trees, drinking the lemonade and *chai* that she paid for. She was not unaware of the sly looks in her direction, though she was careful not to make it obvious that she was looking at them.

The house was just a skeleton of timbers reaching up two floors, built on the burnt ruins of the one before. When she had returned home the previous spring the land had not been cleared. Only the remains of her parents' bodies and the staff that had died with them had been taken away. She had left again as soon as the legalities had been dealt with, returned to Barbara Makepeace-Flynn at the Fortress in Ceylon.

Then things had occurred, events that had been difficult to deal with. It seemed that the more she pushed thoughts of Valentine away, the more he became stuck in her mind. *He is so irritating*, she thought, *even when he's not here*. But she would never see him again, and that was unquestionably for the best.

When she had returned home, her mother's parents gave little more than a frosty welcome to their granddaughter. They had objected when her mother married a Scottish engineer even though there had been no demand for dowry. But the one thing Barbara had taught her was the importance of family, even if they were barely tolerable.

So she had paid for the ground to be cleared, to be cleansed and blessed, then found a French architect who was sufficiently civilised to work with a "native woman". Her French had come back to her swiftly, and he soon learned she, young as she might be, was not to be underestimated. But she remembered the way that Barbara dealt with tradesmen and tried to be like her. She did not find manipulation to be a pleasing activity, blunt honesty was more her style than subterfuge, but there was less heartache than simply riding roughshod over people's wills.

Amita touched her arm and Maliha shook herself from her reverie. She had promised the site foreman that he and his men would be rewarded for swift completion and perhaps that was working.

She turned away from the partially built home and climbed into her steam carriage. It was a new French model she had bought from a trading company in the heart of the city. Designed to be driven by its owner rather than a servant, the driving position was integral with the passenger interior. This model was also open to the elements but had a cloth cover that could be deployed in the event of rain.

To make the vehicle even easier to pilot, it burned very fine coal-dust which flowed like a liquid to the furnace. The wheels were driven by electric motors powered from batteries, themselves recharged by the generators driven by the steam boiler. This arrangement ensured the vehicle was always ready and did not require time to build up pressure.

She picked up the helmet, woven from flax since it would be inappropriate to wear one of leather, pulled it on her head and then pulled on the goggles. Maliha took her seat and tucked her sari under her so it would not catch on the controls. Amita sat behind beneath the integral parasol.

Maliha engaged the electric drive and the vehicle moved off smoothly, with a slight lightening in weight as it also possessed a low power Faraday device. She steered down the baked and rutted mud of the road. As she turned out on to the main street, paved in stone and thus much smoother, she recalled flying in Valentine's air-plane. Something that was so much more pleasant than talking to him.

There he was again. If only he would stay out of her mind. She really needed something to occupy her. Perhaps a murder to be solved. She shook her head. No, that was another thing that she must put aside along with Valentine. It was not an appropriate thing for a Brahmin girl of good family and at a marriageable age to be involved with.

The road swept up over a bridge that stretched across one of the many rivers and inlets that composed Pondicherry. Along the banks were the huts and houses of those who made their living on or from the water. There were those who fished just in the rivers, tidal though they were, and those further toward the coast with boats that harvested the seas for food.

When she had been at Roedean she had been able to see the English Channel, and the reminder of the true ocean had made her heart ache for home each and every day.

She crossed the island and took the next bridge. There were no other mechanical vehicles on the road, in fact few people were out at all, which made the journey even more enjoyable.

However all enjoyment had to end and soon she was moving through the more opulent surroundings of the Indian upper classes. She shut down the flow of coal to the furnace, and noted the water was in need of replenishment. It pleased her to operate the machine as efficiently as she could. The furnace would stop supplying steam to drive the generator, but the batteries had sufficient power to bring them into the long sweeping drive of her grandparents' home.

She brought the vehicle to a stop at the side of the house. The other advantage of disengaging the furnace and boiler early was that the electric motors on their own were far less likely to upset the horses. The main part of the house was built of white stone on two tall floors with wide windows that stood open. A shaded verandah went all the way around the building.

She took off her helmet and allowed Amita to help her down from the vehicle. There were a few moments of fussing while Amita sorted out Maliha's hair. The maid was tall and did not make an attractive girl but she was very adept at sewing, make-up and hair. She also had the advantage that she made a very effective bodyguard.

When Amita finally decided that Maliha was ready they headed back to the front of the house and went up the steps. The door was opened to them as they approached by one of her grandparents' many staff.

Maliha, with Amita in tow, was shown through to one of the airy reception rooms at the rear of the house. A *punkhawallah* stood to one side pulling rhythmically on the rope that moved the waving fan in the ceiling. Maliha disliked such ostentation; a mechanical *punkha* machine would be more efficient and cheaper but her grandparents, just like many of the Westerners, preferred to use real people.

Her grandparents had visitors. Another man and woman, the deference of the woman suggested she was the man's wife. Maliha slowed down from her preferred purposeful, and unladylike, walk. She may have been away from India for many years but she had not forgotten. She knew exactly what this was.

This was a bride viewing, and she was the victim.

She touched her grandmother's feet and received her blessing, then her grandfather's. She pressed her palms together in greeting to the others.

"She has good manners," said the woman.

"Though she was away for many years, she has not forgotten," said her grandmother.

The man, the quality of his clothes marked him as being in trade, though still rich, looked at her and then let his gaze slide away. "She was at a school?"

Maliha felt the anger rising within her. To be treated as an object in the room was bad enough but the man's contempt for learning was infuriating. But she held her tongue and sipped from the cup of tea, made in the English style, even with milk. She kept her eyes down just as a proper woman should do.

"It was by request of the father."

The father. Now he was gone they could make their displeasure at their daughter's choice of husband obvious. Marriage to an influential British engineer was seen as a good thing in the class in which they moved. But personal prejudice was another thing altogether.

She stared out the window and studied the trees, trying to block their conversation from her ears. They were saying nothing of importance. She would not be marrying anyone that she did not want, and at this moment there was no one she had the slightest inclination to marry.

She thought of Valentine, and slammed the teacup into the saucer in sudden annoyance.

Conversation stopped abruptly. Her grandmother was frowning.

She wanted to shout at them and that desire alone confused her. She never shouted to make her point. Instead she placed the cup and saucer down carefully and rose to her feet. She pressed her hands together and bowed her head. "I am so sorry. I am afraid I am overcome. If you will forgive me?"

And before they had a chance to respond she turned and walked out of the room at full speed. Amita followed.

Maliha headed upstairs to the small suite of rooms that had been set aside for her when she had arrived in Pondicherry. She flung open the door and went to the window. She heard Amita push the door closed behind her.

Maliha slammed her fist against the wall. It relieved nothing. She slammed it again and again and again until it hurt, and still the frustration did not escape.

She wanted to scream. And she wanted desperately not to cry with her suppressed anger.

But she did not scream. And tears slipped down her cheeks.

It was not the longest wedding in the history of Pondicherry, but at four days it was one of considerable ostentation. They were now into day two and Maliha had suffered three changes of sari already today.

But still, not as bad as the bride, Renuka. So far Maliha had succeeded in staying clear of weddings and other social events. After the disastrous bride-viewing even her grandmother seemed to have given up on trying to control her, at least for now. But Maliha had no dislike of her cousin Renuka; they had played together occasionally when they were children and Aunt Savitha had been allowed to visit with members of her family. Sometimes her aunt would be accompanied by her husband, Uncle Pratap. Her perfect memory recalled Uncle Pratap only too well, how quick he was to punish his daughters for the slightest misdemeanour, and even Maliha when he saw a chance.

During the first day Maliha had only had to turn up for the present giving and, apart from introductions, had not been required to talk to anyone. Though there were plenty of glances in her direction.

She had thought returning to India would save her from all the stares. To be in a place where her skin colour did not draw comment, in fact having such a light tone was a measure of her high status. But she had been naïve. While she took after her mother's skin and hair, her facial features contained an unmistakable echo of her father.

Too Indian for the British; too British for the Indians.

The line echoed through her mind as she sat amid the giggling female relatives and close friends, although Aunt Savitha was absent. And succumbed to having her hair thoroughly oiled and henna patterns drawn on her skin.

After the initial shock at Amita's height, the girl's artistic skills, as she drew across Maliha's hands and arms, attracted attention. It made Maliha the centre of attention that she did not want to be.

"Your father was British?" The girl who asked the first direct question was no more than twelve, one of Renuka's younger sisters, Parvati.

"A Scot," said Maliha. The girl frowned in confusion. "Yes, he was British."

"How did they meet? We only have Frenchmen here."

"He was an atmospheric engineer. They were brought in by Grandfather."

"But we have no atmospheric."

"No, it did not happen."

"Have you ridden an atmospheric?"

"Yes."

"What about a flyer?"

"Yes, I have, many times."

Another older girl, Maliha had not been introduced so did not know her name, interrupted. "I heard you touch the dead."

The room went completely silent. Only untouchables dealt with the dead.

"My cousin is an avatar of Durga Maa, Charvi. She brings justice and revenge to murderers." Renuka's hair glistened with oil and had been wound into complex knots intertwined with flowers and leaves. Her feet and hands were covered in henna patterns. "I am sure you would want someone to avenge you if you were murdered."

The laughs that followed came in two varieties: the younger girls thought it was just a joke; the older ones recognised its true meaning. Charvi joined in too, after a moment. Maliha looked into Renuka's brown eyes and saw a sadness that mirrored her own anger.

"Come," said Renuka. "I forbid any more of this at my *sangeet*. I want to talk to my cousin alone. We have not spoken properly since we were children. Your Amita can work her wonders on someone else for a while. Honestly, Maliha, I would steal her away from you if I could.”

Renuka took her by the arm and led her through to a balcony overlooking the city. The dazzling sun shone off the waters highlighting the spires and minarets of the temples, mosques and churches. There was an easel set up on one side and in the dim light Maliha could see a reproduction of the city.

“I am sorry about Charvi. She is unhappy.”

“Lots of people are unhappy, Renuka, that does not mean they must make life miserable for others.”

“Truth is not a popular concept, when applied to oneself.”

Maliha did not respond. She went to the painting, ran her fingers across the pots of paint and compared the image to the world it depicted. The hills were not complete.

“This is quite good.”

Renuka came up beside her. “Thank you for saying so but I have to get some more green.”

“At least it doesn’t matter with oils,” said Maliha. “You could leave it a year and then come back to it.”

“Why did you come back, Maliha?”

Maliha knew the correct answer to this question, and reeled it out without difficulty. “This is my home.”

“This place is nowhere.” Renuka smiled. “I read the British newspapers to practise my English. I know what you’ve been doing. The murders and the detecting. But the newspapers did not say why you came back here.”

Maliha felt tears well up again, and cursed herself for it. Valentine always made her so angry, even when he wasn’t present.

“Here,” said Renuka, holding out a very Western lace handkerchief. “It was a man, wasn’t it?”

Maliha looked out across the city. *Yes*, she thought to herself, *but I'll never tell you who, and certainly not why.*

"If I had your life, I wouldn't run away from it, Maliha. Even if my heart had been broken a thousand times."

There was something about the way she said it. A strange catch in her voice when she said "run away" that made Maliha alert. She dabbed away the tears so she could see more clearly.

"You want to run away?"

"I always wanted to run away. I wanted to escape and board a boat to England to join you."

"You don't want to marry Balaji?"

"You've been away too long, Maliha. You forget we have no choices. His family are decent enough, so this is my chance at escape now. I will return with him to Madras which is a big city, not like this place. And it is British. We visited a couple of weeks ago and *amma* and I had some time and so we went to the shops. They are so big, and there are so many things to buy. Mama even let me go off with Balaji's sisters."

"Why do you need to run away, Renuka?"

At that moment Parvati burst out on to the balcony. "Françoise is here."

Renuka placed her hand on Maliha's forearm and gave it a gentle squeeze. "I must talk to Françoise." She turned and went back into the room with Parvati at her heels.

Maliha watched them go. The sounds of the women talking and laughing drifted out to her, making her feel separate once more. It had always been that way.

Leaning against the stone balustrade, Maliha looked down into the courtyard below. The sacred *tulsi* grew in the shade and a tree stood in the centre. All was as it should be. There was a sudden flurry of movement and half a dozen seagulls that had been roosting in the shade burst into the air with their raucous cries.

A very dark-skinned woman staggered into view from one of the doors of the outer buildings, used for storage and as living quarters for servants. At first Maliha thought she must be low caste, her skin was almost black, then she remembered the Negro woman she had encountered back at the Fortress—the servant of Constance Mayberry.

Maliha frowned, what was a Negress doing here? It was not as if there was a shortage of servants. And besides, this woman was dressed in a single wrap-around cloth, nothing a servant would wear. There was the sound of a woman's voice; Maliha could not make out the words but the voice seemed to be angry. As the black woman crept back towards the building every muscle seemed tense. She disappeared inside.

There was something about the way she had moved that made Maliha's skin crawl. She was like a dog that had been beaten so many times it feared every command, which it dared not disobey, would result in more pain. What was worse was, if Maliha was not mistaken, the woman was heavily pregnant.

She was not sure how long she continued to stare down into the courtyard hoping, perhaps fearing, she might understand what she had seen.

"Maliha?"

She realised that someone had spoken her name several times. So she turned and for a moment thought she was seeing a dead woman standing next to Renuka; someone who had been hung for murder a year before.

Renuka was the one who had been calling her name and she still wore a smile though it was slightly tainted with a frown.

"I'm sorry I was miles away."

"I wanted to introduce my friend Françoise," Renuka said. "You see, I have become *cosmopolitan* as well." She used the French word.

The woman appeared to be about twenty-five and had a great deal of make-up to accentuate her eyebrows and lips. She did not wear the kind of French fashions that Temperance Williams had worn, and that Maliha herself had adopted, for a short time. She was dressed in the heavier fabrics of an earlier time, though perhaps not enough layers to cause discomfort in the heat.

She held out her hand. "Françoise Greaux, *Mam'selle* Anderson. I am pleased to make your acquaintance." She stumbled over the words as she spoke.

"Your English is very good," Maliha said. "But we can use French if you prefer."

"*Merci.* Your French is no doubt better than my English."

"Françoise is a missionary," said Renuka. "She wants us all to become Roman Catholic. I said I would be anything she likes if she would bring me her European magazines to read."

"Who was the black woman in the courtyard?" Maliha asked in Hindi.

Renuka's smile dropped from her. She grasped Françoise's arm for support, for a moment, then pushed her away, turned and fled through the room. Cries of surprise, anger and then concern followed her.

Françoise looked at Maliha with a frown. "What have you said, *mam'selle?*"

Maliha turned to look down into the empty courtyard. "Something I should not have, I think. But you cannot un-see a thing, can you, *Mam'selle* Greaux?"

"And what is it you've seen?"

"I am not sure."

For three evenings prior to the wedding there had been a *sangeet*. As a close relative Maliha had no choice but to attend, or suffer the not-so-silent indignation of her grandmother. There was little else to be done than suffer the singing both good and bad of the other women, smile when spoken to and avoid being forced to sing herself. She did not know any of the songs.

This final night there was some relief in the presence of the French woman who was equally out of her depth, perhaps more so since she did not understand the language either. But at least she did not have to avoid making a fool of herself: No one assumed that she would sing.

When Françoise Greaux entered across the room from Maliha, and after Renuka had greeted her, the woman stood uncertainly, holding a glass of squeezed orange. Her eyes lighted on Maliha standing on the opposite side of the room and Maliha could see the relief in her as she made her way over.

It was an odd sensation for Maliha, to be thought of as someone to talk to. This must be how those with better social talents must feel all of the time.

"*Mam'selle* Anderson?"

"*Mam'selle* Greaux."

"Please call me Françoise."

"Maliha."

An awkward silence developed. Maliha watched the women and girls laughing and talking. Grandmother was in deep conversation with another older woman whom Maliha did not know. The bride's mother, Aunt Savitha, loitered near her daughter. She was not talking a great deal and did not seem particularly happy.

"I believe we should engage in small talk," said Françoise.

"It is not a skill I have learned."

Françoise gave Maliha an intent look. "Are you always so honest?"

"I try to be."

"That must make it hard to make friends."

"On the contrary, I find the friends I have made are those that you would want to have, rather than mere acquaintances that profess to friendship but would not offer genuine help when needed."

Françoise took a long drink, and looked around the room.

"Is Renuka a friend?"

"She's family, it's not the same."

"Could I be your friend, do you think?"

Maliha looked at her face. "I don't know. Would you help me move bodies?"

The initial shock on the woman's face dissolved into laughter, which dried up when she realised that Maliha was not laughing.

"You're not serious?"

"No?" said Maliha. "You know what I do?"

Françoise looked down in embarrassment. Maliha continued. "Of course you do. No doubt my activities have been the subject of gossip. It doesn't matter how young they are, they had nothing in their lives to excite them until I returned."

"I don't have the prejudice against touching the dead that your relatives have."

"No, but you haven't answered my question."

"Do you require a test of me? Do you have a body you want me to move?"

"Not exactly, Françoise," said Maliha and watched as the woman's humour evaporated for a second time. "But there is something I would like to do which might be considered inappropriate, under the circumstances."

Parvati ran up to them. "When are you going to sing, cousin?"

Maliha put a smile on her face. "Another time, little one."

"But everyone has to sing and this is the last *sangeet*."

"There will be other *sangeet*s; you will be married one day. Run along. I am talking to Françoise and it is rude to speak Hindi in front of a guest who cannot understand. Off you go."

Parvati pouted, glanced at Françoise and ran off. The French woman frowned. "What was that about?"

"A much stronger reason to be away from here. Come."

Maliha set off around the edge of the room with Françoise following, and slipped out the door without being accosted by any other guest. Though Maliha was fairly sure that Grandmother would have noticed, still she was unlikely to do anything.

The *sangeet* was in a room on the second floor. Maliha took them to a small staircase in one of the wings which curved round in a long sweep to the ground floor where corridors led off in both directions. Maliha was wearing sandals but Françoise wore heavy Western shoes that echoed on the stone flooring.

"Take your shoes off," Maliha said quietly and noted with satisfaction that the woman did as she was asked without question.

"This is about what you saw in the courtyard?"

"Yes."

"What was it you saw?"

"A black woman."

"Is it so unusual to see a dark-skinned woman in India?"

"An African black woman."

Françoise was silent and followed her until they reached the courtyard. It was empty. The moon was high and full, filling the space with its pure light. The single tree grew at its centre and the *tulsi* grew in a pot where it would be shaded from the sun for most of the day. Maliha looked at the plant for a few moments.

Without saying a word to Françoise she went over to the pot and slipped her hennaed feet from her sandals. She touched the plant and breathed in the sweet basil scent, then offered up a prayer.

She was torn. It was not that she believed the plant to be truly holy, or that there was anyone listening to her prayer, but she knew she would be wracked by guilt if she had not done so.

She put her sandals back on. Françoise was watching her, head on one side.

"I did not take you for a religious woman."

"Neither did I."

Françoise changed the subject. "Where did you see this black woman?"

Maliha looked up at the main building that enclosed the courtyard on two sides. Many of the rooms above had balconies. She frowned in concentration and then recognised the room that she must have been in. She walked across the courtyard until her back was to the wall below the room.

"What do you want me to do?" asked Françoise.

"Keep a look out at the door." The woman retreated to where they had come in and faded into the interior.

Maliha studied the layout of the courtyard and recalled where the woman had appeared from. She stared hard; there was no door.

She went across and touched the wall. It was solid stone and rough to her touch. She ran her fingers across its surface. There were the joins between the blocks but nothing to indicate a door of any kind.

Maliha growled to herself. She knew she was not wrong. The woman came from here. She wanted to pound on it. Instead she pressed her ear against the stone. There was no sound except for distant laughter and music.

And someone speaking French. A man.

Maliha slipped away from the wall and headed back to the entrance to the courtyard. The voice was coming from inside, Maliha stepped into the dark interior and could make out two figures, one was the size of Françoise, the other larger.

"*Mam'selle* Anderson, can I introduce Father Christophe?"

"Good evening, *Mam'selle* Anderson," said the man. "I would shake your hand but I fear I would not find it in this dark. I hope you don't mind?"

"One might wonder what a priest is doing wandering a Hindu home in the middle of the night?" she said, and heard Françoise's sudden intake of breath at her rudeness.

"I imagine for the same reason as you," he replied, his voice betrayed no irritation. "It is a fine night and the courtyard is a pleasant area to relax and contemplate."

"You are a friend of the family?"

"I would not walk the corridors of a stranger's home, *mam'selle*. Yes, I am a good friend of the family."

"Of course, I'm sorry; I did not wish to offend. Please don't let me detain you."

The shadow of Father Christophe ducked as he bowed his head in the half-light and made his way through into the courtyard.

Maliha, with Françoise following behind, made her way back to the well-lit entrance hall. The sound of two *sangeet*—the other being the men's—filtered through the house and mingled in a gentle cacophony.

"You cannot speak to a priest like that."

Maliha sighed. Françoise was Roman Catholic and Maliha had absorbed the British dislike of that particular religion and its devotees, despite her lack of adherence to any. Her extensive reading did not endear the Roman Catholic Church to her as a whole; throughout their history they seemed far too worldly—to say nothing of their treatment of women—though the Franciscans seemed decent.

However she did not think Father Christophe was a Franciscan.

She glanced at Françoise who had *mehndi* applied to her hands and wrists but only simple designs and patterns. To her it would be an experiment, a way to do something her friend would like. For her it held no symbolism. Religion was about symbols and meanings. The priest was a symbol.

"I am sorry if you were offended by my attitude," said Maliha and found that perhaps she was sorry. "My manner is always direct. If it is something you are unhappy with then perhaps it might be better if we remained mere acquaintances rather than attempt to become friends."

Françoise laughed. Maliha frowned. There was far too much about Françoise that was reminiscent of Valentine. Neither of them seemed to take her very seriously which was quite vexing.

And then Françoise threw her arms around Maliha and hugged her. "You are a most fascinating and delightful person, and I would be pleased to make the attempt to be your friend."

iv

There were no repercussions from the events of the previous day from either the woman in the courtyard or her encounter with the priest. It was as if nothing had happened at all.

In her suite of rooms Maliha got up and stared at her unfamiliar hennaed arms and legs. Amita rustled up yet another sari. Maliha was familiar with the concept of wearing different dresses for different events during the day. This was perfectly normal behaviour for British women in well-to-do families. But this was a dozen times worse, because each sari would never be worn again.

It was a waste, regardless of how much money she, or her grandparents, had.

Today's itinerary involved the actual marriage ceremony. She would have to endure an hour of socialising beforehand—though that might be less annoying with Françoise—they must witness the event, and then there would be several hours before she could escape and not have to worry about this ever again.

She yawned as Amita wound a section of her hair into a plait. She had not slept well; the pregnant black woman preyed on her mind. The woman's terror was enough to pique Maliha's interest, but Renuka's look of horror was branded into Maliha's mind. It was the same terror she'd seen in the black woman.

And the missing door was annoying. Clearly it was hidden and she would have to examine the wall in daylight. Well, the wedding ceremony would take place in the courtyard so there would be plenty of time for that.

Renuka called her the goddess of vengeance and victory. Maliha was fairly sure she did not believe in the gods; they were too like people and she wanted more from a deity than the ability to indulge in whatever emotion they chose. The Christian God was better and she had had seven years of enforced worship at that altar. And unlike the majority of his devotees, she had read their Bible. Several times.

But Renuka was right, since those last days at school she had become an avatar for what was right. And whatever it was Maliha had seen happening in the courtyard, it did not represent justice.

If she had been back in Ceylon she would have consulted with Inspector Forsyth who would have been curt and sarcastic, and then pursued the issue. And she would have talked to Barbara who would advise, or perhaps just listen.

Valentine would have followed her anywhere and done anything she asked of him. And even if he had stolen her victory from her that last time, at least there was still the vengeance. She shook herself. Ridiculous, she was no more an avatar of some mythical god than Amita was a ballet dancer.

"Amita," said Maliha. "When we get to the wedding, I need you to ask the servants something. But you'll have to be delicate about this one I think."

The horse-drawn carriage came to a stop in front of the house. Its white walls combined traditional Indian design with Roman columns to make it all the more imposing. She allowed her grandparents to descend first and then followed them in. The place was crawling with servants: more ostentation to show the guests just how rich the family were.

While her grandfather went off with the other men to witness the finalising of the dowry arrangements, Maliha and Grandmother went through into the suite of three reception rooms. They were already well filled with guests and more were arriving all the time.

Grandmother had boasted there would be nearly six hundred in all. That number included the entire upper echelon of Pondicherry Indian society, which contained a number of very eligible young men with families that would overlook her mixed parentage in order to marry a woman who provided excellent connections and a considerable dowry.

In the past, dowry had been intended to provide the wife with financial security, now it was simply the price for taking a worthless daughter off their parents' hands. Maliha had no intention of being bought and sold at her grandparents' whim; however they seemed to become deaf whenever she said it.

The sari that Amita had chosen for today revealed considerably more of her midriff than she found comfortable but she could not fault the colour; Amita was a rebel of course and had chosen a midnight blue with gold trimmings. It was important not to outshine the bride herself—not that that was likely—but while Amita had kept Maliha's jewellery restrained, the bangles, anklets and hairpiece she wore were of the highest quality gold.

For over seven years Maliha had been told she was ugly, not just by the other girls at school but the teachers as well. She accepted the truth of it compared to the flawless white skin and perfect hair of her peers. And now she was here, dressed as well as she ever would be, and the looks she received from both the men and women were unnerving. Grandmother seemed to want to introduce her to almost every older woman they met—each one, no doubt, a potential mother-in-law.

The tortuous hour wore on. Light refreshments—of the finest quality of course—were served and Maliha was able to hide behind the process of eating. She found herself searching the crowd for a friendly face. Children ran in and out of the adults. She could not hear the words people were saying, there was just too much, but she could make out the emotions—anger, fear, happiness, sympathy—more and more layering on top of one another.

She took a sip of lemonade, its sharp tang distracted her for a moment but the overwhelming press of people took her again.

"Maliha?"

She tried to compensate for the chaos about her by studying the Frenchwoman's face. She had what, in the Western world, would have passed for heavy eyebrows but in India could be described as delicate. Her eyes were hazel, her face quite round and her skin olive of the Mediterranean, barely lighter than Maliha's own.

"Are you all right?"

Maliha studied her mouth as her lips shaped the words. But still the noise of the room battered her.

"I am not comfortable in crowds," she said.

Françoise took her arm and guided her to a corner where several grandmothers were gathered, discussing how weddings were not the way they had been in their day. This was all show and lacked true spirituality.

Françoise sat Maliha down then stood in front of her, blocking the view of the crowded room.

"My grandmother will be most displeased to have lost me."

"I have been here long enough to understand what your grandmother wants." Françoise was smiling. "Will we be pursuing your investigation of the mysterious woman today?"

"When the ceremony is over. I can examine that wall in daylight."

"Very good."

* * *

Overnight a huge awning had been erected in the courtyard shading most of it from the sun's intensity. The holy bush had been moved— no doubt with great reverence—to a position where it could watch over the proceedings without risk.

At seven minutes after two o'clock, the time indicated as most auspicious by the horoscope, the bride appeared. She was radiant in her red sari and weighed down by necklaces, dozens of bangles round her arms, and anklets pressing on her feet. A silver hairpiece entwined and contrasted her black hair. A single teardrop sapphire rested on her forehead, and the henna patterns stood strong and dark on her skin.

"She is beautiful," said Françoise. Although she was only a friend of the family she had stayed with Maliha when she was brought to her seat near the front. With everyone seated and only talking in subdued tones the mass of people was far less oppressive. Maliha looked around the sea of expectant faces. Françoise was the only white person there, apart from herself and she only counted as a half.

There was a flurry of activity near the gate in the courtyard on the far side. The gate was flung open and there was a blur of white as Balaji galloped in on a beautiful white horse. Maliha raised an eyebrow; she might not be able to ride but she could see when someone was a good horseman and Balaji was not. He barely managed to get the horse under control before it flew right past the wedding group and might have ended up in the house itself.

Maliha turned to look back at the gate. Two men she guessed to be his brothers were sharing a laugh. A practical joke then; they were lucky it had not turned sour. The gathered family and friends were impressed however.

With the assistance of a servant, who came running up looking quite upset, Balaji dismounted without mishap. The horse was led away and the groom surrounded by the male members of his family.

Once seated beside Renuka they began the rituals which were going to take the rest of the afternoon. Servants moved among the seated and standing guests with drinks to ward off the heat of the sun.

Françoise asked her to explain what was happening and Maliha passed the time explaining the various rituals in French; recalling the significance of the fruit and the rice as they were given to the couple.

After two hours they had reached the stage where the presiding priest was about to entwine the two with the unbreakable cord when there was a motion behind the wedding group. A shadow moved under the balcony resolving into a dark-skinned girl moving awkwardly.

A murmur ran through the crowd on Maliha's side of the courtyard; they were the only ones that could see. And Maliha was the only one who recognised who it was. She stood up.

Out of the shadows, wrapped in a coloured cotton wrap tied across her bust but stretched open across her pregnant belly, came the African. Now that she saw the girl more clearly Maliha realised she was no older than Maliha but her arms and shoulders bore long scars, some old, others still red raw. The Hindu priest saw her and pulled back. He called out to her telling her to go away. Maliha doubted the girl understood Hindi.

The wedding party broke in panic, some moved away, a couple of the brothers tried to shoo the girl away as she was clearly untouchable. The congregation nearest to the front started to push back, chairs were overturned and people fell. Then there was screaming and panic.

Maliha stood firm as others brushed against her. An older woman fell against her knocking her to the side. The African girl shouted something in a language that sounded German. Maliha was sure that cursing was part of it. The bride and groom had not moved. Renuka stared at the girl who now stepped down into the space recently occupied by the bride's mother and father. They had not run but retreated. Aunt Savitha was imploring Renuka to move back and away.

Maliha saw the African held a small glass object in her hand; she raised it to her lips, cried out a single word *Marten* and threw the contents of the container down her throat.

Silence fell across the courtyard like the dropping of a veil.

Maliha was galvanised into action. She pushed her way to the centre as the African crumpled to the ground. Maliha grabbed a bottle from the collection of wedding offerings, thrust her arm under the girl's neck and lifted her. She brought the bottle to the woman's mouth and poured it down her throat to either dilute the poison or force her to regurgitate it.

But she knew she was too late. The girl's body convulsed, she coughed blood and a trickle of it emerged from her nose. The girl's eyes were severely bloodshot and her lips were turning blue.

The girl convulsed again but she focused on Maliha's face. She reached up and touched Maliha's cheek. Maliha let the bottle drop and held the girl's hand. The girl convulsed once more and ceased to move.

Someone somewhere was wailing but Maliha doubted it was for the dead girl.

The courtyard fell quiet. All Maliha could hear was her own breathing rasping in her throat as if she had been running.

"The baby," said Françoise.

Maliha looked round at her, not understanding.

"You can save the baby, Maliha." Françoise knelt beside her. "I do not have the words, you must tell them to save the baby." The Frenchwoman took Maliha's hand and placed it on the girl's belly.

Maliha shook her head. "They will not touch her."

There was a movement beside them. Renuka pulled the ceremonial knife from Balaji's waistband and offered it to Maliha hilt first. She took it. The gem-encrusted hilt was slick.

"Do you know what to do?" asked Françoise.

Maliha looked at her feeling numb. "I've read books."

Françoise gave a humourless smile. "Then you are more qualified than I."

There was a movement beside them. "You cannot do it, the blood will corrupt the sanctity of the courtyard," said Uncle Pratap.

If she was in doubt before, his command gave her resolve. "I will not do it here if you want to move her, Uncle, and I truly think the purity of the courtyard is already contaminated by her suicide, don't you?"

She gave him a moment to reply but it seemed he had nothing with which to respond. With Françoise's help they removed the wrap from the girl's body, it was a simple rectangle of cloth, and Maliha gently laid the girl back.

The courtyard had become silent. The guests had all escaped leaving only the immediate family. Balaji and his parents still stood there looking on in horrified fascination. Renuka remained with Aunt Savitha but they would not help. Amita had appeared and stood nearby. At least there would not be too many witnesses.

Maliha had read the books. Her insatiable appetite for the written word had consumed every one she could lay her hands on, including many that would have been forbidden, if anyone had known. And she forgot nothing. But reading was not the same as doing.

The ceremonial knife was sharp and there was very little blood when Maliha cut into the skin of the girl, in a line across the lower part of her abdomen. The heart was no longer pumping so there was no pressure to force it out. Maliha did not know how long she had but she dared not hurry lest she cut the child.

The burst of liquid when she broached the amniotic sac made her jump. And there was a groan from someone, she guessed it was Uncle Pratap, but she was nearly there. She dropped the knife and plunged both hands into the girl's body. It was filled with wetness and the baby's skin was slippery. She took hold as firmly as she dared and eased the baby from its mother's womb. Françoise had retrieved the knife and cut the umbilical cord.

The child wriggled, coughed and cried.

v

Françoise took the baby girl from Maliha and swaddled it tightly in the dead girl's wrap. The child made little crying sounds.

"Is it all right?" asked Maliha, studying the dark, wrinkled skin, big eyes and flat nose.

"I think so." Françoise got to her feet. Maliha had only her sari on which to wipe her hands. "She will need a wet-nurse"

"*Dhai*," Maliha said absently. She ran her hand across the shoulder of the girl, feeling the ridges on her skin. There were scars from many beatings. Some were ridged and healed, but others were softer bumps suggesting they were more recent.

The girl was not undernourished so whoever had done this was feeding her. Maliha put her arms under the shoulder and pushed her up. She ran her fingers down the dead girl's back; there were scars all the way down the spine. The girl had been whipped consistently for a long time but not enough to cause serious harm.

She let the body down again. There was no indication of recent bruising, but there were marks from old burns and cuts across the rest of her body. The face was untouched and, Maliha ran her hands across the girl's head, no lumps, and the bones in her arms, hands, legs and feet all looked normal—except perhaps her left ankle which did not lie normally.

"What are you doing, Maliha?"

Maliha looked up at where Françoise held the baby, moving it from side to side. Françoise gestured with her head. Maliha looked around at the family standing a few yards away watching her every move.

"I am examining the body before the police arrive and ruin everything."

"No police," said Uncle Pratap. "The shame of it."

Maliha jumped to her feet, then staggered slightly, the strain of being bent down for so long had weakened her thigh. Only those who knew her well, her friends at the Fortress in Ceylon, knew how bad she had been before, and that until a couple of months ago she could not get around without her walking stick.

If she had been anywhere else, if it had been her aunt, anyone other than a man, she would have rounded on them. But she was only a woman; she could not tell her uncle what he must or must not do, especially not in his own house.

She kept her eyes down and said quietly. "A woman has died in your home, Uncle. Do you know who she is?"

"Of course not."

"Then the police must be called."

"But she is not Indian, she is not even European."

Maliha sighed. "She was a living, breathing person. She had a name, perhaps she had a family," Maliha turned and pointed at the baby. "She has a family."

"I will not permit it."

Keeping her gaze down, Maliha stalked towards him. He and the whole family drew back. She was tainted by touching the dead; they did not want her close. As they drew back they opened the way to her real target. The holy plant stood overlooking the whole event.

"What are you doing?" said Pratap.

Maliha stopped before the sweet-smelling plant. "If you do not send for the police I will touch the *tulsi*." The thought of committing such a crime had her own soul rebelling. She did not want to do it, but was sure she would not have to.

"You would not dare."

Maliha lifted her arm and stretched it out towards the leaves. She could not imagine what Françoise might be thinking.

"Very well."

She stopped but did not lower her arm. "Very well?"

"I will summon the police."

"You will summon the police immediately. You will insist that all the guests remain in the house, and those that have already left must return. The police will want to interview each of them." The baby gave a weak cry. "You will find a wet-nurse for the child."

"The baby is nothing to do with me."

"I will deal with the baby but you will find an *dhai* to take care of it."

"Yes."

Maliha dropped her arm and turned as her uncle gave orders. She heard him say something about cleaning up. "No! The courtyard must be left exactly as it is until the police have completed their investigations."

"As you say."

Maliha let herself relax and sighed.

* * *

Commissioner Abelard of the Sûreté, Indian Prefecture, arrived an hour later. In the interim, a *dhai* had been found and the child delivered into her care for the time being. Water had been brought so Maliha and Françoise were able to clean off the blood, and at Maliha's insistence a cloth found to cover the poor girl's body as some protection against the flies that had gathered.

The commissioner was accompanied by a brigadier and two guardians, one of whom was quite young. None were Indian and the youngest blanched at the sight of the dead woman.

Maliha watched them carefully. Abelard barely glanced at the covered body and went straight to Uncle Pratap. His wide, plump fingers enclosed Uncle's as they shook hands.

"A terrible business, my friend, we'll have it cleared away as soon as possible," said Abelard. "We will send your guests home."

"Are you not going to interview them?" Maliha said. Uncle still backed off as she approached, because washing away the blood did not cleanse the corruption.

Abelard, a rotund man with a fine moustache and a winning smile, turned to meet her amiably. "We do not have the staff for such an undertaking, *mam'selle…?*"

"Anderson. Maliha Anderson."

She could have sworn that the man flinched as he absorbed her name, but he recovered fast and held out his hand. "Of course, *Mam'selle* Anderson, the schoolgirl detective."

"I am no longer a schoolgirl, Commissioner, and if you know of me by that event you will also know of my other successes in bringing murderers to justice—" *the one where I failed, you have no knowledge of, and where you think I succeeded I was not permitted to hit the target, but no matter "*—and if there were not more pressing issues I might enquire as to the progress you have made in determining how my parents came to die." This time he really did flinch. He hid it by scratching the side of his neck. "But leaving that aside, for the moment at least, may I enquire when the medical examiner will be arriving to take charge of the body? There are many aspects of this death that make it worthy of investigation."

Seeing his discomfort increase, she pressed home. "And, foremost, regardless of the fact that this was apparently suicide, are the questions: How is it this African girl was here at all? How did she gain entry during the wedding? And most important of all *who is she?*"

The silence that followed stretched interminably. Abelard forced a laugh that was unlikely to convince anyone of its sincerity.

"What you do not understand, *mam'selle*, is that what you see before you is almost the entirety of the Prefecture of Police for our small portion of India. We do not have the resources for the scale of investigation that you may be used to with the power of the British police force at your back." He relaxed into his words, expressing them with a calm authority. "All these things you speak of will be done, but as and when they *can* be done. After all, the death of some African slave is hardly worth spending time on."

"What about the medical examination?"

"Yes, very well, that is a good point, after all she's not going to last the day in this heat."

Until then Maliha had been facing the commissioner head on, confronting him face to face, though he was more than a head taller, with her body held tense like a coiled spring. She let the tension go, relaxed, looked down to the ground. When she spoke again her voice was quiet, almost coy. "I understand that you and your men have a great deal to do, that you are very busy. I'm so sorry to be strident and unladylike."

A paternal smile took over the commissioner's face. "That's all right, *mam'selle*, it must have been very traumatic for you."

"Thank you for your kindness. I know I probably won't be able to discover much but perhaps you will not mind if I do some of my own detecting work. Perhaps I might be of some small service?"

"Of course, you may do as you wish. Just don't be getting in the way of the real investigations."

Maliha curtsied, an outrageous thing to do when wearing a sari, but it clearly flattered him. "Thank you again, for your kindness."

She turned away and headed towards the gate in the wall. She would not upset her Uncle further by contaminating the house with the taint of death. She heard Françoise following her. One of the servants opened the door, and even he tried to keep his distance. She paused beyond the gate as Françoise and Amita caught up.

Amita showed no indication that she was upset by the contamination that now hung about her mistress. Maliha instructed Amita to find the baby and nurse and have them go to her grandfather's house. "But don't take them inside; find somewhere that won't offend anyone until we can sort out some better accommodation."

Amita went back through the gate and it was closed behind her.

"*Don't be getting in the way of the real investigations,*" Maliha mimicked, contempt dripping from each word. She turned towards the east, inland and took the main road.

"What is the problem with that?" asked Françoise.

"Not a problem at all," said Maliha. "How can I get in the way of an investigation that does not exist?"

"You think he will do nothing?"

"It will be passed to the Examiner who will collate the evidence and decide it was suicide which, though a mortal sin for you Catholics, cannot be punished since she is already dead."

"She will go to hell."

"Perhaps, but I think she has been living in it for long enough that she may not know the difference. You saw the violence that had been done to her."

The main road started to rise towards a bridge over one of the many rivers. Maliha turned off and headed down the side towards the river bank.

"Where are we going?" said Françoise.

"To wash."

They reached the river bank. The tide was in and seagulls wheeled overhead. There were fishing boats out while, on the bank, women worked to repair nets.

"But we have already washed."

"It requires more than a bucket of water to wash away the taint of death. I'll be needing a priest at some point but the river will be a good start."

"I don't understand."

Maliha pointed at the slow-moving water. "This is the Kaveri, or, at least, part of its delta," she said slipping off her sandals. Françoise's face still indicated a lack of comprehension. "This is the second holiest river in India. Bathing in it washes away all sin; only the Kaveri and Ganges can do that. Even the Ganges is said to seek the Kaveri in order to cleanse itself of the sins of all those who wash in its waters."

Without removing anything else Maliha waded into the water and kept walking until only her head was above the water and then ducked down into the silence beneath. She wished all her sins and troubles could truly be washed away so easily.

CHAPTER 3

i

Grandmother had taken some persuasion to let her into the house, even after she had explained she had bathed in the Kaveri, but banished her to her rooms until a priest could be fetched to arrange proper cleansing.

Françoise had accompanied her. Since she was a foreigner she did not come into the rules at all—just as the African girl did not—she could neither be clean nor unclean no matter what she did.

"The room has a pleasant outlook," she said, looking from the window out on to the lawns.

"I will be glad to be away from here," Maliha replied.

Françoise turned. "Don't you love your grandparents?"

"They are ashamed of me."

"What for?"

"Existing."

It felt odd having a visitor and Maliha was not entirely sure how to behave. She had pulled a sheet of paper from the bureau preparing to write a letter to Barbara but then put the top back on her fountain pen and pushed the paper away from her. She could not write a letter with so many distractions. And it would be impolite with Françoise there.

Amita appeared and informed Maliha that the baby and the nurse had been put into one of the gardening sheds. Maliha gave her some money to fetch the basics. She did not enquire whether Amita knew what those basics were; she had no idea herself.

Françoise had helped herself to the lemon-flavoured water, and sat down in one of the armchairs, facing Maliha.

"You were very brave."

Maliha raised her hand as if to push the compliment away. "It is not bravery, only doing what must be done."

"Isn't that what bravery is?"

Maliha wasn't sure. She considered the way she had sacrificed her body to Guru Nadesh; how she had allowed herself to be caught by the Dutch spy; and entered the den of the Welsh lioness on the Sky-Liner. And the things she had done before that.

Were those actions bravery? She thought she was just reckless. Even Valentine had said she was courageous. Though she did not think he had quite the same opinion of her encounter with the guru. She shook her head in denial.

"So what is to be done?" asked Françoise.

"Done?"

"The police will not investigate, you said. We may not have known one another for very long, Maliha Anderson, but I do not believe you will allow this to pass."

I should not get involved, thought Maliha. *I came here to get away from all those things, to become a normal woman. Perhaps even to marry.*

But not now, because now there were so many questions that needed to be answered before she would be able to settle. It was in her nature. As if she was an avatar of vengeance and victory.

"No, I cannot let it be," Maliha said, and a smile filled Françoise's face.

"Talk to me, tell me what you are thinking."

"Did you see a door in the wall?" said Maliha. "The one I examined the previous night?"

"I did not even look."

"There were distractions."

Françoise raised an eyebrow at the word but the smile did not leave her face.

"We cannot return to my uncle's house until I have been properly cleansed."

"But you know where to start."

"I think we should begin with a *devadasi*."

*   *   *

The wind whipped Françoise's fine brown hair across her face and into her mouth. She would have to get herself a driving hat and some goggles if this was going to be a regular occurrence.

Maliha was driving her carriage at full speed through the streets of Pondicherry, apparently careless of the people, horses, carriages, bicycles, cows and carts. Every time the traffic increased to a level that looked dangerous Françoise pulled the cord Maliha had given into her charge—and the steam whistle would blare its warning scattering pedestrians and other traffic to the sides of the road and out of their way.

Only the cattle seemed oblivious, and those Maliha drove round at break-neck speed. It would have been terrifying if it had not been exhilarating. Up to now her life in French India had been quite dull. She had been trying hard but had few friends other than Renuka. At least pretending to be a missionary was getting her into the women's houseswhich was a good start.

The carriage careened directly towards another of the rivers on which Pondicherry was built. Maliha twisted the wheel and the vehicle juddered round to the left, its wheels slipping on the stones. There was a crowd up ahead gathered around a group of fruit stalls. Maliha steered around them but Françoise let off the steam whistle just in case someone in the group hadn't noticed the puffing monstrosity.

Françoise jumped when another steam whistle, a dozen times louder, with a deeper tooth-rattling tone roared nearby. She looked out on to the river to see a steam paddle-boat thundering along parallel to the road. A man, the ship's pilot, standing high up in a cockpit waved to them. Françoise waved back.

The journey came to an end as Maliha brought the vehicle to a smooth stop outside a towering building of red stone. Its enormous columns were adorned with sculptures of men and women, some of them intimately entwined. But there were animals too, and gods and goddesses with a dozen arms. In her time here Françoise had learnt the Indian gods were just as complex in their relationships as those of the Greeks and Romans, and apparently were of a greater vintage.

Maliha had pulled off her scarf and goggles. Françoise ran her fingers through her hair in a vain attempt to straighten it. At the very least she would need to put it in a plait to avoid the depredations of the wind.

Amita climbed out and helped Maliha down. Françoise was very impressed with the loyalty of Maliha's maid. It was clear the girl was devoted to her mistress. Françoise could understand that because despite knowing Maliha for only a short time even she felt some attachment. Maliha had that effect.

Having received a brief reorganisation of her hair and clothing from her maid, Maliha strode off towards the temple doors.

Françoise ran to catch up, glancing back at the carriage now surrounded by Indians staring but not touching, as the smoke stack still emitted a trail of black smoke and the engine wheezed, hissed and clicked as it cooled. The paddle-boat was rounding a turn in the river, its twin stacks disappearing from sight.

Maliha had already disappeared into the dark interior as Françoise climbed the steps, worn smooth and dipped by countless feet across untold generations. The doors stood open before her but from the outside she could see nothing inside. She took a breath and entered. Her eyes adjusted. It was an open and echoing space. She saw Maliha's sandals on the floor and removed her own.

Back in Dijon she had worn stockings but the heat here in India was too much. The stone was cool as she walked across it.

The temple was old. Its massive columns were carved in the semblance of elephant legs supporting the high ceiling. The openings around the walls admitted streams of light that glowed on the brightly painted colours of the sculptures.

As she crossed the floor of the temple she saw Maliha bow down and touch the feet of a man, perhaps in his forties, he laid his hand on her head. The touching of feet was a strange custom; she had trained herself not to avoid it when children did it to her in the houses she visited, and to touch their heads. It pleased the parents when she responded as expected.

Amita had not approached the man, so Françoise came to a stop next to her. She assumed the maid didn't speak French as Maliha had only spoken to her in Hindi, and Françoise couldn't speak the language beyond a few simple words. The man started quite friendly but apparently Maliha said something he was not entirely happy about as his words became abrupt.

Even so he seemed to give some directions and then turned abruptly and walked away, without any goodbye that Françoise could discern.

"Better get this over with," said Maliha as she came up to them. "What's a little more corruption to my already tainted soul?"

"I don't understand," said Françoise.

"Later."

* * *

Maliha slipped her sandals back on and went out into the sun that now sat low in the sky, though its heat still beat upon her skin.

She glanced across at the steam carriage and decided to leave it. No one would do it any harm. She headed in the other direction, the way the priest had indicated, however reluctantly.

Was he less a hypocrite now than he would have been twenty years ago? She wondered. Once upon a time being a *devadasi* had not simply been a matter of being a temple prostitute, it had had religious value. That was before the British had decided prostitution was a bad thing and suppressed the women that were sold to the temple.

The British were so naïve. Before they came, yes it was true that a *devadasi* was a prostitute but they had other duties, and sometimes sex was not part of it. But when the British decided to crush the institution, the women were left with nothing except the streets. And what happened in British India found its way into French India, though the governing French cared little for what happened in this little piece of the world.

She led the way along a street with residencies on both sides, counted three alleyways and took the third one on the right. The smell was disgusting but no worse than the shanty town outside the Fortress. She glanced back at Françoise; perhaps she would not be able to tolerate the human sewage that ran in the gutters. But though she held a kerchief across her nose she picked her way along the alley. Amita was unconcerned.

They reached an unremarkable wooden door set in a wall. Maliha pounded on it.

For a long time there was nothing. Maliha beat her fist on it again. There was the sound of a bolt being drawn and the latch rose. The door scraped against the ground as it was pulled open a few inches. A woman with grey in her black hair and wearing a sari that had been washed too many times peered out.

"I am sorry. You have the wrong house."

"If you would be kind enough to let us in, I wish to speak with you."

"Please. You do not wish to do that. You don't know what I am."

"I know, and I will pay you for your time."

The woman paused. "Please wait." She pushed the door shut and there was the sound of movement and the grinding scrape of a pottery lid. Then the door was pulled open enough to give them access.

They entered into a very small courtyard. Off to one side was a kitchen area and a sleeping space with a straw mattress, and that was the limit of it. There was a pot for flour in the kitchen and another for rice. Both were dusty.

The woman withdrew to the far side of the yard. It seemed very small and crowded with all four of them. Amita pushed the door shut. Above them were windows to other apartments but all was quiet for now.

"I am enquiring about the African girl."

The woman looked nervously at the door then back at Maliha, with her gaze to the ground at Maliha's feet. "I do not know her."

ii

A year ago, Maliha thought, she had been naïve and self-righteous. She believed she understood the world and the people in it. She thought she was like Sherlock Holmes from Conan Doyle's tales. A year of death had disabused her of that idea. Things were never the way they were portrayed in stories. The only thing she had was her ability to see when something was missing.

She had not known what she really expected. There had been the stories when she was young about the glamorous *devadasi* who won the heart of some powerful man and lived happily ever after. But they were just make-believe.

The truth was a broken woman who may have been attractive once but had been used, no doubt abused, and now approached middle-age with no one to support her.

A year ago Maliha would not have cared; she would have been strident and punished the woman for trying to mislead her. But not now. Instead Maliha found a stool and sat down.

"What's your name?"

"Sumangala."

"I am Maliha," she said quietly. "I think you are lying to me, Sumangala." A look of fear crossed the woman's face, Maliha held up her hand. "It's all right. You have nothing to fear from me."

Sumangala relaxed a little. Françoise shuffled around behind Maliha, obviously she had no idea what was being said.

"How old were you when you came to the temple?"

"I was sold when I was six."

"Have you ever seen any girls from another land in the temple?"

Sumangala shook her head, looking down.

"But there have been girls who were not Indian."

Keeping her head down, Sumangala gave a very slight nod. It could have been nothing. But it wasn't.

Maliha opened her reticule and retrieved a few coins. Not too much because that would attract attention, but enough to make the woman's life a little easier for a while. Sumangala followed the movement of Maliha's hands, and the coins.

"You know where the slaves are sold."

Again the almost invisible nod.

"Half a year ago did anyone come by asking where they could buy a slave?"

There was a slight hesitation, then. "No, *sahiba*, no one asks."

Maliha stood and left the coins on the stool. As she turned back Sumangala bent down and touched her feet. The action caught Maliha by surprise; she expected it from a child but not a woman so much older. She laid her hand on the woman's head and muttered a blessing.

Maliha was the last out the door. She paused. Sumangala was wringing her hands, Maliha waited.

"*Sahiba*, do not beat me."

"I won't."

"Half a year gone, a high-caste woman came asking."

"Was she young?"

"No, *sahiba*, she was older than I."

"Thank you."

Amita pulled the door tight behind them and they picked their way back up the alley. They finally reached the main street with the sun almost touching the tops of the taller buildings across the river.

"Did you learn anything?" asked Françoise.

"She knew about the slaves and someone who came asking," said Maliha. "But I think she's been paid not to say anything."

"By whom?"

"Doesn't matter for now."

"So this dead girl was one of the temple prostitutes?"

"That is not likely since she was not native." There was a thought nagging at the back of Maliha's mind, but it refused to form into a coherent idea. Well, it would come in time.

They made their way back to the carriage. The crowds around the carriage had gone; there were just a few hangers on, mostly children.

"Where is the man to drive the carriage?" One of them shouted as Maliha climbed into the driving position.

"I do not need a man to take me," Maliha replied in a pleasant tone. She could have driven off immediately but decided to give them a show. She pumped the lever that forced puffs of coal dust into the furnace. It roared into life and smoke billowed from the stack. It would take a few minutes to return to full heat.

I do not need a man. She thought of Valentine then glanced across at Françoise: perhaps she should take a woman instead. Although her only previous experience of a woman's love had involved Temperance Williams trying to kill her. Well, not entirely the only experience; she had, after all, attended a girls' boarding school for seven years. But while such things happened there, they had not involved Maliha.

She shook herself and put on her cap and goggles.

Françoise laid her hand on Maliha's arm. "I wonder, Maliha, if you would not mind, perhaps we could go a little slower?"

Maliha frowned, then remembered Valentine said she frowned too much. So she smiled instead. "I'm sorry. I do like to go fast. It's almost like flying."

"I found it somewhat discomforting, I'm afraid."

"We're not in a hurry."

She engaged the gearing and as the carriage moved forward she turned the wheel hard to the right to bring the nose round. She disengaged the drive quickly when she realised there was a bicycle in the way, leaning against the temple wall.

"A man could move that bicycle," she called out to the boy. He grinned, went over and pushed it further along the wall. There was barely an inch of space between the carriage and the building as she pulled it round. She waved at the boy and accelerated away.

"It would be a blessing if they were to put in gears to allow motion in either direction," commented Maliha. She had to put in a very deliberate effort not to drive as fast as she was able.

* * *

Maliha drove through the French quarter. It resembled pictures she had seen of the south coast of France. The buildings were large and looked out on to the Bay of Bengal, filled with fishing vessels and seagulls wheeling overhead in their thousands. They passed the great Victorian lighthouse built eighty years before that had become almost redundant when the ships took to the sky. Now it was used by the sky-pilots as a marker.

Françoise guided Maliha along smaller tracks off the coast road, past residences built on an increasingly grander scale. She drove the carriage up the driveway of one impressive construction and stopped in front. "You live with your parents?"

"My cousin, he has a trading company."

"And you're here to spread the word of God."

Françoise laughed. "Something like that."

"You don't understand India. She is old and has seen religions come and go. She doesn't mind if you want to come and talk about yours, she will smile politely and listen with half an ear. But she will not change."

The woman let out a sigh. "It is as I feared."

"When will you be visiting with my aunt again?"

"We did not have a date, with the wedding everything was in uproar and uncertain."

Maliha nodded. "Perhaps you could send her a letter and ask to meet tomorrow after lunch."

Françoise eyed her suspiciously. "And you would like to accompany me?"

"I will be properly purified and as fit for company as I am ever considered to be."

"*À bientôt, Mam'selle* Anderson."

"*Au revoir, Mam'selle* Greaux."

Maliha found herself smiling as she turned the puffing carriage towards home. She had not had a female friend of her own age for many years.

Her grandparents did not greet her or ask for her when she arrived so she headed out the back of the house and, guided by Amita, made her way to the gardener's shed.

The light was on and she pushed open the door. The *dhai* was feeding the child. Maliha felt a wave of embarrassment wash over her. She looked away and then looked back. Why should she feel awkward? The child lived because of her—and Françoise—it had a roof over its head. Even if it was a shed it was more than most had. And it was because of her. The giving of sustenance to a child was natural. Why should she not witness it? One day she might do the same.

Which made her think of Valentine and that put a dent in her good humour.

The baby was tiny yet a perfectly formed human being. Her hands and toes exact miniatures of her mother's. Her skin was as dark as her mother's but her eyes, closed now, had an oriental look. She sucked rhythmically but seemed to be slowing down. After a few moments she stopped completely.

The *dhai* pulled the baby gently away from her breast and covered herself. She wrapped the baby tightly and then offered her up to Maliha.

Maliha felt awkward; by default the child was hers. But she did not know what to do. If she had stayed in India, there would always have been children of different ages to look after, to see, to play with. If she had been full Indian.

Seeing Maliha's uncertainty the *dhai* stood up and brought the child to her. Maliha found herself wrapping her left arm under the little girl and taking the weight of the head. She put her other arm around the girl and stared down at the face.

She did not understand when she found she was crying and her tears fell on to the baby's wrapping.

* * *

Later she lay in her bed. The window was open with the screen pulled down. In the silence of the night she could hear the waves breaking steadily on the beach. She reached up and touched her cheek where her tears over the baby had dried.

There was so much loss in the world, things ripped away in life that it was hard to understand how anyone could continue to live. She had grown up knowing that life was not fair but did that mean it always had to be pain? She wondered what Valentine was doing and the thought occurred to her that perhaps she should not have driven him away quite so completely.

And it was thinking of him that she fell asleep.

iii

"The commissioner himself said he did not mind me investigating this case." Maliha found herself in the unusual position of almost pleading with the man.

"I am very sorry, *mam'selle*, my findings are confidential."

Maliha cursed her luck, to find one man in the French bureaucracy who had principles and kept to them. And for it to be the only one with whom she really needed to talk.

"Over what period of time do you think she was being whipped?"

Dr Gimbert was thin and in his sixties, but still active. His body may have aged but his mind had not. "I am not willing to discuss it with you."

"I think it was six months but no more than once or twice per month."

"*Mam'selle* Anderson, you are trying my patience." He placed his medical bag on the table and gathered up papers into a folder. "I have visits to make."

"I saved her baby's life. The child has no name, and no family. When she is grown and asks who her real mother was, what shall I say, *monsieur*? Shall I say that I was unable to discover the truth because a doctor would not discuss the matter?"

The doctor paused, the folder half way into the bag. "I do not believe there is much I can tell you."

"My estimate of the beatings is correct?"

"I think perhaps a little longer, and more frequent, but yes."

"And whoever did the beating was careful."

He looked up at her. "Careful?"

"They wanted to hurt her, but not do permanent damage. Perhaps a follower of de Sade?"

"What would a young thing like you know of such matters?"

Maliha sat down in the hard-backed chair on the opposite side of his desk. "I am very well read, Dr Gimbert. But I can assure you my interest in it is purely academic."

Following her hint, he sat down and moved his bag to the side so it did not come between them.

She continued. "You agree that would fit the damage done to her?"

He nodded as if unable to commit himself in spoken words.

"And she was well fed?"

"She was not suffering from any form of malnutrition, but my examination of her joints indicated that she was probably underfed for most of her life."

"I did not see any lash marks on her belly."

He shook his head.

"What do you think was used to strike her?"

"Oh, almost certainly bamboo cane; the indications were quite clear."

Maliha sat back, deliberately, and placed her hands in her lap, and the doctor followed suit, relaxing as he did so. "But there are other, older injuries?"

"You are very observant," he said. "Those older injuries are of a completely different nature. A combination of cuts and burns, which I estimate would have been received in the month before the whipping began. They are overlaid by the flaying marks but none of them are on top of any whipping scar." He paused.

"There was something wrong with her left ankle."

He nodded. "It had been broken and not reset properly."

Maliha looked down at her hands so that he was not too embarrassed by her next question. "The cuts and burns, they were of a sexual nature?"

She could imagine the look on his face but she continued to examine her hands.

"While they were present across her body, there was a concentration on her genitalia."

There was a long silence. Maliha stood up and went to the window. The doctor's office looked out on to a narrow well rising the height of the building, intended to allow light and air into a set of offices. There was another office directly across from his that seemed to be an examination room. The bottom of the well was dark with shadow but there was a hint of green, probably mosses and ferns.

"How common is slavery here in French India, doctor?" she said at last.

"It's illegal."

She hesitated in exactly the way that the old Maliha would not. She had always imagined that age and experience would add to her certainty. She found quite the opposite to be true.

The doctor saved her from having to say anything further. "But I believe it continues, underground, of course."

A sex trade, thought Maliha, as it had always been.

"Have you been able to determine the nature of the poison she used?"

The doctor opened a drawer in his desk and withdrew a small glass bottle. He placed it on the table. Maliha squatted down and examined it in the light from the window. It was about four inches tall. The base and body resembled the bulb of a flowering plant while the opening looked like petals. The glass was thick and cut in an Italian style. The inside of the neck had been ground to provide a tight join with the missing stopper.

Maliha picked it up in her left hand. It was lead crystal so heavier than it appeared. She lifted it to her nose and using her right hand she wafted air from the neck to her nose. She frowned and then stared down inside; there was the merest trace of a green stain clinging to the bottom.

"Cyanide?"

"Apparently."

Maliha returned the bottle to the table. "It looks like a perfume bottle."

"That's what I thought, perhaps Italian?"

Maliha retrieved her reticule and made her goodbyes.

*　*　*

Her grandmother had been right about one thing, thought Maliha as she pulled the white cotton sari closer about her body, trying to cover as much skin as possible: A well-advertised purification was the correct approach. After delivering a baby from a dead woman's womb the taint she had received so publicly made her virtually outcast. The only way she could counteract such notoriety was with an equally visible bath.

The entire family had been summoned to the banks of the river that, by popular choice, contained the highest proportion of the Kaveri River in the delta.

Renuka was also to receive the priest's cleansing since it was her wedding that had been interrupted. Balaji and his immediate family were not there having made their own arrangements.

All the other wedding guests had also been invited with the likelihood that the entire gathering would end up in the water for a mass blessing just to ensure they were not affected by the terrible events of the wedding.

"And that," said Grandmother, "is how you deal with these things. We pay the temple, anyone who thought bad of us gets a blessing for free, and we will provide food and a little music.

"Besides," she continued, "we need this public so the parents of eligible bachelors will still call."

At which Maliha had growled to herself and made her exit.

As it was the middle of the day, there were not as many of the original guests as there might have been. But the total number of people lining the road that ran along the bank of the river exceeded those that were officially invited. No one avoided a chance at a free blessing and lunch.

But it was Maliha who went first. The tide was in. The chosen location was sheltered by a promontory pushing out into the main flow. The beach here was pebbles and they pressed into Maliha's feet as she walked barefoot down to the edge of the water where small waves lapped.

The priest was a relatively young man. His long hair was tied back. He wore a white *dhoti* and was already standing out in the water waiting for her. Maliha pushed ahead. At every step the water rose up her legs, then past her hips. When she reached the priest the water had reached her ribs. She smiled at his theatrics. He must be standing on a rock because he was much higher in the water.

Maliha was fluent in English, French, and Hindi but the priest was quoting passages of Sanskrit that she could not follow, though the occasional name of a god or goddess came through.

The priest got to the blessing itself. He placed his hand on her head and pressed her down. She allowed herself to sink below the salty water, taking a deep breath as she went. It was unlikely much of the actual river water reached the banks; most of it flowed down the middle of the channel, while sea water flowed up the sides.

But it was what people believed that mattered. Besides, who was she to claim that a goddess couldn't also be in the sea water part of the river?

The priest's hand stayed on her head, holding her completely submerged. It seemed to go on for a long time. When the pressure released from her head, she pushed herself up to the surface. Her ears were full of water and at first she thought the noise she heard was the distant rumble of an engine. Then the sounds became clearer and it was a chant.

She wiped her eyes with her fingers and turned. A group of onlookers, younger ones, had moved to the edge of the water and were chanting *Durga Maa*—the name of the goddess of victory and vengeance. In the middle of the group, through the water dripping from her, she could make out Renuka.

And then the priest gave her a final blessing in the name of *Durga Maa* and a cheer went up. Maliha could make out the scowl on her grandmother's face, deeper than she had ever seen before. Maliha sighed. She doubted many women would want an avatar of vengeance as a daughter-in-law considering most mother-in-laws treated their sons' wives as little better than slaves.

Perhaps something good would come of this after all.

iv

Françoise waited at the window of an upstairs lounge. The view looked out on the front of the house, and the driveway. She had not gone to the ceremony. She knew of it but had not received an invitation. Attending uninvited was not something that crossed her mind.

She was aware that her upbringing had been sheltered in some ways. She had lived in Dijon with her mother in her parents' home. She had received an education appropriate to the female offspring of a successful businessman, which is to say arts and proper devotions to the Holy Mother and, apart from her one secret, she tried to do the right thing.

She was a good daughter of the Republic, except she read romances. She justified these to herself because most were in English and it was important to practise her English as often as she could. It was not the relationships in the books that thrilled her, it was the locations.

Some of those romances, particularly the English ones, took place far from the shores of France, or even England, in the far-flung parts of their Empire. She liked the ones set in India best of all where the stories usually revolved around a young English woman who would fall for some exotic Indian prince, but there would always be the good English soldier who would be the ultimate prize. She always imagined herself in the role of the soldier because she found the women so ineffectual.

However India had failed to fulfil her expectations. It was hot and dry, except when it was wet and hotter while the type of romance she sought was nowhere to be found, just the odd flirtation. Then she had stumbled across *Mam'selle* Anderson who trailed excitement in her wake.

Françoise had surprised herself when the poor *Africke* had died in front of her. It was a terrible thing and the memory of the event made her feel queasy. But, at the time, her head had remained clear. It was she who had thought of the child, unborn and dying in the womb, even if it had been Maliha who had carried out the task.

And she had been ready to take the babe and comfort it. It was as if she and Maliha had both become mothers to the same child. Of course that the *Africke* had committed suicide was a difficulty. She would be suffering in Hell for the mortal sin but, though the Old Testament taught that the sins of the parents were visited on the children, she did not see how the Holy Mother could possibly allow it. And all the stories of Blessed Jesus showed God's forgiveness. How could it be right to curse the innocent?

Or did she want that to be true because then, perhaps, her own secret would not consign her to Hell?

A line of puffing smoke appeared over the roofs on the road. There were so few steam carriages in Pondicherry she knew this must be Maliha.

With a light heart she picked up her hat and veil, to keep off the worst of the sun, and trotted down the marble stairs and was out the front of the house as Maliha's carriage turned into the drive and crunched up the gravel driveway.

*   *   *

The steam carriage pulled up outside the house where only two days before Françoise had been enjoying the wedding, though it did take an interminably long time.

Maliha climbed down awkwardly. Françoise was under the impression that Maliha required a walking stick due to some accident. That was how she'd been described in the newspapers. But apart from a very slight limp that occasionally manifested, and the fact that her maid was always there to assist her, Françoise could not see that she needed one.

"Perhaps you would get us inside?" said Maliha.

Françoise climbed the steps to the door and knocked. There were a couple of glances from the staff but all three were admitted: Françoise in her conservative Western dress, she preferred the corset to the new fashions, Maliha in a sari. Françoise admired Maliha's figure. Her skin was scarcely dark at all and had the bone structure close to a Westerner. She could easily be mistaken for an Englishwoman gone native.

They were guided through the house to a set of rooms set aside for the women, the *zenana*. Maliha had referred to her as a *zenana* missionary, but that term was reserved for the Baptists.

Françoise had managed to persuade the younger members of the family not to touch her feet, but when Maliha entered every woman, including the older ones, went through the ritual with her. Françoise was confused since she understood that it was reserved for elders, not to say that Maliha was happy with it. She stood there stoically receiving their obeisance and handing out blessings—as if she were a saint.

Finally it was over. Françoise was brought a chair, which she had indicated she preferred on previous visits, while the rest sat on floor cushions. In truth it was a practical thing. She could not sit on the floor in the boned garments she wore.

Renuka sat beside her to act as translator, so that she could practice her French.

"Has the marriage been rescheduled?" asked Françoise.

"The astrologer cannot find a good date," said Renuka.

"But I thought you had perfect compatibility?" Françoise said. Using astrologers to determine the best time for such things was another heretical activity but it seemed a lesser one.

"We have chosen a new astrologer," said Savitha. "To make such a terrible mistake, how could we continue to use the first one?"

"I don't think you should reschedule a wedding until I have completed my investigations, Auntie Savitha," said Maliha.

"But if the new astrologer says next month?" said Renuka. "I should be married now. I don't want to wait."

"Do you like Balaji, Renuka?" asked Françoise.

Savitha did not give her a chance to reply this time. "That is not important. She will come to like him."

But Renuka smiled. "My mother is right, of course, but she thinks that if a wedding is to be arranged then the bride and groom should not like one another, so that they can learn to be in love. She thinks it means their love will be stronger."

"So you do like him?" asked Maliha.

"We are perfect for one another," said Renuka. "And I do like him, but more importantly the astrologer told me we were born on the same day in the same place. We cannot be more perfectly matched."

"And Renuka's dowry is very valuable," chimed in Parvati.

"You be silent, little one," said Savitha. "Your elders are talking."

"Can I touch the goddess?" asked Parvati, looking at Maliha.

Françoise frowned when Renuka translated. "Goddess?"

"She misunderstands," said Maliha. "It's just Renuka called me the avatar of *Durga Maa*, the goddess of vengeance, as a joke. And the priest decided it would be clever to give me a blessing in her name. I don't know what he thought he was doing."

"Sadaiappan Sethi is a troublemaker," said Aunt Savitha. "He has ideas of independence."

"And what's so wrong about that, *amma*?" said Renuka. "They stole our country from us, why shouldn't we have it back?"

"You are too young to understand."

"I am old enough to be a wife."

Maliha cleared her throat, and the room went silent. "I wonder if I might have some more tea?" she said.

* * *

It was all very interesting, Maliha thought sipping her *chai*, but it is getting us nowhere.

"Auntie," she said turning to the elder. "I would like to speak with you in private."

Savitha paused for a moment and then nodded. She stood and headed towards a room in the back. Maliha followed but Parvati grabbed her arm. Maliha turned to prise her off but Renuka was already there.

"Let us get some lemonade and we will play some games while *amma* talks to the goddess."

Maliha sighed. What had Renuka started? She saw Françoise stand and look as if she were going to follow them. Maliha was about to tell her to stay behind, but then thought better of it. She wanted to help, but without the ability to speak Hindi she had no idea what was going on around her most of the time.

Maliha gestured for Françoise to follow and went through into the other room after Savitha.

This room was furnished in the Western style with expensive French sofas and armchairs. A strange luxury, thought Maliha, for such a traditional family.

Savitha did not stop in the room but threaded her way around the furniture and out on to a balcony. This was inward facing to prevent the possibility of the women folk being spied on by men. That theoretical logic was thwarted by the fact that the room was overlooked by the taller buildings opposite.

A haze hung over Pondicherry spread out across its river islands. The boats were like toys. Two squat flat-bottomed air-ships floated down from the north, the air faintly buzzing with the sound of their distant engines, towards the small air-dock at the south of the city. They were most likely carrying ice which was in constant demand and fetched a good price at this time of the year.

"I hope you will forgive me, Auntie, but I must ask questions."

It was different when you asked strangers awkward questions about their private lives, thought Maliha. There was a certain distance between you and once the events were over you would never see them again. (Though Barbara put a lie to that assertion.)

"You are no goddess to me, Maliha. I bounced you on my knee when you were a babe, even though your grandmother frowned."

"Even so, I must ask. For the poor dead girl."

Savitha turned away at the mention of her. "I will not discuss it. It was a shameful thing to happen to our family. It is a miracle that Balaji's family have not called off the wedding."

"Why would a slave girl commit suicide at Renuka's wedding, Auntie?"

"Do not press me, Maliha." Savitha's words were harsh but there was no strength in them. It was more as if she were in pain. She leaned against the balcony.

"Please, Auntie, what is it you will not tell me?"

Savitha did not respond but her fingers gripped the stone as if she were going to tear into it.

Maliha took a breath and stepped forward. She placed her hand on her aunt's. "Is it that Uncle owned her?"

There was a long silence until Savitha spoke, her words no more than a whisper. "Leave my house."

v

It took a few minutes to take their leave of the family and the children in particular; Parvati wanted to play. But as Maliha and Françoise were closing the door Savitha had come through smiling as if nothing had happened. She did not say goodbye.

"I did not understand any word of what happened," said Françoise.

Maliha had always found it best to ignore rhetorical statements and questions. People either got to the point or let it drop.

"She became very upset," Françoise continued.

They continued down the wide staircase to the ground floor. The number of servants was back to normal levels, with all the additional wedding staff having been dismissed.

"What did you say to her?"

Maliha stopped in the main entrance hall.

Instead of heading out the front she went through the back. They passed the reception rooms where the wedding events had been held and along the passage that led to the courtyard.

The holy plant had been returned to its usual position and seemed none the worse for having been moved or witnessing such terrible events. Maliha crossed to it, slipped off her sandals, touched the leaf and offered a quick prayer. Well, if there were someone listening perhaps they might at least help her find out why the girl died.

"What did you say to her, Maliha?" asked Françoise again, as Maliha put her sandals back on, hooking her finger into the strap at the heel.

"I went to see the medical examiner this morning."

"Without your loyal assistant? I am hurt."

Maliha went behind the holy plant and looked at the wall. "Have you read de Sade?"

The pause that followed was sufficient to tell Maliha that, at the very least, her innocent French friend knew the nature of the man's writings. "I have not *read* them," Françoise said finally.

"Very good. The girl was most likely a slave, and had received systematic whipping over a period of months. Sufficient to cause pain and injury—you saw her back—but not enough to damage her permanently."

"So she had reached the limit of her tolerance, and got her revenge by committing suicide in the middle of the wedding?"

Maliha glanced over her shoulder. "Perhaps."

She ran her fingers along the crease between the stones then stepped back with her head on one side. "I believe this is a door."

"A secret way into a torture chamber?"

Maliha felt herself go cold at Françoise's words. That was precisely what it was. But she only had to know it was there, she did not have to go in. She turned away and headed for the entrance back into the house.

"Where are you going? Don't you want to gain entrance?" called Françoise after her.

"It's not important."

*   *   *

Françoise could not believe her ears. How could it not be important? She chased after Maliha but did not catch her until she had already entered the house.

She had to choke back the questions that boiled in her mind as Maliha walked briskly back to the entrance and was let out the front door.

Françoise chafed in silence as Maliha went through the steps to get the vehicle running. She drove at a relatively sedate pace down the drive and accelerated out, heading south.

"Why isn't the door to the torture chamber important?" she finally exploded when she was sure that Maliha had no reason to avoid the question.

"What emotion drives the French?" said Maliha.

"What?"

"What drives you, Françoise? What makes you French?"

Françoise looked out at the buildings flashing past. At first there had been the houses of the rich, but after a while they changed, became smaller, more close-packed. Now they were the homes of the well-to-do.

What drove the French? "Patriotism. We are a proud people, and we are proud of everything that is France."

"What do you know of the Nipponese?"

"What does anyone know? They keep to themselves."

"Honour and duty," said Maliha. "To them life is nothing without those things. To lose them is to die."

Françoise thought hard. "I do not understand why we are discussing this."

"You have lived here for a short while: Do you know what makes India?"

"I have not thought about it."

Maliha paused as she concentrated on a junction blocked by an incident that appeared to involve several bicycles and an elephant. Almost without slowing Maliha threw the vehicle into a sharp turn and drove it down an alleyway behind the main buildings.

The smell was most unpleasant and Françoise judged the vehicle would need a good clean quite soon, or perhaps it should take a blessing in a river. The alleyway was quite narrow but Maliha managed not to knock the wooden fence on the right, nor catch any of the stone walls on the left. Though she did give a sleeping dog a shock as the machine thundered past.

At the end Maliha turned left and then right. Françoise looked behind and saw the elephant incident retreating into the distance. The buildings around them were becoming ramshackle and in a very poor state of repair. They came out on the bank of the estuary with the sea to the left and rolling breakers running up the beach.

"What is it that makes India?" Maliha asked again.

"No, I do not know," said Françoise. She was not interested in these games; she simply wanted an answer to her question.

"Shame."

"Is this important?"

Maliha sighed and reduced speed. She brought the vehicle to a halt and climbed down before Françoise had a chance to move. Maliha pulled off her scarf and goggles, threw them on to the seat and headed away towards a stand of trees on a piece of land that stuck out into the sea.

Françoise leapt lightly on to the sandy ground and followed her. She caught up with Maliha as she stood on the edge above the sea twenty feet below them. The waves beat against a chaotic pile of rocks at the base of the small cliff.

"You cannot make your way in India without understanding that simple fact," said Maliha. "It is hopeless to even try."

Françoise was not entirely sure how to respond and Maliha saved her the need.

"My Aunt Savitha was ashamed when I pressed her on the subject of the dead girl. I had already established that she was a slave and had been beaten, apparently for pleasure." Maliha stopped and left the words hanging in the air. Françoise knew this was a test.

She thought for a moment, tried to put herself in the older woman's position to imagine herself feeling guilt and shame. "Your uncle?"

"Most likely."

"But he would not have given her the poison to kill herself, would he?"

"Unlikely."

"Your aunt?" Françoise was horrified at her own words, to condemn someone she had known for so long, who had given her hospitality.

"That would be the assumption of the police, if they managed to get past the idea that my uncle had done it, if they bothered to investigate."

"But it's still not murder, is it? If someone commits suicide, it was still their choice."

"No, it's not murder. But to convince someone to kill themselves? That is far worse."

The conversation died there. Maliha stared out to sea. Françoise watched Maliha. She was almost impossible to read, not that Françoise thought she was skilled at understanding how a person thought, but Maliha held everything inside. Except, perhaps, on those rare occasions when it became too much. She cried for others, but did she ever cry for herself?

"Renuka said you came back to Pondicherry because of a man."

The long pause suggested to Françoise that the girl was right, until Maliha finally spoke.

"Have you ever kissed a woman?"

Françoise's heart pounded. Did this question mean what she thought it might?

"My mother, my sisters, cousins, relatives, friends. The French kiss a lot in comparison to the British, I understand."

"As a lover."

Françoise's mouth went dry but she managed to croak. "Why?"

"The only woman who wanted to kiss me like that tried to kill me."

Françoise hesitated. "Did you want her to kiss you?"

Maliha shrugged. "Not really, I knew she was a murderer by that time."

"Do you want me to…"

Maliha turned to face her. For some reason all that Françoise could focus on was the red *bindi* in the middle of her forehead. "Yes, I would like to give it a try."

Françoise found no words so after a few moments of silence she stepped forward and pressed her lips against Maliha's. And then backed away.

Maliha raised her eyebrows. "Is that how you kiss a lover, Françoise? I may not have any practical experience, even with men, but I am aware that there's rather more to it than that."

Françoise was also fully aware there was more to it. She had some experience of kisses that had been very passionate and long-lasting. She remembered them with a great deal of pleasure.

Maliha smiled. Françoise was astonished; she had never seen Maliha smile and it transformed her face. She opened her arms and Françoise stepped forwards into her embrace. As their lips met a second time she enfolded Maliha, feeling the silk of the sari soft against her skin.

She closed her eyes and felt the warmth of Maliha's lips.

"*Sahiba!*"

i

After Maliha had returned from the city earlier that morning, Amita had braided Maliha's hair into one plait that ran straight down her back, dressed her in the simplest white cotton sari and placed the sandals on her feet ready for the purification ceremony.

Then she prepared to carry out her mistress's instructions by changing into her oldest, cheapest sari with faded colours, and released her hair from its pins, allowing it to hang loose around her shoulders.

Leaving Maliha's grandparents' house by the rear, and attracting disapproving stares from other staff, she made her way along the back alleys towards the nearest market. She allowed her head and shoulders to droop, and she met the eye of no one.

It was a perfect disguise since no one would give her more than a moment's attention. Once they decided she was an untouchable, she ceased to exist. Maliha had given her some money. Though it would be difficult finding someone to carry her, it was the task she had been given.

Amita did not find it hard to take on her old behaviour again. She had been with Maliha for less than a year but her mistress treated her as an equal: a servant, yes, but as a real human being. When Maliha said *Namaste* she meant it; it was not simply mouthing a word of greeting.

The alley led down a slope that led into an open area crammed with market stalls. The air was filled with the cries of the traders and the smells of fruits, flowers and spices. Amita kept out of people's way as much as possible but was still jostled and pushed by those who were, she understood now, afraid of her status.

She made her way across the market to where men lounged by bicycles and carts. There was even one with a steam-driven truck. The picture of the airship, and the name *Pooranankuppam* on the side, suggested it might be traveling where she needed to go.

They had agreed that she would need some justification for travelling quickly. Normally an untouchable would be expected to just walk wherever they were heading. Maliha had given her a letter addressed to an air-cargo company. It even contained a letter in French that had a genuine request, just in case she found herself forced to hand it over.

Her mistress thought of everything.

Amita approached a group of men and squatted nearby. There was a man boasting to those gathered round him about the functioning of his most excellent steam vehicle. She waited while he told them it could carry six tons of fruit. This elicited praise and envy from his admirers, and one dissenter.

"Six tons of fruit? It would collapse beneath the weight."

The vehicle owner grinned, as if he had been hoping for the remark. "I will show you! Jump up on the back."

"I will not go near it, Sushrut; it will probably explode like Gunveer's root masher did last month."

That got laughs, and the man called Sushrut frowned; he was losing support.

"I will ride your machine, if you will allow," piped up Amita, but still keeping her gaze averted. "It has Faraday, no?"

They ignored her.

"Come on, one of you will do it."

They shook their heads laughing and began to wander.

Amita stood up and went behind the men to the other side of the truck and pulled herself easily up on to its flat back. Some of the men noticed and pointed at her laughing. "There, Sushrut, there is your assistant."

Sushrut held up his hands and joined in the laughter. "Woman, can you lift that case?" He pointed at a wooden carton, some yellow fruit could be seen between the slats. To Amita it smelt as if the fruit were going off.

She reached around. "With those arms she could wrestle a tiger," shouted someone and there was more laughter. Amita lifted the box with some difficulty, less because it was heavy and more to do with its awkward shape.

"Put it on that other box and then lift them both," instructed Sushrut. Amita did as she was told but could barely even lift a corner of the two together with her cheek pressed hard against the wood and the rotting smell strong in her nose.

"All right," said Sushrut. "I say that in less than five minutes she will lift three of those boxes."

"All full?" said the dissenter.

"All full, Ashraf," Sushrut said and turned to Amita. "Woman, put another box on top of those two."

As Amita strained to do it, Sushrut took bets.

Then he climbed up to the truck's cabin but before he went inside he looked at Amita. "You know what Faraday does?"

She nodded, and he grinned. He slipped inside the cabin. The steam engine that had been puffing quietly to itself roared deafeningly into life and a cloud of smoke and steam poured from the chimney. Amita steadied herself against the pile of cartons as the steam whistle gave one quick blast. He was warning her.

Amita had never travelled on a flyer of any sort, but she had experienced the Faraday effect in an atmospheric train several times, though the first time had been a shock and she had embarrassed her mistress by crying out because she felt as if she were falling.

So she was ready when the steam truck's Faraday device was engaged. She did not think she was an expert but she was sure this was not as powerful as the ones on the train, or even in the lift they had travelled in at the Fortress. But whether it was or not, she was suddenly a fraction of her original weight, as were the cartons.

Sushrut climbed down from the cabin and stood with his friends, rubbing his hands. "Any last bets?" There were no takers. Sushrut turned to Amita. "When you're ready, woman, pick up all three."

In her previous employment, if you could call it that, Amita had learnt that men liked a show. Even if she did not really care whether they saw her body or not, they liked it more if she seemed shy or unwilling. They liked to be tantalised and led on; they even believed it.

She squatted down beside the boxes. She reached round as far as possible on each side and got her fingers between the slats. Whatever the fruit was, these were too far gone for sale and her fingers caught on more than one and forced out the juices that ran over her fingers.

With a great show she pretended to try to make the boxes move; she even managed a quiet groan as if exerting her utmost effort. She could imagine Sushrut's face. There was growing laughter and demands to be paid. She relaxed back for a moment, not too long because she was still an untouchable and likely to receive a beating from him if she were not careful.

Then she made the effort again and with extreme slowness lifted the boxes.

"There you see," shouted Sushrut. "She is lifting them."

"Call it quits, Sushrut." It sounded like Ashraf. "You only have to see her arms to see she's strong as an ox, she's simply lifting it normally. Did you set this up?"

Sushrut grumbled but sounded as if he was going to give them their money back.

Amita was standing erect and she shifted her right arm, hidden
from the main view, so that it was beneath the boxes and taking all
the weight. Then she turned toward the crowd and took her left arm
away completely and held it out as if she were a dancer about to take
a bow.

"Look," said someone in the crowd. There was a moment's
astonishment, laughter and Sushrut received many claps on the back.
Even Ashraf was laughing.

After she climbed down, Sushrut was almost friendly. He
offered her some of the winnings. She took what he handed her—
perhaps a tenth of what she had earned him—divided it in two and
handed half back.

She maintained the submissive posture and did not look him in
the eye. "My mistress has message I must take to air-dock, will you
carry me in steam carriage?"

"I must go anyway, so I will take you," he said and then as a
generous afterthought. "You may ride in the cabin."

To his clear relief she declined and simply clambered back on to
the rear.

They travelled swiftly through the city, though not at the break-
neck speed that her mistress tended to employ. She could not criticise
her mistress, of course, but Amita would have preferred to go at a
slower pace. In order to keep from panicking she often simply closed
her eyes and prayed to any god that might be listening.

After only a quarter of an hour they reached one of the main
rivers. This one was far wider than most of the others and had not
been spanned by a bridge. She had little doubt the British would have
built a crossing, but the French seemed less inclined to indulge in
civil projects.

But there was a steam-ferry with great paddle wheels on either
side crossing towards them as they arrived. There were already a large

number of pedestrians, people with donkeys, goats and a couple of old nags; the only other vehicles were a cart and some bicycles.

Amita leaned on the cab of the steam truck and watched the boat thunder towards the jetty, with its single stack belching smoke. It seemed to be travelling too fast but then the paddles stopped turning and dragged in the water. Then they began to turn in the other direction and the boat slowed until it was barely drifting.

It floated up to the jetty, lines were thrown, tied off, and the front opened up. People poured off, intermingling with the animals and vehicles. It was cleared in a few minutes and the waiting passengers went aboard.

Sushrut greeted the sailors who ran the ferry and tossed them a coin as he drove aboard. He did not stop but drove through an opening under the boat's superstructure and out the other side. He brought the truck to a halt opposite a closed ramp identical to the one by which they had come in.

Though she had never been on a boat Amita did not think it would be good to climb down. The other pedestrians would not appreciate an untouchable in their midst when there was nowhere to retreat, either for them or her.

The boat cast off, the engines roared into life and the paddles churned the water driving them forward. They did not seem to be making much progress but when she looked back they were already a long way from the northern shore.

Across the river, and further inland, a cigar-shaped object lifted from the ground into the still, warm air. Her mistress would have known instantly what sort of vessel it was and what country it came from. For Amita it was simply an airship. She knew there were different types. She understood they flew because of the Faraday—that even now made the steam truck, and her, lightweight—but more than that, she did not really care.

It was not long before the boat carried out the same manoeuvre as before and came up against the jetty on the southern shore. The ramp was lowered and moments later the truck rattled off on to dry land.

ii

Sushrut let her off on a main road where the streets were lined with offices and shops. It was not busy. If this had been the Fortress the roads would have been teeming with traffic, pedestrians and sailors. But Pondicherry was a small city, and completely cut-off from the rest of India because it was, in effect, a different country.

She was not sure where she should start looking for information but this wasn't the area. This was too business-like, too clean, and too upmarket. She needed the dives where the sailors went. There were always such places, as she knew from her previous life.

Making a decision she crossed the almost empty street and took a turning that led towards the air-dock. She kept to the side of the street, taking her time. One of her caste would never give the impression that they were moving with too much purpose.

Her route took her along streets that were primarily offices. She could hear the sound of typewriters and the low buzz of conversation floating from the windows. As she went further the buildings changed to brick-built warehouses. Workmen lounged outside. The sun was moving up in the sky and would soon be at its highest. The strongest heat of the day would follow. Maliha had said she would meet Amita on the road back into the main city, just the other side of the ferry.

She pulled her sari up over her head. There was the occasional shout directed at her, usually an insult, telling her that her kind was not wanted. She would have liked to have retorted but that would not do any good.

- 97 -

She reached a junction where she had to either go left or right. At last she saw what she was looking for: a drinking establishment for foreign sailors. She approached it slowly. This one was out on a main road so would not be the sort she was looking for.

The building was on a corner with a much narrower road, and people spilled from it almost as if it was ejecting them. She glanced at their faces. Most were Indian but there were a few whites and Chinese among them.

She turned down the smaller road and into a sudden melee of people. Though the Indians steered clear of her, the foreigners took no such precautions and people bumped and brushed against her.

The street was lined with shops, tea shops and coffee houses with no space between them. The further she travelled from the main street the dingier and smaller the shops became. The buildings here were much older. Alleyways broke off the road and wound away into mystery. She spotted a prostitute down one of them. Now she was getting somewhere, even if it was the end of nowhere.

Still it was going to be difficult finding out what her mistress wanted to know. She needed a very particular alley, providing a very particular type of service. The one that she used to supply.

She walked more slowly and glanced down each side alley, trying not to look too interested. It was odd, now that she was not in that business she found it difficult to recognise those who were. She was getting towards the end of the street. It ended in a square with a desultory tree dropping at its centre.

At the entrance to the last alley on the right a young girl stood. She was no more than twelve or thirteen but she was looking for business, just as Amita had at that age, just about the time she had realised what she really was. She had been wise enough to know her family would never understand her desire to be a woman.

The memories did not hurt anymore. All the teasing he had received before he left had not been intended as cruel. That his older sisters always wanted to put make-up on him because his face was so feminine. That other boys teased him about his lightness of voice and how it had not become like a man's.

Then the day when the fun had become serious when, as a dare, Bhanu had kissed him as if he were a girl. Something had happened; both of them knew it. There had been a feeling that had passed between them, as if the same thought had joined in them. They had broken away from each other. The other boys had laughed thinking the two had been so disgusted they could not stand it. The difficulty was exactly the reverse.

He could not resist touching his sisters' saris; he wanted to wear them, and to look beautiful, as they did. To be admired by the men. Bhanu avoided him, when all he wanted was to kiss Bhanu again.

So he had run away from his home, from the village, and reached the Fortress, though he was almost starving and could only survive by stealing. He had gone there because his father had said the Westerners were corrupt. Well, he was corrupt and so that should be the right place for him.

But he could not get through into the Compound and had lived in the slum city that surrounded it. He found the other *hijra*, changed her name and had a new home. She had grown up like this one who leaned against the wall in her old and torn clothes.

"Business not good?"

The *hijra* blinked twice. "I don't know you."

"My name is Amita."

"This is my patch."

"I don't want your business."

"But they will want you more than me, you're clean."

"I won't be staying. I have questions." Amita saw the look of disgust on her face.

"I have no time for questions."

Amita glanced around; there were no potential clients anywhere near. She raised her eyebrows. The younger one corrected herself. "I don't answer questions."

Amita pulled a coin from inside the folds of her clothes like a magician and flicked it across to her. She caught it, slightly awkwardly.

There was the low hum of humanity around them, talking, working.

"My mistress wants to know about the slaves. The Africans."

"Africans?"

"Blacker than you or I, their noses are flat and their hair is curly." She twisted her straight black hair into ringlets to demonstrate.

The girl nodded. "I know that sort. Some sailors are like that."

"What about slaves, girls to be used for sex?"

"Does your mistress want one?"

"My mistress is Brahmin."

The girl shrugged. "Never known it to matter. They all come here. Even women sometimes."

"I know," Amita said. "What's your name?" She didn't say *what do you call yourself.*

The girl looked at her for a long time and turned the coin over in her fingers. "Shashi."

Amita took out another coin and stretched out her hand holding the coin between her fingers. Shashi hesitated and then took it, her fingers brushing Amita's.

"African girl slaves?" Amita asked again.

"I don't know where they come in. But a sky ship doesn't have to land in an air-dock, does it?"

Amita shook her head.

"Didn't think so."

"Every few weeks there's a market. Girls, boys, others I suppose."

It was in the nature of India for the people to say what another wanted to hear. Amita had done it herself many times, though she learnt that her mistress was not happy unless the words were true. So she always told Maliha the exact truth.

She found, listening to the girl, she had also learnt when someone else was being accommodating to her. "And how do you know this?"

"I see them," said Shashi. "Sometimes."

"Where?"

"They bring them to places here. For—" she hesitated, "—things."

"How do you know they are new slaves?"

"Because I see their eyes, and they are afraid."

Amita nodded. This was the truth. She knew that look as well. It was something you understood when you had felt it yourself.

"Amita? What are you doing here?"

iii

Amita looked at the man who now stood a short distance away. She went cold thinking it might be someone who had known her before. But most of those had come and gone. There were few repeat customers, and she was sure she did not recognise him.

He was dressed in the casual loose, but strong, clothing many air-sailors chose when there was no proper uniform for a ship. So he was an independent. His hair was roughly cut and he had a beard untidily trimmed. But his eyes. There was something about them that stirred a memory.

"She's not working here." Shashi was annoyed. "This is my patch."

"If you want service," Amita said quickly. "I don't do that anymore. Shashi can supply your needs." She tossed Shashi a third coin then with her head down she turned back up the road.

The man put out his hand and caught her by the arm. "Is Maliha here?" His tone was one of anger and resentment.

Amita jerked her arm free but turned to face him, recognition burst in on her. "*Sahib* Valentine?"

A fist came from nowhere and struck Valentine in the jaw. He staggered to the side. Amita saw a man she guessed to be Shashi's pimp, flanked by two heavies, one of which was pulling back his fist to hit Valentine a second time.

Amita did not hesitate. Her foot lashed out and found its target in the man's groin. His desire to hurt Valentine was quenched by pain, all his focus became inward looking, and he folded to the ground with a whimper.

Valentine had not fallen, but was not fully aware. The second thug was about to move when the pimp gently touched him on the arm and he paused. As Valentine lifted his gaze and took in the situation she saw his hand go into his pocket. There was something large and heavy there.

"No, *sahib*, do not draw gun," she said quietly. "Unless you wish to bring police."

They stood in a tableau, Valentine and Amita on one side, the broken thug, the one standing with his master, and Shashi to the other. Valentine and the pimp were locked eye-to-eye. Amita realised nothing good would come of this unless she acted.

"I am sorry, Master," she said in a high-pitched whine. "Please do not beat me." She prostrated herself in the muck of the street and touched Valentine's shoe.

There was a long pause.

"You deserve every beating I give you. And you will receive another for running off again."

Amita was surprised, the *sahib* managed to sound quite genuine, as if he truly despised her. From previous experience she had not thought he had it in him to be unpleasant. She uttered an abject whimpering noise and kissed his shoe.

"What has she done now?"

"*Sahib*, your servant has damaged mine."

"Your servant struck me without provocation; he got what he deserved. Now tell me what this piece of filth has done." said Valentine. "And *if* I think you deserve recompense I shall consider it."

"Well, *sahib*, she has spent time with my girl and I have not been paid."

Amita stopped fawning over Valentine's shoes and squatted beside him, keeping her face down but still able to see what was happening.

"How much?"

"Ten rupee, *sahib*."

Amita reached out and put her hand on the back of Valentine's thigh. She dug her fingers in and squeezed hard. His leg muscles twitched with the pain. He had very strong legs, she noted, no fat.

"Ridiculous."

It was ridiculous; ten rupee would keep a family for a long time. But there were other considerations.

"She's not worth more than one *annas*."

A bit low, but a good bid.

"There is my time, *sahib*, and that of my men, as well as my proportion of the whole. As well as wear and tear."

Valentine said nothing. Good. Let him suggest.

"Five rupee, *sahib*."

"Since I did not touch your—" Amita knew he was too refined to call Shashi what she was, a whore "—servant. And as discussed, the wear and tear is not my concern. There is my own injury to take into consideration."

He did not make a counter-offer. Silence dragged out. The sounds of the streets filtered through to them but Amita noticed that the square and the alley had become empty of other people. They were quite alone.

"Two rupee."

"Two *annas*," said Valentine. Amita stroked his thigh to show she approved of his bid.

The pimp laughed; it was not a pleasant laugh, and carried danger. The first thug was recovering. Was the pimp buying time?

"Please, master, can we *go* now?" she whined as if unaware of the tension. She hoped he understood her meaning.

"One rupee," said Valentine and pulled the coin from his pocket. He flipped it through the air towards the pimp and turned to go. Amita scrambled to her feet.

"And beating."

Valentine paused. "What?"

A grin spread across the pimp's face. "You beat her now."

Amita closed up on Valentine and clung to his arm. "Please beat me now, master." She made her tone as seductive as possible, loading it with sexual pleasure and perversity. She saw an uncertainty flash across his face. She gave his arm two quick squeezes. She was sure he was better muscled than he had been. Not that she had touched him before: only looked, when no one saw her.

"Yes, excellent idea. We will find a room."

"I have room," said the pimp.

Amita squeezed his arm twice again. There was no way out of this.

* * *

Valentine had managed to get them alone, at least. The room was on a second floor. It was small and dirty, and smelt of unpleasantness he had come to know too much in the last few months. There was a window.

He had no sooner pushed the door shut—there was no lock and the pimp was not far away—than Amita was wrestling with his belt.

"What are you doing?" he hissed. He pointed at the window. "Let's go."

"Give me your belt, *sahib*," she said quietly. "Quickly. We must give them what they expect first. If we are silent they will come back."

He undid the belt and pulled it free. She took it from him, folded it in two, and then handed it back.

"You beat me then we make sex."

"I will not beat you and we will not…do that."

Amita smiled and touched his cheek. "I would kiss you, *sahib*, you are good man. But you are not mine to kiss."

She grabbed the hem of her ragged sari firmly and pulled. It ripped loudly. She nodded to herself then pointed at the belt and indicated he should strike his hand with it.

He did and the sound of the folded leather striking itself gave a satisfying slap.

Valentine nodded and moved to the pallet. He knelt down beside it, lifted his arm and brought it down on the straw-filled mattress. The sound reverberated through the room. Amita moaned quietly, and gestured for him to do it again.

He struck, she moaned louder. He listened with almost wonderment at how she seemed to make the sound of pain and yet, somewhere hidden in its depths, make it seem like pleasure.

She ripped her sari more. He slapped again at steady intervals and her moans grew louder. Valentine had not been a complete innocent when he had known Maliha in Ceylon; the last few months had torn away whatever innocence remained in him. He had encountered situations and people he wished he had not, discovered things that he could never un-know.

He knew there were people who took pleasure in pain. And listening to the way Amita groaned, even though she was pretending, he could almost understand it. But the fact remained: He had no desire to cause pain to those he cared about.

Even though he had unwittingly done so.

In his sudden anger at himself he slammed the belt down repeatedly very hard and ripped up the flimsy cloth on the mattress. Amita's eyes widened in surprise and she screamed in pain. Valentine stopped abruptly fearing that somehow he had actually hurt her in his sudden frenzy.

She squatted beside him and laid her hand on his arm. "Good," she said quietly. Then she choked out a few loud sobs. "Now we sex." She smiled at his obvious discomfort. "You know sounds, *sahib?*"

He nodded and tried to swallow but found his mouth to be dry. Damn woman was grinning. He wondered, not for the first time, where Maliha had found Amita. She did not behave like the usual agency staff. Knowing how perverse Maliha could be when it came to doing "normal" things, it was almost a certainty that Amita was anything but typical.

He turned away from her and threaded the belt through the loops of his trousers. He grunted. And felt a hot flood of embarrassment in his face. He did it again, and stopped. It was too much, he could not do this. He looked at Amita with a pained expression and shook his head.

Amita slapped him hard on the cheek, and gave a choking sob as if she had been the one to be struck. She grabbed his hand and held it to her cheek. He shook his head and pulled away. She slapped him again and sobbed.

He closed his eyes and groaned. She made a small noise. He growled. She joined in. They began a rhythm, a dance of sounds. He hated himself, but the embarrassment ebbed away; he opened his eyes and saw Amita was smiling.

It became a game. He would make a guttural sound and she would respond, like a call and answer in a song. She was still holding his hand. He allowed his noises to become louder, and a little faster. She became more excited in her responses. He broke away from her and moved across to the window, still groaning. His breathing was short and each in-drawn pant croaked in his throat before re-emerging as an animal snarl.

He looked out the window sidelong so that his voice would remain within the room and not fade. There was a short drop to a roof protruding from the lower floor and then way across between two houses to what looked like an alley or maybe a street.

His attention was dragged back into the room when Amita started to screech in time to his grunts and shout something in Hindi. She was still smiling in between the sounds. He came back to her and took her hand. He had not noticed the designs painted on her skin before.

Together they reached a crescendo. Amita screamed and jabbered some words. Uncertain, Valentine gave a final loud groan. And they went silent.

Amita's face was serious now. She put her head beside his and whispered into his ear. "We must go."

In a moment of impetuosity, just as she was pulling back, Valentine leaned in and kissed her on the cheek.

They crept across the floorboards to the window. Amita was not a weak female and did not require any assistance climbing from the window and levering herself down on to the roof below. She was already between the opposite buildings by the time Valentine was on the roof.

She gestured for him to hurry. There were voices coming from inside, asking if they were finished. Valentine stumbled across the roof and made his way between the buildings. There was a shout from behind. He glanced back and saw the pimp leaning out the window. Valentine waved and jumped to the street below. The two of them ran.

iv

Valentine seemed to know his way around and Amita followed as he led the way through the streets and alleys away from the market.

After a few minutes they had entered an area with low residential buildings all the same, recently built by the style and the use of brick. They were utilitarian but not slums and the streets were clean.

It was building number eight where Valentine turned in and climbed the steps. He pushed through double doors into the hot interior. An ineffective fan running on electric was set in the ceiling. It did not seem to move any air.

There was a white man at a desk, but he looked up from a newspaper as Valentine came through. He nodded, threw a momentary glance at Amita then returned to his paper.

They climbed two flights of tiled stairs and into a short corridor. She watched the numbers growing as they followed the passage until Valentine unlocked a door and held it open for her.

"I am sorry for the impropriety," he said. "The man downstairs will think you are a prostitute or, at best, a woman of easy virtue."

Amita was certain Maliha had never told Valentine of her origin, so she simply smiled and accepted the honour of being treated like a lady. Valentine had barely given her a second glance when Maliha was in the room, which was the way it should be; Amita was only a servant.

The room was simply furnished with a single bed, armchair, straight-back chair by the writing desk, wardrobe, chest of drawers, and table. There were bottles with a couple of glasses on the back of the writing desk, and a newspaper open on the bed.

"Please sit," he said indicating the armchair. She could not bring herself to do it, and perched on the hardback one instead.

"Maliha is in Pondicherry still?"

"Yes."

"Is she all right?"

Amita hesitated, unsure of how much she should reveal. "She is investigating murder."

Valentine gave a half-laugh and the beginnings of a smile touched his lips. He was such a beautiful man, even when he had this mess of hair.

"Who's dead?"

"Slave girl with no name and no one knows where she has come from. She is African."

"The girl who suicided at the wedding?" He glanced over at the newspaper.

"Yes."

Amita was not sure how much she should tell him. Her mistress had broken off the relationship between the two of them after he had killed the guru. She had not been pleased with him. Not that Amita understood what their relationship had been. Only that Valentine adored her, and she was always angry with him—but never missed an opportunity to be with him.

"You were helping with her investigation?"

"Yes, *sahib*."

"So she's replaced me already."

"Yes, *sahib*, but not with me."

His head jerked up. "She's found another man?"

"Oh no, it is Frenchwoman, called Françoise Greaux."

He relaxed. "I see."

There was an awkward silence. Amita glanced around the room but there was little to notice and it had not changed from the last time. She looked back at him with his untidy hair.

"Excuse me, *sahib*."

He roused from wherever his thoughts had taken him. "What?"

"Do you have scissors?"

"Scissors?"

"Your hair, *sahib*, it is untidy."

He looked over at the mirror behind the door though he was not in a position to see himself in it. "You want to cut it?"

"If you would like me to," she said. "I can make it tidy."

He seemed to contemplate this for far longer than it should have taken to make a simple decision. "You wouldn't mind?"

"Of course not, *sahib*."

"In there." He pointed to the drawer beside her in the writing desk. She pulled it open, and found it was almost empty save for scissors and writing paraphernalia.

She took them out and moved the chair to the open space between the end of the bed and door. He stood up from the bed and sat down on the chair holding himself stiff.

Amita laid her hand lightly on his shoulder, feeling the gentle reflexes of his muscles. "I require comb also."

He almost leapt from the chair, opened the wardrobe, fumbled for a moment within and pulled out a tortoiseshell comb.

"A present from my mother," he said, handing it to her. He sat down again.

Amita ran the comb through his hair a few times to untangle it. She began to trim it, starting at the top and working down. At first she tried not to touch his scalp but as they both relaxed she rested her hand on his head as she combed and snipped.

She could almost see the tension leaving him as time wore on. His hands that had grasped one another tightly in front of him loosened and he adjusted them so each lay along his thighs instead.

She moved around to the front of him. As intimate as lovers. She combed his fringe. She knew her mistress would want to know he was in Pondicherry, and what he was doing here. Just as he had wanted to know about her. Though he was too polite to press the point. Amita, however, was not polite and pleasing Maliha was her main concern.

Now that he was relaxed she tried an opening gambit. "I did not expect to see you here."

"I came in on a trader."

"And you are going out again?"

"When I have finished what I'm doing."

They were face to face, their noses inches apart as she carefully cut along his fringe. His eyes were blue. So very beautiful.

"I did not know you liked *hijra*, *sahib*."

He frowned. "What's *hijra*?"

"Women who are men."

She pulled the scissors away as the shock of realisation went through him. She was surprised, did he really not know of such things? She continued to regard him as he did what the British do when faced with an emotion too strong to show. He buried it.

He forced himself back under control. "That girl was a boy? Like Lochana Modi?"

"Yes, *sahib*," she said and decided she would never tell him the truth about herself. She treasured the intimacy they had had, though it was an illusion, and the kiss he had given her was like a memory of honey. If he were to know, it would hurt him and destroy the memory. "You did not know?"

"No."

"That would be difficult."

He seemed confused by her words, then understood. "Oh, no, I was not—" She watched him wrestling with the thoughts that he could not express. "I only wanted to ask some questions."

"What about?"

"Ships landing and taking off but not leaving a cargo. Ships taking too long to travel from one place to another."

Amita had finished cutting the hair on his head and turned her attention to his face. In the months since he and Maliha had worked together he had become tanned on the exposed skin of his face, under the beard his skin was still white.

She gently ran her fingers through his beard, then the comb and cut off the longer hairs. She wondered how far she might push him.

"What would *hijra* selling herself on street know about such things?"

"I make enquiries where I can, Amita. Sometimes people know things that might seem unconnected and yet when taken together, they are pieces of a jigsaw you didn't even know you were making."

"Jigsaw, *sahib*?"

"Puzzle."

"You must understand, *sahib*, these people who sell themselves on street, they have owners, masters, who expect money always. They are not good men."

"I know," he sighed. "I was not getting anywhere and became careless."

She stopped cutting; she was finished. She put the scissors and comb into one hand and brought her other hand up and rested it on his cheek. "You are good man, *sahib*. You should not deal with such people. You should return home to England, find good girl and work for King."

He lifted his hand and laid it over hers, not pushing it away.

"I found the girl I wanted, Amita, but I did not understand her. I drove her away from me, and now I am trying to make it up to her in the only way she will understand."

* * *

Amita stood on one side of the ferry, away from the other people so as not to upset them. Her disguise made it difficult to get things done and had proved to be almost useless.

Before they had parted Valentine had made her promise not to tell Maliha he was in Pondicherry. He did not know how much longer he would be there so it would not matter.

She watched the river churning away as the hull of the ferry ploughed through it. The paddle wheel, three times her height, threw up water that made rainbows in the sun. Seagulls followed the boat and dived into the water behind looking for fish disturbed by the passing vessel.

She disembarked from the ferry last, as befitted her place. There were a number of shops and houses around the jetty but they soon fell behind as she walked along the long road back towards the city. She did not know where Maliha was going to be. She hoped it would not be far. And that her mistress had not been delayed.

The road climbed up into a small range of hills and she looked back across the river that curved round with it. Then down the other side, coming around a corner she saw a steam carriage parked by the side of the road. She smiled and hurried.

It was empty but there were trees on a spit of ground that poked out into the river. She thought she saw a splash of colour there. She reached the vehicle and confirmed it belonged to her mistress; the head scarf and goggles lay on the seat. She turned towards the promontory and walked through the trees.

She stopped short. Her mistress stood with her arms around the Frenchwoman. They were kissing. A riot of emotion went through her. Her initial confusion was replaced by jealousy, then anger at this Françoise who presumed to take the place of Valentine. And finally a great feeling of sorrow for him. She did not think her mistress to be so fickle, and yet here she was.

Well she could and would stop this. She pushed through the trees and bushes.

"*Sahiba!*"

CHAPTER 5

i

Françoise catapulted out of her arms and turned away from the approaching maid. Maliha considered the experience. As she had never kissed Valentine she had nothing to compare it to; in fact she had not kissed anyone so intimately. Even with Guru Nadesh, since kissing had not been part of his repertoire, only inducing paroxysm, and even that had been interrupted.

Of course relationships between women were frowned upon as much as those between men—when they were acknowledged at all. Maliha knew what physical passion felt like; the guru had achieved that much at least. While the kiss had not been unpleasant she had not felt the same passion with Françoise. Perhaps there was more to it. She looked across at Françoise who was looking particularly discomfited and had the red flush of embarrassment in her cheeks.

Amita reached the two of them and pressed her palms together at her forehead to indicate her deference and their high position above her. Maliha nodded to her.

"Did you find anything useful?"

"Very little, *sahiba*," said Amita. "The person I spoke to has seen African slaves around the air-dock but did not know details."

Maliha looked at her thoughtfully; if she were not mistaken her maid was hiding something from her.

"And?"

The look of discomfort that crossed her face, the slight shuffling of the feet and the way her hands gripped one another tighter confirmed it but she did not respond.

"What happened?"

"There was trouble, *sahiba*." Amita glanced at the French woman, but they were speaking Hindi and she could not understand their words. "I spoke to *hijra* on street. Their pimp—"

"Pimp?"

"Owner, manager, *hijra* work for them and they give up all money to them."

Maliha nodded and remained silent for Amita to continue.

"The pimp wanted money for her time. I had to run," Amita said. "I am sorry, *sahiba*, I have failed you."

Maliha waved her hand. "All information has value. Did you find where they landed?"

"I am sorry. She said she did not think they came in at air-dock. A ship can land anywhere?"

Maliha nodded. Although, she thought to herself, it would most likely be day otherwise it would be difficult to find the place. And if it were night there would have to be recognisable landmarks for the ship's pilot or navigator, and lights to land by.

They could not make such landings without being seen whether it was day or night. And if they could be seen then someone would talk about it.

* * *

At the wheel of her steam carriage Maliha headed back into the city. It was mid-afternoon and two days since the girl's death, and what did she have to show for it?

Françoise sat beside her but had not spoken since being discovered in Maliha's embrace. She was a good Catholic girl; it was probably very confusing for her, particularly if she had enjoyed the kiss. Then Maliha thought of Valentine again. He was always teasing, never serious. And she felt a smile creep across her lips.

"Let us review the situation," Maliha announced in French as they approached the first bridge into Pondicherry. Françoise jumped at her words.

"Review?"

"The facts such as we know them. You start."

The woman sat up straighter in the seat and looked out at the approaching buildings as they went over the top of the bridge. "A pregnant African girl poisoned herself in the middle of a wedding."

"Good. The poison was some green form of cyanide which was in an Italian-made lead-glass container. What else do we know about her?"

"We believe she was a slave."

Maliha nodded. A small herd of goats scattered as they rumbled past. "And she was being beaten."

"Yes."

"In fact beaten constantly, regularly and severely for six months or so, but on the other hand she was being kept healthy, her wounds treated, and she was well fed."

There was a long pause. They passed a field where a water buffalo was pulling logs into place for the construction of a fence.

"Amita was able to determine the slaves are probably not brought in at the air-dock, but they do pass through it. I do not think it would be too hard to discover where they arrive."

"Is that something we should do?" asked Françoise. "It sounds dangerous."

"It probably isn't necessary for this investigation," said Maliha. "So who did *not* commit the murder?"

The French woman paused again, as if she were not used to having her rationality tested in such a fashion. Perhaps it was unusual.

"The bride and groom?"

"One or other of them might have had a reason to prevent the wedding from taking place."

"The parents?"

"Same argument."

"I do not know how to answer your question."

"Exactly," said Maliha. "We have no motive."

"But," said Françoise, "whoever owned her killed her because she was pregnant."

"In some ways that is the reason why I do not think the girl's master—or mistress—"

"A woman could not do such a thing."

Maliha thought about the cases she had dealt with. "Françoise, I like you very much but I must tell you, from personal experience, that a woman is very capable of such a crime. I have known three women who were killers and quite cold-blooded in two cases."

"The one that wanted to kiss you as a lover?"

"No, she only killed on the spur of the moment, in a moment of passion."

"This was not a moment of passion."

"No. This was calculated. The poison. The timing. The fact the poison was self-administered," said Maliha. "Everything says that this was carefully planned."

"You are saying the girl must have been instructed to poison herself."

Maliha did not respond.

"*Sacre bleu*," Françoise said in a barely audible whisper. "It is a terrible crime, to force someone to commit a mortal sin, to throw someone else into hell for eternity."

Maliha engaged the brake. She had pulled up at the front of Françoise's cousin's house.

"We are here?" Françoise seemed surprised.

"We are also taking the pregnancy for granted," said Maliha.

"The girl is murdering her own child in the womb. Another mortal sin."

"You are thinking like a Catholic, Françoise."

The woman turned and looked directly into Maliha's eyes. "You make me wonder whether you are sent by Satan to tempt me, Maliha Anderson."

"I am not insulting you, Françoise," said Maliha. "Your beliefs are your own concern. When I say you are thinking like a Catholic I just mean that you are ascribing your own thought processes to others, when you have no right to do so."

"I do not understand."

"Do you think the African girl was a Catholic?"

Françoise opened her mouth as if the act of doing so would bring the words into her mind. But there were none and she closed it again without speaking. Then she brought her hand to her mouth. "I see."

Maliha smiled.

"Would you like to come in for some tea?" said Françoise.

Maliha's automatic reaction was to resist; she was not the sort who engaged in social niceties if she could avoid it. But she had not finished working through her thoughts yet, and it was refreshing doing so with someone as innocent as Françoise. It was like writing in chalk on an untouched blackboard.

"That would be acceptable."

She engaged the engine once more and moved the carriage to a shady spot and placed it such that the sun would not touch it all the rest of the day. In her disguise Amita was forced to remain in the car.

Together she and Françoise walked up the steps and into the house.

"The servants have the afternoon off," said Françoise.

"All of them?"

Françoise apparently had not heard her and led the way to the kitchen where she prepared the tea.

They carried the teapot and cups, along with a selection of cakes to a cool room at the back of the house. It had tall windows that looked inland, towards the hills.

"There are many questions that still present themselves," Maliha said having taken some Battenberg cake, which she adored. "What do you think they are?"

Françoise seemed to prefer the small round cakes with sugar toppings, and was midway through consuming one when Maliha asked the question. She continued to eat the cake slowly while she looked for answers.

"If it wasn't the slave master who killed her, it must have been someone who knew she existed."

"Good."

"Someone who wanted to disrupt the wedding."

"Most likely, but why do we know they wanted to disrupt the wedding?"

Françoise searched for an answer but Maliha could see she was not going to come up with anything. Eventually Françoise shrugged her shoulders. "I do not know."

"If the intention was simply to kill the girl, there are far easier ways of doing it," said Maliha. "Do you think the girl would have tried to escape if she had been able?"

Françoise looked up suddenly. "Perhaps she liked the pain as well—are there people who like pain?"

Maliha nodded. "If you can imagine it, someone somewhere will have done it."

"You make the world sound like a terrible place."

"You are naïve, Françoise."

"You insult me again."

Maliha smiled. "No, a simple statement of fact."

"I am older than you by five years but you speak to me as if I am a child. I am not sure I want to live in the world you inhabit."

Maliha put down her cup. She stood and brushed the crumbs from her sari with delicate flicks of her fingers. The patterns of *mehndi* still showed on her hands. Amita had painted her fingernails blue to match the sari she had worn to the wedding, but that was long gone; bloodstains would never come out of the silk. It had been burned.

She went to the windows, opened them, and stepped out on to the paving stones that led across to the garden proper. She heard Françoise come up behind her. She felt her close by, Françoise's blouse sleeves brushed against Maliha's bare arm.

"What do we do now?" asked Françoise.

"That depends on whether you want to continue to be involved with me. You are not wrong, my world is not a pleasant one."

Françoise seemed to consider her words. "I think I would like to follow you."

"Even if I lead you down roads where you do not want to go?"

"You have done so much more than I."

"Though I am your junior by five years."

Françoise laughed, but it was more of a chuckle. Maliha realised she had not heard her laugh before. It was not at all a proper laugh for a woman. Too throaty, too … provocative. "I am a naïve girl from the French countryside who has seldom questioned what she has been taught."

"And I am an agent of Satan sent to tempt you from the one true path."

"Sorry."

"Perhaps I am."

Françoise took Maliha's hand and pulled her round so that they were face to face. "I do not believe that. I do believe that perhaps my education was not as broad as I may have believed."

"And you want to learn from me?"

"I believe that would be a good thing to do."

Maliha pulled her hand from Françoise's and stepped away from her. She spotted a seat set into a tall hedge, out of the sun and she sat in it. It was out of sight of the windows of the house. Away from prying busybodies. Françoise followed and sat beside her, close but not touching.

"Think about it, Françoise," said Maliha. "Whoever provided the means for the girl to kill herself, who persuaded her to do it, who arranged for her to escape from her torture chamber—this person knew all about her. They must have had her confidence and yet did this terrible thing. But this person was most likely not the same one that had been beating her all these months."

Françoise looked into her eyes; it seemed as if she were mesmerised by them. "But the person who committed this crime is truly evil."

"Sadly no. If only it were that simple," said Maliha. "I think that with the right pressure a desperate person may do almost anything."

Françoise made no reaction but reached out and took Maliha's hand again.

"At present," continued Maliha, "we are a moth fluttering near the truth, but soon we will become a wasp and we will be able to sting. And then this person will direct their murderous attentions to me. If you are also there they will surely try to kill you as well."

"They will try to kill us?"

"That has been my experience in most cases."

"But you did not die."

Since the answer was obvious Maliha remained silent. Françoise smiled and squeezed her hand. "I had scarlet fever when I was young and almost died of it."

"It is different when someone has the power of life and death over you and truly desires to bring your existence to an end."

"You cannot dissuade me."

"You do not understand the truth of it."

"I have faith in you."

Maliha opened her mouth to protest at the choice of word, but Françoise silenced her with her lips.

ii

Valentine tested the weight of the gun in his pocket. He knew it was oiled and loaded. There would not be any mistake this time.

Six months had changed him. Ever since Maliha had rejected him for daring to rob her of her prize, though he had only acted to preserve her honour. An honour she clearly did not value, since she was willing to discard it to bring the dregs of humanity to justice.

That piece of slime was better off dead.

Valentine pressed back into the shadow of the doorway he stood in. Two men walked past, their loud voices echoed between the dark buildings. By their clothing they were air-sailors but he did not recognise the language. Something oriental.

He envied Maliha's command of language, but then he could not match her memory; her mind was like a camera and everything she saw was indelibly imprinted.

A door opened and closed. There was raucous laughter from somewhere away in the night. From the far distance the thunder of waves forever breaking on the shore. There was so much less noise in the night that every sound stood out.

After Amita had left he had returned to the market and watched the pimp. He saw which children he ran and where he went with the money. The child Amita had been talking to could not have been more than twelve, but some were even younger.

Every fibre of him wanted to leap out and slaughter the monster that forced them into such labour. He wanted to release the anger piled up inside him. Once upon a time he had seldom been angry, and when he had he would simply *be* angry.

But since she had rejected him, it was as if a dam had been constructed within him and the anger grew behind it. He did not know how much longer he would be able to keep it there before it broke free and consumed everything in its path, including himself. All he could do was relieve the pressure.

The lights in the building across from him were extinguished. Not long now.

The dark windows emitted the sounds of sex. The anger boiled in him.

He strode across the square and pushed on the door. It did not move. He went to the window. It was open. No one would dare steal from this house. He sat on the window ledge and slipped his legs up and over. He pushed off and landed lightly on his toes.

He pulled a small electric torch from his pocket. He flicked it on and its feeble beam penetrated the dark illuminating the furniture. He moved through the door to the entrance hall and climbed the wooden steps, keeping his feet to the supported edges to minimise the possibility of creaking.

As he approached the landing, he flicked off the light and allowed himself time to adjust to the dark. There was the steady animalistic grunting of a man, and a lighter tone in response. It filled the air, reminding him of the incident with Amita.

The room from which the sounds emerged was at the far end of the landing, perhaps ten feet. There were doors on both sides. Valentine reached behind him and pulled a long knife from his belt. He moved to the first entrance and scratched the tip of the knife down the door, making a slight scraping sound.

Nothing happened. He kept at it, slightly increasing the pressure. The sounds from the far room were reaching a crescendo. All the better.

The door handle turned, Valentine stepped back, flat against the wall, knife ready. The head of one of the pimp's heavies poked out.

Valentine's knife slipped smoothly into his neck cutting through his carotid artery, slicing through his oesophagus and trachea.

He kept the knife in place as the man's hands groped for the knife and he choked, unable to breathe. He staggered forwards as the creature in the far room reached his peak.

Valentine grabbed his victim by the arm and dragged him to the floor. He twisted the knife trying to slice between the vertebrae. Metal scraped on bone. Finally he whipped the knife away using the prone man's arm to shield the burst of blood from the artery.

The man on the floor shuddered twice, choking on his blood as it filled his lungs, then lay still. Valentine noted he was naked. And then he headed across to the room opposite, and listened at the door; he did not think the death had been heard. From the room at the end came panting that declined in volume.

"*Hey.*"

Valentine whirled round. The second heavy was behind him *in the same room*. His naked body outlined against light filtering in from a window, his faint shadow across the fallen body in the doorway. Valentine covered the distance between them in moments.

The big man's arm hit him across the left side. Valentine fetched up against the wall and tumbled noisily to the ground. He still held the knife as his opponent reached down and grabbed Valentine round the neck: the huge hand squeezing, crushing his windpipe.

Valentine lashed out but his knife hand was under him, limiting his movement. His lungs cried out for air that could not reach them. Desperate, Valentine pulled his legs in and curled into a ball, pivoting on the hand that crushed his neck he twisted and lashed out with both feet.

They made contact. His assailant's legs were pushed from under him and the man fell on top of Valentine, pinning him down, but the pressure on Valentine's neck was gone. He jerked upwards with his knife, and slid it in deep. But now, with the man's full weight on him, he could not pull it out. The thug gave a long low groan and vomited blood into Valentine's face, and ceased to move.

Valentine lay still beneath the body but there were no sounds of alarm. In fact, no sounds at all. His neck hurt and every breath was a pain. Swallowing felt like trying to force a tennis ball down his throat.

Making as little noise as possible, Valentine pushed himself out from under the body. There was a thud as the head slipped from his chest and struck the floorboards.

Wearily, Valentine climbed to his feet. He glanced around the room and almost jumped out of his skin when he saw the two naked women in the bed. The moonlight from the window highlighted their curves. They were watching him, but did not seem concerned he had just killed the two men who had, most likely, been their lovers less than five minutes before. He went to the basin and rinsed the blood from his face.

He ran his finger across his neck and squeezed slightly, testing the bruising. The skin was inflamed and would no doubt bruise terribly. Every muscle in his body was weak and he leaned against the wall breathing deeply.

In the distance the sound of lovemaking grew in volume again. He was not discovered. He walked to the bed. The women still did not react but stared at him with a dreamy gaze that barely focused. He wiped the blade of his knife on the bed clothes. One of the women reached forward and touched the bloodstain then brought her bloodied fingers to her mouth.

Valentine watched in horrified fascination. She did it again but this time offered her fingers to the other woman who grabbed her hand and licked the blood from them.

Then they smiled at him, inviting him.

He turned away in disgust. He stepped past the bodies and back out into the hall. He sheathed his knife and took out the gun. He crept to the door at the end, timing his footsteps to the moans and groans. He placed his hand on the door handle, and when the next groan floated out he turned it and pushed the door open a little. He took out the torch and ensured he had a firm grip on the gun.

He kicked the door wide and shone the light in.

The bedroom was lavishly decorated—out of place in the building they occupied—there were hanging curtains with tassels, furniture with fine quality upholstery, and delicately carved figurines and statues. But there was too much of it; the place was crammed like an Aladdin's cave of tastelessness.

In the middle of the room was the bed. It was bigger than any bed Valentine had ever seen and the way the light reflected from the sheets they must have been satin. The bed was piled high with cushions.

The months Valentine had spent in the underbelly of society had inured him to the horrors that the dregs of society engaged in. Or so he thought.

The pimp was on the bed, lying on his back, his head was towards Valentine so he had it twisted back and was looking at Valentine upside down. Sitting on the pimp's hips, in the midst of intercourse, was the girl that Amita had been talking to earlier in the day—who was not a girl at all.

Though he tried not to look, his gaze was inexorably drawn to where their bodies were joined. The girl pulled herself away from the pimp, terror in her face.

Sodomites.

Valentine took three steps into the room, slamming the door shut behind him. He waved the gun at the…boy. "You, on the floor, don't move."

She threw herself to the ground face down. Valentine could see her quaking with fear. He looked back at the pimp. Valentine wanted nothing more than to shoot the slime through the head and rip his miserable life from him. He deserved nothing better.

But Valentine needed information. He crossed the remaining distance and held the gun to the man as he lay on his bed, the barrel placed against the middle of his forehead.

"*Sahib*, do not kill me."

"That depends."

"I give you everything. I give you all I have. You want Shashi, you can have Shashi. I give her to you. No charge."

"Shut up."

"Treasures, women, men, boys, little girls: you can have them all. Just do not kill poor Jabir."

Valentine hit him across the temple with the gun. "I said shut up!"

The pimp whimpered with pain.

"What do you know of the slave market?"

"Slavery is illegal, good *sahib*."

Valentine whipped him across the other temple. This time drawing blood which dripped on to the satin sheets.

"If you do not give me a straight answer next time," the words dripped like venom from his mouth, he leaned down close to the man's ear, "I will rip your manhood from you. Do you understand me?"

"Yes, *sahib*, yes, master."

"Where do the slave ships land?"

"In the hills, near Odiyampathu."

"Where exactly?"

"I do not know." He cringed as Valentine raised his gun to strike him again. "It is truth, master, I do not use slaves, I do not know."

Valentine hit him again.

"Why, master?"

"Because I didn't like your answer."

"But it is truth."

"I believed you."

Blood seeped from the pimp's nose. He sniffed and then choked.

"How do they sell them? By auction?"

He nodded.

"Where?"

"I do not know."

Valentine pressed the gun hard into his forehead. The man's eyes crossed as he focused on Valentine's trigger finger.

"Where?"

"It is truth, I do not know. I do not know. I do not know. In the city by the water, is all I know."

"Why shouldn't I kill you?"

Valentine watched the man's face as he tried to find reasons but realised with every thought he had that it was not anything that would sway the man who held a gun to his head. Finally he sobbed. "I have family, *sahib*."

"But you sell children on the street and sodomise this boy?"

"Oh no, *sahib*, Shashi is not boy, he is *hijra*. Woman-man."

Valentine felt sick. "Your family would be better with you dead."

But he could not kill him, he knew that. He could kill someone who was trying to return the favour. But to shoot someone in cold blood, even if he were such an appalling low life. It would make Valentine as bad as the scum in front of him. Besides, he was very tired. The fight had taken away all his energy.

Valentine could see the pimp was confident he was going to be allowed to live.

"Get on your knees."

The look of horror that came over the man gave Valentine a moment's pleasure.

"But, *sahib*, have I not answered your questions with truth?"

"Just do it. I don't have all night."

The man held the side of the bed and lowered his ugly frame into a kneeling position. He broke out into a sweat which stank. Valentine grabbed a satin-cased pillow and placed it against the man's head. He pressed the index finger of his left hand into the pillow, pressing hard against the pimp's skull.

He pointed the gun at the sole of the man's foot.

"Goodbye."

The pimp let out a desperate whimper. Valentine pulled the trigger and shot a hole in his foot. The pimp screamed and went limp, slumping to the floor. Blood flowed from his foot. The boy-girl looked up expecting to see the brains of her owner splattered across the room and stared at the man lying there.

"If he dares warn anyone or comes after me, I will kill him. You tell him that."

The boy-girl nodded.

Valentine stalked out.

iii

Maliha stared into the mirror as Amita oiled her hair, combed it out and plaited it. She knew she needed to stay focused on the dead girl but there was too much happening. It made her uncomfortable.

It was not that she had any objection to Françoise's affections, or indeed to returning them, it was just that the woman was probably suffering from the same sort of "pash" as Valentine had. Although how it could be that two individuals could both feel like that about her she really had no idea.

"The Mistress has asked that you attend her this morning, *sahiba.*"

"All right but we need to visit Aunt Savitha again, perhaps without Françoise. I can't believe she didn't know about the slave girl

- 130 -

hidden in the house." Which reminded her. "The day of the wedding, did you manage to get any information from the staff?"

"Very little, *sahiba*, it was very busy. When I asked about girl, I was ignored. But no question made that she existed."

"So everyone knew," said Maliha. "I may be able to get some of it out of Auntie but she will try to protect anyone she can."

"Yes, *sahiba*," said Amita. "Can I help you with your sari?"

"No, you go and get the carriage ready. Do you think you could get the furnace hot and the steam pressure up?"

"Yes, *sahiba*, and if I have difficulty I will ask Suraj to help."

Maliha looked at her maid in the mirror. "Suraj is one of the gardeners."

"He is very skilled with steam engines."

Amita put down the brush and comb and tied off the yellow ribbon she had intertwined with the plait. She pressed her palms together and left. The sari that she had put out for Maliha was blue and yellow. Maliha spread it out and found the undecorated end. Even after a few weeks of practice it was not second nature after so many years of English clothing.

She needed to practise but preferred to do it without Amita hovering and wanting to help. After a couple of false starts she finally got the pleated *pallu* over her shoulder and headed downstairs.

Her grandmother sat in a chair under an awning in the courtyard. Maliha stood obediently beside her waiting to be spoken to.

When she was young, Maliha had not had a great deal to do with her grandmother. Although, on the one hand, a pale-skinned Glaswegian engineer would have once been a fine catch, things were changing. The British no longer looked favourably on such marriages, and the fact Maliha's mother had gone behind Grandmother's back and been married in a Christian church over the border in British India did not go down well.

Grandfather, as far as Maliha could understand it, had mixed feelings. He had not had to hand over a dowry, which he was happy about. But again, while her father may have been a Scottish engineer, he did not have any connections in French India, so did not advance Grandfather's social standing.

Not that it had anything to do with Maliha, at least not in theory. In practice, since her parents were no longer around, all their reasons for disliking Maliha's mother were visited on her.

"Sit down, Maliha."

She placed herself in a chair as far from her grandmother as possible. It was not unheard of for the old woman to lash out with her walking stick. She did not require it but she affected the need.

"The neighbours are all talking."

Maliha bit her tongue to avoid a sarcastic retort. "Oh?"

"I do not like them talking."

A seagull flew overhead, its shadow moving across the courtyard like an arrow. Maliha knew exactly what her grandmother was fishing for and she was not going to escape this interview without suffering through it.

"What is it they are saying?"

"They are saying that you are unmarriageable."

"That is not something that affects me."

"Not affect you?" The anger burst from the old woman like an explosion. "You shame this family with your ways, your disregard for tradition, and with the insults you lay at the feet of those who come to see your suitability."

"If you had no regard for what they say, Grandmother, then there would be no shame."

"We have a position to think of. How do you think your grandfather can carry out his business if the men he does business with have no respect for him?" Her grandmother lifted up her stick and jabbed the end at her. Maliha was thankful she had chosen to sit sufficiently far that the stick could not reach her.

"A girl has been killed, a child, grandmother."

The old woman waved her hand dismissively. "She was nobody, nothing."

Maliha clenched her fists to hold in her anger. She stood and pulled her arms around herself. "What is it you want, Grandmother? If you want me to take part in your attempts to marry me off, then yes, I will be a good granddaughter and I will sit there." Her vision blurred with tears. "But you will not stop me from finding the truth about the girl."

"I will not bargain with you."

"Then I will move out."

"You have nowhere to go."

Maliha shook her head as if by jumbling the logic of her grandmother's arguments they might fall into a pattern that made sense.

"Grandmother," she started with heated passion. Then she stopped and calmed herself. "Grandmother, you know I love you. But you must understand, I am able to go anywhere, and do anything, I please."

The woman in the chair seemed to deflate. "You will be my death, let alone my shame."

Maliha brushed her tears away with the back of her hand and then knelt on one knee before her grandmother. "I will be a good granddaughter and see the families of your prospective husbands. If I like one of them well enough, and I may, then I will not oppose a marriage. But I will not stop investigating this crime."

The old woman looked her in the eye. "I am tired."

It was a dismissal. Maliha stood, pressed her palms together and headed away.

"A husband will control your foolishness."

No husband of my choosing, thought Maliha as she went inside, she thought of Françoise. *Or wife.*

Then she wondered, if two women lived together as lovers, would they both be wives?

*   *   *

Aunt Savitha was waiting for her. The house was full of life, just as Maliha's grandparents' house was empty of it. Always there were children running about. Relatives visiting.

Once more her aunt took them to the room that looked out inland, and over the courtyard. Maliha went to the window and looked down. The part of the building where the hidden door was situated was single story and not wide. It might be possible to enter it from the outside through a window. She would have to check.

Chai was brought and the two of them sat comfortably on chairs beneath a fan that circulated the warm air.

"Grandmother is insisting I marry," said Maliha.

Aunt Savitha smiled. "She is trying to make up for her failure with your mother."

"My father was a good match."

"But she did not arrange it; she did not oversee it. She could not boast to her friends about how it was all due to her skill." Aunt Savitha took a sip of *chai*. "She was not in control."

Maliha nodded. "She does like to be the one that makes it all happen." She took a drink and then continued. "Renuka said that she and Balaji were born on the same day?"

"More than that, almost the very same time, and in the same place too," Auntie said. "That is why the signs were so positive."

"The same place?"

"The Lady Lansdowne Hospital in Madras," said her aunt.

Maliha shook her head, not understanding.

"The British Queen sent her servants to better the medical services for the women of India. It is a hospital they built."

"But Madras? Was there not one closer?"

"It was thought best." Her aunt's reply was curt.

Maliha returned to the earlier issue. "But the astrological signs did not predict what happened at the wedding."

Auntie's face fell at the reminder. She shook her head and took another drink from her cup.

"You would think something so catastrophic would show up in the chart."

Her aunt did not answer but her grip on the cup had tightened with each word.

"Who was she, Auntie?"

Aunt Savitha held her hand up to ward off Maliha's question and looked away from her niece. Maliha put down her cup and got to her feet. Just as she had with her grandmother, she knelt down in front of her aunt.

"Grandmother has a lot to say on the subject of shame, Auntie," said Maliha quietly. "She blames me for everything bad that happens in the family. I would not be surprised if she blames me for what happened at the wedding."

"No, Maliha, that shame is not yours." Then, as if she were forcing the words out through sheer will power: "That fault is mine."

Maliha had had enough experience with people confessing their deepest secrets she knew that now was the time for stillness. The truth would come. She could almost see the desperate need to speak wrestling with the shame of the words to be spoken. Aunt Savitha glanced up at her face and looked away again when she saw Maliha looking at her.

"It is my shame, Maliha," she said finally, the words coming out in fits and starts then all in a rush. "I am not the wife your uncle wanted."

"Uncle takes pleasure in beating women."

Savitha jerked her head up and looked at Maliha, almost as if she was going to deny it, but then she bowed her head and nodded. Maliha studied her aunt's shoulders and realised her blouses always covered her entire back. Maliha had not noticed before because that was the way it had always been.

Without asking permission, Maliha reached up and lifted her aunt's blouse away from her neck. She slipped her hand beneath it and ran her hands across her aunt's skin and felt the scar ridges.

Tears ran down her aunt's face and fell to the floor.

"You let him beat you—for how many years?"

"Always."

"Why?"

"If I had not he would have beaten another, perhaps Renuka, or Parvati, or Purvaji. I had to protect my daughters," she said.

"Did you enjoy it?"

Her aunt hesitated, she glanced at Maliha. "I…I don't know. At first I did it because it was my duty—"

"Duty?" Maliha could not keep the outrage from her voice.

"I was young, Maliha. I did not know about men, about life, about husbands. And after a while, I came to believe I did like it. It gave my husband pleasure, and is that not what a wife must do? Give her husband what he desires?"

Maliha bit her tongue on what she wanted to say, instead she said. "What happened?"

"It was an accident. He struck me and something broke, inside." She held her hand to her midriff. "The doctor came and said I had an internal injury. That it must stop."

"The doctor *knew*?" But, of course, how could he not know? That explained why Aunt Savitha had travelled to Madras to bear her children, otherwise too many people would find out.

"My shame is beyond all, Maliha."

"So Uncle bought a slave that he could beat instead." She did not hide the contempt in her voice. But her aunt shook her head.

"No, he did not.

Maliha frowned.

"You must understand, Maliha, he would have beaten my girls. He would have done it to Renuka."

Maliha blinked. "*You* bought the girl."

Savitha hung her head. "And now I must let him beat me again, otherwise he will do it to Parvati. She is only ten years old, Maliha. I cannot let him do that. You see that."

"No." Maliha stood up, shaking her head. "No, I do not see that, Auntie. This is madness. It is you who does not see."

Maliha looked down at her aunt. She seemed so tiny, and shrivelled up, as if she had no substance. Nothing like the woman who used to fill the house with her presence.

"It is Uncle Pratap who must stop. He is the one who carries the shame, not you."

"I am insufficient as his wife."

"No. You are strong. You bore the pain all those years. You have committed sins, yes, but only to suit his perverted needs. He is the wrong that must be undone."

Aunt Savitha held her head in her hands. Her voice was hoarse with crying. "There is nothing that can be done."

"If you let him beat you and he kills you, who will protect Parvati and Purvaji then?"

"You must protect them, Maliha. You are strong."

"No, Aunt Savitha. I love you, and I love my cousins. But I will not let you sacrifice yourself because you think they will be protected. You must protect them; you are their mother. Not me."

Maliha turned away and went to the door. She paused and looked back.

"Did she have a name?"

The tear-stained face of her aunt looked up in confusion.

"The girl, did she have a name?"

"She said her name was Riette."

Maliha pursed her lips and nodded, then without another word, she left the room. She had not lied, of course, only implied she would not step in. If her aunt died at the hands of her husband, no force upon the earth would stop Maliha from avenging that death as well. Her cousins would be completely safe.

iv

"I'm sorry, Grandmother, I will not be available."

Maliha sat at the table with her grandparents. The sun was low in the sky and its light angled through the windows throwing long bright patches and wide shadows across the tiled floor.

"What do you mean?" snapped her grandmother. "The Nayyars are a prestigious family and their son is very handsome. They are doing us a very great honour by ignoring the trouble you've been."

"Yes, and I'm sure they are thinking of a considerable dowry to compensate."

Maliha glanced at her grandfather but he was studiously ignoring the conversation around him. He was a good businessman, and as such he knew when to keep his nose out of a conversation.

"I am going to Madras for a few days."

"Madras? Why? How will you get there? You promised you would make yourself available to interested in-laws."

"As to why, Grandmother, I am investigating the girl's death, as you know."

"In Madras?"

"Wherever it takes me."

"So your promise means nothing?"

Maliha bristled. "I will keep my word. But you will have to rearrange the meeting for when I return."

"It will take you a week to get there and another week to return," said Grandmother. "Unless you plan to take that monstrous carriage of yours."

Maliha smiled. It would take a week if she was walking, and the steam carriage would have problems since the roads were not built for a heavy machine like that.

"I'm flying," she said, and enjoyed the silence. "I'll be back in three days."

* * *

Amita rode in the back of the carriage as usual; it was preferable. When her mistress had driven the vehicle on to the ferry, scaring goats, children and some adults, Amita had prayed the brakes would work. She knew that her fear was not the fault of her mistress, who seemed to have excellent control. But that was the difficulty: Her skill meant that she had no fear, and she was quite incautious.

It reminded Amita of the way she had been after flying in Valentine's air-plane. Amita thought of him as Valentine, though it was very presumptuous of her. But it was only in her mind, as long as she never addressed him that way. But her mistress loved to fly; it made her so happy.

Now they were approaching the air-dock. The second time for Amita, though this time she was not wearing rags and was unlikely to be mistaken for a whore.

She hoped they would not encounter Valentine, after seeing her mistress kissing the French girl—and Amita suspected they had been kissing again when they went to the girl's house and the two of them had disappeared for a considerable time. Her mistress had returned with a slightly breathless air. Valentine was still very unhappy about what had happened, that much was clear, and if Maliha had found someone new? No good would come of this.

That they were now going to fly did nothing to settle Amita's mind. She had heard the phrase butterflies in the stomach, now she understood it. It was not as pleasant as the words might suggest.

Maliha brought the vehicle to a rumbling halt at the gate of the air-dock and conversed for a few moments with the uniformed guard who directed them along a road that ran parallel, but inside, the fence that enclosed the air-dock.

There was a large Zeppelin tied down on the main field. The skin of its envelope rippled in the light wind. Amita had seen her mistress with the captain of the *Hansa*. It was a huge vessel that plied the passenger routes from Indonesia to Germany. And at the Fortress there were the British liners and military vessels with their huge rotors. This Zeppelin was not as big as any of those.

They passed behind a warehouse and the next gap revealed a set of smaller ice cargo ships, they all had the same colours painted on them so must belong to one company. Again her view was blocked. At the next junction Maliha turned right towards the airfield. They came around the end of another building and stopped.

In front of them was a machine that looked like a huge bird, with a chimney emitting wisps of smoke. Amita did not have time to stare. Her mistress disengaged the Faraday and normal weight returned. Amita opened her door, jumped lightly down from the carriage and opened the door then took Maliha's hand to help her descend.

While Maliha no longer needed her walking stick—the strange encounter with the guru had improved her injury in some fashion— there were still situations in which she was awkward and getting down from the carriage was one of those. Amita glanced at the metal bird. It rested on three wheels and there were steps up to the entrance. Maliha would need help there as well.

Françoise came around the front of the carriage. She wore a practical dress with a corset, entirely appropriate for travel. Her mistress was travelling light but Miss Françoise had four large pieces of luggage.

Maliha strode off across the grass towards the winged air-plane. Amita studied it, the resemblance to a bird was not just passing, as it even had feathers. The wings were folded back with the ends resting on the ground, but at the rear it had propellers.

Three men emerged from the building. Amita was pleased to see they were all Indian. There was something satisfying about having her people in command, instead of the British—or French.

Amita unloaded the luggage from the carriage as her mistress and her friend spoke to the men. There was lots of smiling. She saw Maliha gesture in her direction and one of the men broke away from the group and came over.

"*Namaste*," he said, and pressed his palms together. She nodded and copied him. She turned away to hide the smile she couldn't keep from her face. He was a handsome and strong fellow. "Which of the bags shall I take?"

Amita could barely get over the thrill of being spoken to as a person. The gardener was nice but even he had a certain superior attitude in the way he spoke with her.

She indicated several of the bags, the ones belonging to Françoise. He managed to get them all, with one under each arm and one in each hand. Maliha had a single large case and a small one for extras, while Amita just had the one. She did not own a great deal— though even what little there was was far more than in her past.

The rest of the party made their way to the vehicle, as Amita drew near. One of the men wore a captain's hat that had seen better days. He climbed aboard first. The other man handed Maliha and Françoise into the ship before climbing in himself.

Her man had gone around the other side of the bird and was loading the luggage into a smaller compartment. She handed her items to him. His hand brushed hers and she glanced away demurely. It was only a game, but one that she was enjoying. She looked up and saw Maliha's head through one of the wide windows forward of the articulated joint where the wing went into the body of the air-plane.

There was a whirring as the propeller at the rear started up. It ran up to speed quickly and whined. The man grabbed her hand. She looked at him—there was too much noise for speech—he pointed round the front of the vehicle. He did not release her hand and they went at a run round the front. Then he handed her up into the interior. There was a short corridor. The sound of a whirring engine came from the right. He pushed against her as he climbed aboard, and she moved to give him space.

He pulled the door shut and pointed forward. She took a few steps and went through into a cabin with four pairs of seats. Maliha and Françoise were sitting together at the front. Amita's mistress was looking intently at the controls and talking to the pilot. It seemed to Amita that Françoise did not look comfortable perched on the interior seat, only able to see out of the front window.

Amita sat at the back in the rearmost seat that backed against a wooden wall. She could feel it vibrating with the energies of the air-plane's steam furnace and…whatever else it had to drive it.

Her man was also a pilot because he took the second seat at the front. He took up a sheaf of papers with maps and many circular lines drawn on them: The navigator.

The vehicle shuddered and a shadow went across the window. Amita jumped and looked out. The wing had lifted from the ground and was moving up and down. Practice flaps, she thought, to make sure it's all working properly.

Her navigator jumped out of his seat and spoke briefly to Maliha and Françoise. They looked to be doing something around their waist. She looked and saw there was a belt. She found the ends and buckled them, clinching it tight about her waist. The navigator came back along the seats to where she sat. He reached over and checked her belt, then saucily ran his hand along her leg.

She looked at him wide-eyed as if she were horrified. He just grinned and winked.

He turned away and she breathed out a shaky breath. She realised her hands were shaking and it was not because he had touched her. She was scared.

The air-plane screamed and Amita jumped again, then realised it was just the steam-whistle. The Faraday was engaged and she lightened. While she was no expert this one seemed to be full strength; she was as light as she was on an atmospheric.

The vehicle shuddered, the shadow crossed the window in the blink of an eye and the plane hopped. The propeller engine whined shrilly, the noise penetrating into their cabin. Another sweep of the wings and it jumped again. This time she was pressed back into her seat. She looked outside as the wings beat again and again. The ship surged on every stroke, the ground dropped away and slid backwards. The coastline came into view beyond the dunes and within moments they were crossing the beach and swooping across the sea.

Amita realised she had been holding her breath and breathed out suddenly. She unclenched her hands. The wings ceased to beat and it was as if they were soaring gulls. Amita looked down. There were fishing boats on the water and she could see dark shapes beneath the waves.

She looked up and forward, but could see only sky.

Amita decided she did not like flying.

*   *   *

"Are you comfortable?" said her navigator as he sat down next to her. Maliha had moved up and was sitting in his chair at the front. The pilot was gesticulating and pointing at different controls.

Françoise looked round and glanced at the navigator sitting next to her. It gave Amita a little burst of pleasure to think that Françoise was sitting alone, while she—the servant—was not.

"No."

He smiled. "You would rather be on the ground than soar like a bird."

"Yes."

"Your mistress understands machines."

Amita shrugged. "She understands everything."

He nodded. "Her father was the engineer."

"Yes."

"The one that died in the fire."

"Yes."

"You don't say much."

Amita looked away and shook her head. She was holding her hands together tightly for fear they would tremble and he would see it.

"You're scared?"

She looked down at the wooden floor, scuffed and dirtied by many feet. She felt his hand on her shoulder.

"I have to go back up front in a minute. We'll be landing soon."

She looked back at him. "Already?" She couldn't keep the note of hope from her voice.

"It's only eighty miles, just a little hop for our bird."

She said nothing and his grip on her shoulder became firmer. He gained confidence as she had not stopped him.

"Look, if your mistress does not need you. You could find me. She's engaged us for three days so we'll be doing nothing tomorrow. I could show you the whole ship."

"I don't think…" She had been going to say that she had to stay with Maliha in case she was needed. But she glanced forward and saw Maliha squeezing by Françoise to sit down in her chair again. "I don't know."

He gave her shoulder a final squeeze and stood up. He faced her for a moment. "If you can. I'll see you in a couple of days anyway."

Amita smiled at him. He turned and went forward. She watched him climb into the chair.

The vessel bucked. A wave of terror shot through her and she grabbed the back of the chair in front. The engine's whine descended through the scales until it was a low hum, the wings arched upwards and the weight that remained in her stomach—after the Faraday had taken most of it away—tried to lift through her lungs.

She felt sick, and through the forward window she could now see the coast line and the city of Madras. The ship rocked to the right and the horizon twisted.

Amita closed her eyes and clung to the chair.

It was over soon. There had been more rocking to left and right, dips and climbs as the wings beat or they glided. She heard the roar of something outside and for a moment blinked her eyes open to see a British sky-liner thundering past so close she thought they would be ripped apart on its rotors.

She slammed her eyes shut again.

A few minutes later and motors in the wall behind her roared and there was a series of jerks that seemed to want to push her through the floor, and then quiet. Steam pressure vented with a steady hiss. There was a final creak as the wings moved. She opened her eyes and saw they were in another air-dock. Or was it the one they had left? It seemed they all looked the same.

She tried to get up and realised she was still buckled in place. She fumbled with the belt and got it undone as her navigator came down the aisle and opened the door to the passage. He went out of sight but she heard the outside door opening and the crash as the stairs were folded out.

She climbed unsteadily to her feet. She glanced to where Maliha was talking to the pilot again. She made a decision and clambered out through the door to the exit. He wasn't there so she stumbled down the steps and stood on solid ground.

She took a deep breath. She had not realised how stuffy it was in the air-plane.

A steam carriage detached itself from the buildings ahead and bumped across the grass towards them. It was much larger than her mistress's vehicle. The driver and another man were in uniform in the front. There was a passenger compartment in the middle and the furnace, perhaps with a stoker, at the rear.

"Miss Anderson's party?" said the driver. Amita nodded. "Luggage?" She pointed round the back, and the second man jogged off. Maliha was at the entrance. Françoise was helping her down. Amita scowled.

The luggage was quickly loaded, and the three climbed aboard. It was luxurious with settees and armchairs—though they were all bolted down.

The vehicle bumped off across the grass and whisked them the short distance to a hotel. They had a suite.

Maliha and Françoise went down to dinner. Amita ate in the room.

v

Valentine placed the cleaned and oiled gun on his case, and sat back in his chair. The sun was low in the sky and there were light clouds. According to the almanac tonight was almost a new moon; it would be dark. Clouds would help.

He picked up the map again. The British Ordnance Survey produced excellent maps using their airships, even of Pondicherry. He had circled an area inland: some hills between a lake and the river.

From his own experience he knew that navigating an air-vessel was not easy. In fact it carried the same difficulties as sea navigation and used many of the same solutions. When he had flown all the way to the Americas he had used dead-reckoning over the ocean.

He'd never told Maliha how close he came to ditching in the sea through sheer exhaustion when he'd carried her precious cargo to New York. Only the constant prodding of the Thai princess had kept him awake. He'd planned the return journey more carefully and flown via Russian Alaska and the Japanese islands.

Over land, as long as you had a map and major landmarks to follow, things were easier. Generally you followed rivers, roads and the atmospherics. Or the coastline.

He looked at the map. The information that piece of vermin had provided him with had given a general area. Then it was a matter of asking the question: *If I wanted to hide an air-dock, where would I put it?*

The answer came slowly: Not along any major route, which meant not near the coast, a road or river, and Pondicherry had many of those. The area he had been told about was distant enough from them.

There were no major highlands to avoid but there were hills, and hills had valleys in which ships could be hidden. However even the ships arriving secretly must be able to navigate which meant they had to follow landmarks. And they would be flying at night, which most honest pilots avoided.

So, a smaller river or road running into the hills from a major one, or even better, the sea, would be ideal. The ship would arrive as normal, look as if it were following the usual route, and then turn away. It would head into the hills and disappear.

But there was more than one way to skin a cat. The hidden air-dock would need supplies of coal and perhaps diesel, as well as food.

He stood up, put on his jacket and pocketed his gun. He ran his hand across his chin. He had shaved it all off after Amita had tidied his hair but it had grown again and rasped like sandpaper. No time now.

He folded up the map and shoved it into another pocket. He put his wallet in an inside pocket. A hat was essential in this climate and he had opted for a Fedora when once he would have worn a bowler. He growled to himself as he went out and locked the door.

He had resigned from the Foreign Office but found himself working for them again in an unofficial capacity. It was not that the British Government had come to him; he had sought out Sir Bertram in his club and asked to come back, and he had been accepted as a roving agent on retainer.

It was the complete lack of a proper conclusion to the Guru Nadesh case that was the problem. At least that was what Valentine told himself. He'd killed Nadesh with his own hands, the reason why Maliha had rejected him, but Nadesh had been working for someone else, a Terence Timmons, and he became Valentine's target.

If he could track down this Timmons and bring him to justice then perhaps Maliha would forgive him. He shook his head. What did it matter? She was not the kind to change her mind. She always had to have her own way. She was infuriating, delicate, with a mind like a scalpel, and a tongue like a lash.

He looked up and discovered he'd come to a stop outside the building. He wished she would stop preying on his mind. She was the one who had sent him away. She had pushed him out of her life. If she wanted him back she could damn well tell him so.

He set off in the direction of the air-dock but not for any sort of air-plane.

Near the entrance to the dock was a carriage hire establishment. He quickly negotiated for their smallest trap and handed over a deposit. The horse was put in harness and its eyes covered by blinkers. The animal was a bit on the thin side but Valentine gave it a check; it was fit enough and followed his actions with interest but no complaint. Good, the beast wasn't too nervy.

He jumped up on to the two seat bench. It was padded but the stuffing was old and thin. It didn't matter. He checked his pocket watch. It was a couple of hours before dark, that should provide plenty of time.

He set the mare off at a comfortable trot, a rate that would cover the distance without tiring the animal.

They left the town behind and headed north towards the ferry. The horse must have crossed the river many times and had no trouble with the noisy steamer. Still, with the blinkers it couldn't see the huge paddles turning. Valentine climbed down and kept hold of the bridle, just to ensure it couldn't turn its head.

He'd get this over with, send a message to Maliha via Amita, and then continue with his mission. The cargo ship he was currently signed to lifted in the morning, heading for South Africa. It was one that had missing time on its record. It was one of those things you wouldn't notice unless you were looking for abnormalities. He had spent weeks studying the itineraries and official manifests of Timmons' fleet. And there were discrepancies.

Of course a secret air-dock would be just the sort of thing Timmons would need if his fleet was involved in criminal activities. But there was no specific reason to think his investigation and Maliha's were related.

She was just solving a suicide. He shook his head, almost in disbelief. It was just like her to want to solve a death that was not a murder. She could be quite perverse. Like throwing him out for defending her virtue.

On the far side of the river he turned left instead of heading towards the city. The road was little more than a well-used dirt track but the horse stepped lightly long it and the suspension on the cart was sufficient to make the uneven terrain tolerable.

They passed through several villages, attracting the attention of all the dwellers that probably didn't see a white face from one month to the next, despite the fact they were ruled by the whites. He stopped at one village where the river bank was a gentle slope down to the water. He unhitched the horse, led her down to the water and, keeping hold of the reins, let her go. She walked a few steps into the sluggish current and began to drink. He kept an eye out for crocodiles.

Village children edged nervously down the slope, standing in a group watching him in silence. He smiled at them and their faces broke into grins revealing their white teeth.

The horse had finished drinking. Valentine grabbed the halter and brought her head round. He felt something touch his foot. He looked down and found a little girl bent over double, her hands on his foot.

He fought off the impulse to pull away. He knew it was a sign of respect, but it was so un-British. She didn't move, then he remembered and touched her head. She bounced upright, and stared at the horse then back at him.

"You want a ride?" he said.

She looked at him without understanding. He pointed at the horse's back; her eyes grew even wider. He took that as a yes and lifted her—she weighed almost nothing—and placed her on the horse. She knelt on the wide back then clung on as he brought the horse round and led it back up the slope.

The other children were laughing and clapping and shouting in what he supposed was Hindi. The girl laughed between moments

when the horse's motion caught her off balance and she had to cling
on again.

He lifted her down and she jabbered to the others, some of
whom were looking at him hopefully. But he did not have time. He
shook his head sadly, and their faces dropped. He got the horse
hitched up again and set off, waving to the crowd of children.

There were adults who had watched the whole thing from the
safety of their homes, barely more than shacks. They pressed their
palms as he passed. He had always thought of it as being like a
military salute. Anyway Maliha would have been proud of him, he
thought. If she considered him at all.

By the end of the second hour the light was going but he was
approaching the hills which lay to the north, with the river still on his
left. He looked for a route that would take him into the hills. The
maps were good but they did not have every minor path.

There was a wooden bridge across a tributary to the river and
just past it a rough track leading towards the hills.

He looked at them and wondered at his foolhardiness. Did he
really think he could find the right valley in these hills while on foot?
In the dark? He sighed and kept on; at least he would get as far as he
could before it became too dark to drive the cart.

It reached the point where he could no longer see where he was
going. He'd packed some fruit but nothing more to eat. He shook his
head in dismay at his own unpreparedness.

He unhitched the horse and stripped off the tack, leaving just
the bridle. He created a makeshift hobble from a strap and put it
round the horse's front legs to stop her wandering too far. He
managed to find some bits of wood for a small fire, cleared a space
and got it going.

He ate the fruit and stared into the fire. What was he doing? She
wouldn't appreciate him interfering anyway, so what difference did it

make? Just stay the night here, go back in the morning, and get back on board for the trip to South Africa.

The cart would be better for sleeping in, or on, even though it was small. There were too many ways to die in India what with the snakes and scorpions, not to mention leopards and elephants.

With the night being so dark, the sky was filled with stars and the Milky Way was a creamy strip running across it. He had spoken to a Royal Navy Void-sailor one time who had told him that no matter how many stars you could see here on Earth, twinkling in the night, out in the void there were so many more, and they did not flicker but lay embedded like diamonds in the firmament.

A cloud moved across the sky blotting out a section of the stars. He should probably try to get some sleep, though the cart was far from comfortable. He closed his eyes but something was nagging at him.

He opened his eyes again. The cloud had moved. It had surprisingly regular lines. He watched it gliding across the sky, utterly silent, the way that clouds are utterly silent. He licked his finger and held it up. There was a slight breeze, but only a slight one and it was at almost right angles to the way the cloud was moving.

The cloud was perfectly rectangular. It was big and completely on its own. Not another one in the sky. The moon was not quite new and a sliver of it still showed. And, as the cloud crossed the sky, there was a reflection of the moon along its side.

Valentine jumped up, found his bag, and made sure he had his gun. The ship was drifting towards the hills behind him. He needed to hurry. He took a line on its direction of travel and then chased after it through the dark, stumbling and tripping across the uneven ground.

Although the vessel seemed to be just drifting it soon merged with the hills ahead and was lost to sight. Valentine studied the stars above the point where it had disappeared and spotted the tail of Ursa Minor pointing almost directly at the place.

Of course the constellation would move as time wore on but he hoped he would get to the location before that became a problem. Besides it seemed to be following the course of the tributary he had been following just as he had expected.

Now that he didn't have to keep watching the sky he made better progress. He simply glanced up every now and then to ensure he was staying on the right line. He reached the lower slopes of the hills and climbed steadily towards the summit.

When he reached the top he found he was pointing more west than he intended and adjusted his route across the gently rolling hill. It seemed reasonable to assume they would have patrols so he took out his gun, though in the silence of the night he would rather not use it.

He reached the summit, still without any sign of life, and started down the other side.

Finally he reached a point where the slope of the hill was such that he could see down into the valley. Or rather, in the dark of the night, he could see there was not a single light in the thick blackness that lay there. Only the strip of the river was visible, reflecting the sky as it wound its way up the valley.

He sat down, setting the gun down beside him.

He should just go back. *Giving up so easily, Valentine?* That was easy for her to say, what would she have done? *Not gone traipsing across the countryside without information or a plan.* Yes, well, she wasn't here. He was tired. And having an imaginary conversation with his ex—

whatever she was—really was of no help unless she was right. Was there something he should be thinking about?

He stood up and looked at the hills and the valley.

If he was right about following the river then there was no reason they should stop here, just at the entrance to the valley. In fact that was exactly the wrong place; they would easily be visible since that was no small vessel. It must have been the size of a big Zeppelin at least.

All right, so they follow the river and not stop until they've at least gone round the bend. He looked further up the valley, to where the dark line of the river turned to the right. Just there.

I'll go that far and if there's still nothing, I'll go back, he thought to himself.

He set off along the hill rather than go down into the valley: too much chance of meeting another person, or stumbling into a marsh.

Thirty minutes later the constellations had moved several more degrees in the sky and he was reaching the point where he would be able to see around the bend in the valley. His tiredness was getting to him. He drifted off a couple of times even as he walked. The air was warm and, if he wasn't mistaken, getting warmer. Clouds were building slowly from the south. It might not be monsoon but it still rained.

If it started to rain before he got back there was a risk of getting lost, but he'd worry about that when it happened.

The corner of the valley opposite dropped away as he moved forward, revealing the new part of the valley bit by bit. He saw the shadows of trees first, lying long and flat. The light behind them came into view. Under the glow of electric lights stood a fenced compound. It was big enough to accommodate a number of buildings, including an estate house. The ship he had seen lay on the ground, dwarfing the buildings and the house. It was larger than the biggest Zeppelin he had ever seen and was of no design he recognised.

It did not appear to have any national flag or insignia on it that he could make out. The side of the ship had a huge hatch in it which was folded down. A few figures stumbled out. They were tied and dark-skinned like shadows. An armed man drove them forwards. He struck one that was lagging behind the others and drove him to his knees.

Valentine felt a tightening in his throat; the anger welled up. There was perhaps nothing more despicable in the world than slavers. He stood up.

What do you think you're doing, Valentine?

There was a movement in the foreground, at the base of the hill on which he sat. Two men with dogs, and rifles across their shoulders.

What good will you do anyone if you're dead?

Valentine watched as the slaver pounded the butt of his rifle into the back of the prone slave. He ground his teeth. The two guards walked along the line of the hill two hundred yards below him. He could hear the murmur of their voices.

A bark from one of the dogs echoed up the slope. It was a warning. He ducked down so that he was not silhouetted against the stars. The dog barked again and the men stopped, peering up the hill.

Valentine barely dared to breathe. The dog barked again and then yelped as one of the guards gave it a kick. *You should trust your dog*, Valentine thought to himself. Kicking it wouldn't encourage it to do its job right.

The guards walked on.

But then I would not want them to. He looked up again at the compound. He wondered briefly whether this place was British territory. The control of land around Pondicherry was complicated, but even if it was British, the French would most certainly take exception to a raid.

There was nothing he could do here that would not get him killed. The slaves were alive for now.

He took one final look at the ship and shook his head. There was nothing about it that made sense. Its design did not mark it as belonging to any major nation, unless the Chinese or perhaps one of the South American countries were building new types of ship.

The size of it was astonishing and its means of lift and propulsion were unclear. Only the British had mastered complete nullification of gravity, and that was itself a secret—an open secret, it was true, but no nation on earth currently admitted to its existence. And yet though this vessel floated, it did not use any balloon system; the only other vessels that could do that were the ones with the Tesla-Rutherford designs.

Either their secret had got out and was already in use, or these people had a completely new method of flight. Either way they were dangerous and he needed to make a report to his superiors. And again, he could not do that if he was dead.

Reluctantly, he turned away and headed back along the hillside the way he had come.

CHAPTER 6

i

"Are you going to tell me why we're here?" asked Françoise as she helped Maliha down from the carriage.

The hotel had been pleasant. Madras was a much more cosmopolitan location than Pondicherry, a difference that was mostly the fault of French indifference—though the destruction the British had visited on the place had not helped.

"Research," said Maliha. "Information."

"About what?"

"Someone wanted to disrupt the wedding; I want to know why."

"At a hospital?"

"Next door."

Maliha instructed the driver to remain, as she would be requiring further transport, then strode towards the hospital with Françoise in her wake. The Lady Lansdowne Hospital was an imposing Victorian building of polished red sandstone. It was untouched by any thought of Indian sensibilities, and would have been perfectly at home in the centre of Manchester. Sitting next to it was the office of the Registrar for Births, Deaths and Marriages.

"I'm afraid this will all be in English," said Maliha.

"I'll do my best to follow it."

The doors were oak with stained glass windows depicting scrolls with illuminated writing. Maliha pushed one open and entered the open foyer. The Gothic exterior was repeated inside with pillars, tiles, and wrought iron. On the right was a polished oak cubbyhole for the doorman. He was British through and through, probably ex-Army, sporting an impressive and well-trimmed moustache.

"Can I help you, young ladies?" he said. "The hospital for women of Indian birth is next door."

Maliha paused to assess the man. She did not think he spoke out of malice; most women could not read so the opportunity for error was high. Instead of becoming angry she smiled and spoke in her most cultivated English, practised in the most prestigious of girls' schools in England. "Thank you but I can assure you that I am in the right place. I am researching family lineage."

His change of gears was visible. There was a type of person who responded to the right voice from the right class, even if she did not have quite the right colour, and he was one of those.

"Of course, Miss?"

"Anderson. And this is *Mam'selle* Greaux," she said. "If you would be so kind as to direct us to the archives?"

The man gave her directions and they set off through the building. They took the stairs down into the vaults where one of the administrative staff directed them to the shelves for the correct year.

"What are we looking for?" asked Françoise as Maliha lifted down three books covering the right period. She knew Renuka's date of birth but there was no harm in gathering additional data.

"Anything of interest."

"How will I know what is interesting?"

"Something will catch your eye."

"And if it doesn't?"

"Then there was nothing interesting."

Maliha started two months before the births and gave Françoise the registry for the month after. "Work backwards."

They were silent for a while. Maliha ran her finger down each page noting names and children. There were a frightening number of still births, children who died in child birth along with their mothers.

Perhaps having a child was not a wise move, although medicine had certainly advanced a long way in the last few years. Françoise proceeded much more slowly.

One of the staff came by and offered to fetch them some water. There was also English tea and some dry biscuits.

Maliha reached the page that should have had Renuka and Balaji's births. She turned the page expectantly and frowned. She turned back and checked the dates between the pages.

"That's interesting," she said, Françoise looked up. "They're not here."

She lifted the book so she could examine it more carefully, and checked to see if any of the pages had been remove. They had not.

"It will be a mistake," said Françoise.

"No, it's not a mistake. Let me see that book."

Françoise passed it to her. Maliha flicked quickly through the pages and nodded to herself, then checked the other earlier book they'd brought. She held them together and examined their spines.

"Take a look," she said to Françoise and laid out the books open side by side.

The woman looked at the open pages and shrugged. "I do not see."

"Not the individual pages. Look at each book as a complete item."

Françoise picked up each book and flicked through it in turn, she sighed and looked unimpressed. "I see nothing."

Maliha laid them out again, closed. "Just look at them."

Françoise did, and then looked back at Maliha and shook her head. Maliha sighed.

She picked up one of them. "This one, the one that is missing Renuka and Balaji's births, is different to the others."

"I see no difference."

"Look at the handwriting at the beginning, and at the end."
Françoise complied. "Now the middle, look at any page in the book
you like."

There was a long pause while Françoise examined and
compared. "They are the same handwriting on each page."

"Exactly."

"Why would they not be?"

"Look at the others, they change. It's the same people filling in
the book but they change regularly, every few pages. But this one,"
she held it up triumphantly. "The same hand throughout."

The realisation suddenly hit Françoise. "Someone has copied it."

"And left out Renuka and Balaji." Maliha felt the excitement
wash over her; at last they were getting somewhere.

"But," said Françoise. "I think they are the same sort of book."

"Yes, they look as if they're the same age. This wasn't recent."

"Perhaps the original book was damaged and it's just a
coincidence they missed out those two."

Maliha laughed. "A coincidence? I don't believe in them."

"But why would someone do that?"

"To hide something," Maliha said. "Come on."

They took the books back and replaced them. Then Maliha led
the way back to the foyer, walking faster than her walking stick would
have permitted. They went outside into the sun and then crossed to
the hospital and went inside. The two buildings had the same
architect but the hospital was built on a much grander scale.

Instead of a doorman there was a woman in uniform at a
reception desk. She looked up as Maliha crossed the floor, and pasted
a welcoming smile on to her face. It did nothing to improve her rigid
bearing.

"Yes, dear? Do you have an appointment to see the doctor?"
She looked down at a book on her desk. "We're not expecting
anyone; have you got the right day?"

"*I beg your pardon?*"

The woman's head jerked up at the lash of Maliha's outraged and very English tone. Rapidly reassessing her assumptions, she murmured. "Nobody can see a doctor without an appointment."

"Do I look as if I am with child?" Maliha said, spreading her arms, for once pleased that her middle was exposed.

"Well…"

"Let's start again, shall we?"

The woman nodded.

"My name is Maliha Anderson. I am investigating a death on behalf of Commissioner Abelard of the Sûreté of Pondicherry. This is my assistant, *Mam'selle* Françoise Greaux. And just to ensure there is no misunderstanding, I am neither married nor pregnant—" the woman flinched at the word "—and I am here in a purely professional capacity as an investigator. Is that quite clear?"

"Yes, Miss Anderson."

"Good." Maliha allowed herself to relax and spoke in a gentler tone. "Now, I have just been to the Registrar next door and they were immensely helpful, but I have some questions in regard to a birth here a few years ago. So I wondered if there was somebody I might speak to?"

"Of course, Miss Anderson. Perhaps if I were to fetch Matron?"

"Well, perhaps we might not need to bother her yet. If I give you more details you can decide who would be best?" Maliha did not wait for her to agree. "I am looking for a midwife who would have been in attendance sixteen years ago."

"Oh, that's quite a long time. I'll have to get Mrs Wyndham."

Mrs Wyndham turned out to be a lady of some forty years who worked as a volunteer looking after the administration. The whole hospital was a charity based on a command by Queen Victoria when she heard that Indian women suffered considerably during pregnancy and childbirth.

While they waited Mrs Wyndham went through the records. Maliha realised it had been some time since they had eaten and they really must see about some luncheon when they were finished here.

"The midwife was a Mary O'Donnell. She moved on in 1897."

"Do you have an address?"

"I can't imagine she'd still be there."

Maliha smiled. "It's the nature of police investigations to follow every possible lead."

"But you're working for the French, Miss Anderson," she said as she copied out the name on to a pad in a clear hand, gave the ink a few moments to dry and then ripped off the sheet.

Maliha shrugged. "My family live in Pondicherry but my father was Scottish."

"It must be very exciting being a police*woman*."

Maliha folded the paper and pushed it into her reticule. "Sadly not as exciting as you might think. And some of it is quite terrible."

"Oh, I'm sure it is," the tone of prurient delight was unmistakable. "Are you staying in Madras long? I have a circle of friends who would love to meet you."

Maliha stood up, Françoise followed suit. "Unfortunately my airplane heads back as soon as I've completed my investigations here. No time for socialising."

Mrs Wyndham was quite crestfallen, but Maliha was grateful; she could not think of anything worse than being surrounded by a bunch of women panting for gossip. Then she thought of her grandmother's bride viewings. No, even they were less unpleasant; at least she was not required to speak.

"Perhaps another time," said Maliha, which seemed to perk the woman up. Maliha had no intention of returning to Madras.

They took their leave. Maliha made a point of smiling at the receptionist, thanking her for her assistance and saying goodbye; there was no point in leaving someone disgruntled.

As they reached the exit the cry of a baby, new-born no doubt, floated through the echoing halls and made Maliha think of the child she had cut from Riette's dead body.

ii

Maliha gave the carriage driver the address, but told him to go via somewhere they could eat.

That proved to be a problem. Three women on their own, even if one of them was a Westerner, could not be catered for even in a modern city like Madras. This was still India. They ended up back at the hotel where Amita was allowed to sit with them—after Maliha had made it clear to the *Maitre d'* that was precisely what she expected.

An hour later they returned in the cab and were conveyed through the crowded central city streets. The traffic thinned out and the buildings became residential. They had seen better days and while probably originally built for whites were now fully occupied by native Indians; the white middle classes had moved on.

They came to a stop outside an unremarkable set of apartments constructed in a mock Georgian style. All three went inside, and mounted the stone stairs three flights. They followed the numbered doors to the right one. Maliha knocked.

There was a pause and eventually the sound of someone approaching. A bolt was thrown back and it was opened a crack. Maliha saw an Indian woman's face hidden in shadow.

"*Namaste*," said Maliha and continued in Hindi. "I'm looking for Mary O'Donnell."

"I only speak English," said the woman. There was a curious lilt to her voice Maliha couldn't place.

"Mary O'Donnell?"

"She's dead, God rest her soul."

Maliha placed it. The accent was Irish. It seemed out of place in such a face. "She's your mother?"

"She was. She died. Goodbye."

She went to push the door shut but Maliha put her foot in the way.

"When?"

"What?"

"When did she die?"

"Who are you?"

"Maliha Anderson, I—" and she didn't know what to say that would make this woman tell her everything she needed to know, "—I'm like you."

"What do you mean?" The antagonism was unrestrained.

"Mixed parentage."

"I'm not interested in your pity. Get your foot out of my door before I hurt you."

This was the moment Amita barged past Françoise and Maliha, and slammed her shoulder into the door. The force flung it open knocking the woman against the opposite wall.

"Oh for heaven's sake, Amita," said Maliha and bent down to help the woman to her feet. The room was small but not as bad as some Maliha had seen. She noted the images of the Virgin Mary on the wall, the crucifix and rosary beads on the mantle above the fireplace. And black cloth draped on them and a few photographs in pewter frames.

Amita stood behind Maliha with a dangerous look on her face. "She threatened you, *sahiba*."

"Can you stand?" Maliha asked the woman. She nodded but her attention was fixated on Amita as if she was a tiger ready to pounce. Which was not an inaccurate assessment. "I'm sorry about my maid, she's quite…protective."

"She's your maid?"

"Let's sit down," said Maliha using one of the straight-back chairs by the table. "What's your name?"

"Naimh."

"A good Irish name."

The woman frowned. "Try looking like me, with that name."

"I know what it's like," said Maliha.

"You think so?" she said. "You come from money. Look at you with your silk and your maid, and your—" she looked at Françoise, "—whatever she is."

"Associate."

"Is that what they're called now is it?"

Maliha frowned. "You think you had it bad? I spent seven years in a girls' boarding school in England with this skin. At least you could walk down the street and look like you fit in."

They glared at one another, until Naimh finally took a deep breath. "I'm sorry."

Maliha nodded. "So am I." She took a deep breath. "When did your mother die?"

"Two weeks ago."

Naimh stood up and took down one of the frames from under the black cloth and handed it to Maliha. It was a picture of a younger Naimh, perhaps twelve or thirteen, with an older woman with long wavy hair tied back. She was wearing a uniform that was reminiscent of a nurse.

"Your mother?" asked Maliha.

Naimh nodded.

"She was a midwife?"

"She spent her life delivering other people's babies, but they still shunned her."

"Your parents were not married."

Naimh shook her head. "I don't even know who my father was. She never said; I didn't ask."

"But she worked at the hospital?"

Naimh shrugged. "For a time. She said she left because she didn't like it there. They were all protestants, you see. She didn't fit in."

"How did she die?"

"I came home one day, she was lying there—" she nodded at the floor between them, "—she was dead."

"Yes, but *how* did she die?"

Maliha saw the tears forming in Naimh's eyes. "I don't know. She was as strong as a horse. She always went to church on Sunday. I don't know—"

Her voice cracked and she sobbed. Maliha remembered how it had been with Barbara Makepeace-Flynn; she glanced at the other two. Amita just stared at her while Françoise gestured her head at Naimh.

Maliha moved to sit beside the woman and put her arm around her shoulders.

Amita came over with one of Maliha's kerchiefs which Maliha took and gently pushed into Naimh's hand.

The sobbing eventually turned to sniffles. "I'm sorry."

"Nothing to be sorry about," said Maliha. "The police didn't tell you anything?"

"Police?"

"You reported her death?"

Naimh shook her head. "I told the priest and he arranged everything."

"What colour was her skin?"

"What colour..?"

"You came in and found her, what colour was her skin?"

"Pale."

People were so unobservant. "No, there was more than that, wasn't there? She was blue-ish round her mouth, her fingers."

Naimh looked up. "How did you know?"

Maliha didn't respond; she was examining the floor. She got to her feet and pointed. "Show me exactly where she was lying. *Exactly* mind."

Naimh looked at Maliha in that confused way that people so often did.

"Your mother was poisoned. I need you to show me exactly where she was lying when you found her."

"Poisoned?"

"Yes. I need to know exactly how her body was positioned."

"My mother was nobody. Why would anyone poison her?"

"Because of something she knew. Now please, if you would lie down the way you found her."

"I…you want me to lie where she was lying?"

Maliha paused. A year ago she would have pushed the woman, but she had learnt something in the intervening time. "Françoise, would you mind helping my investigation?"

The English was apparently too fast for Françoise to follow, so Maliha repeated in French. "I need you to lie on the floor. Naimh here will adjust your position to the way her mother was lying. Is that all right?"

The French woman did not look too happy about it. "Her mother is dead, the midwife?"

Maliha sighed, it was always the same, everybody else seemed to need it explaining twice or more and couldn't handle more than one thought at a time. "Yes. If you wouldn't mind?"

Françoise complied. Naimh knelt beside her and adjusted Françoise's right arm. She placed it above her head and had her fold her left arm beneath her. Finally she was satisfied, though there were new tears.

"There was no cup or glass on the floor?"

"No."

"Was your mother left or right-handed?"

"Right."

It looked as if she'd fallen from a chair after drinking.

"Not a drop of alcohol ever touched her lips," said Naimh.

Except Communion wine, thought Maliha. "Very good." Then she continued in French. "Françoise, could you sit on the chair there and then fall off and into that position, holding this glass? But let go of it when you land."

Françoise took a couple of attempts to get it just right and the glass went skittering across the floor under the table. Maliha got down on her hands and knees examining the path it had taken. She wetted her fingers in her mouth then rubbed a slight greenish discolouration in the floorboards. The faint smell of bitter almonds wafted up.

She climbed to her feet and gestured for Françoise to do the same.

"What time did you find her?"

"I left early, shortly after dawn and returned in the evening." Naimh dabbed at her eyes with the kerchief. "She was cold."

Maliha nodded at Amita and Françoise, and they moved towards the door. "One final thing, did your mother keep the door bolted?"

"Always, we are not popular."

"But the door was not broken in?"

Naimh shook her head. "It wasn't bolted so I knew something was wrong."

Maliha nodded and they took their leave.

iii

Maliha noticed the looks between the air-plane's navigator and Amita when they disembarked at Pondicherry. She shook her head. It was not that she minded Amita having relations with men. It was Amita's business. However she knew for certain that most men would be very unhappy to learn of her maid's true nature.

Maliha thought of Valentine. It was a conversation that she did not think would go down well with him; the fact that Amita was Maliha's personal maid meant Maliha's body was known to Amita. Not that Maliha encouraged physical contact, after all she dealt with all her personal matters herself, but Amita helped her dress, and undress.

Valentine was unlikely to understand that Amita was probably more interested in him.

She frowned. What difference did it make? She and Valentine had never been engaged, and never would be. She could choose whoever she wished to be her maid and it was no business of his.

The journey back to the city was without incident.

She wished she had Barbara to talk to. Françoise was pleasant enough but lacked the experience of the older woman. And while she might have a sweet smile and lips, she lacked the incisively logical mind that Maliha preferred. Valentine never took anything seriously but one did not have to spell everything out for him.

She swerved to the far side of the road to avoid an elephant in harness carrying some logs.

She debated the best course of action now. She had established that something had happened during the birth of Renuka and Balaji.

She dropped Françoise off at her cousin's house. The woman invited her in. There was an undercurrent of desire in her voice. Maliha declined claiming she needed to rest.

When they were in Madras, Françoise had suggested she stay with Maliha both nights in the hotel. Her forwardness surprised Maliha considering the girl had not even kissed another woman a few days before, but Maliha knew it was just an infatuation and had refused. She needed to keep Françoise under control and at a distance. It was hard to think with the woman mooning over her.

She and Amita returned to her grandparents' house and after a brief visit with her grandmother, just to prove she had kept her word, she went to her rooms where Amita had drawn a bath scented with jasmine oil.

She undressed and sank into it, breathing in the refreshing aroma. Her reverie was interrupted by Amita bringing in a platter with a single letter.

Maliha pushed herself up in the bath and took the letter. Amita passed her an opener. Maliha closed her hand on it absently, studying the handwriting. Slowly she turned it over. There was no sender's name on the exterior but she knew Valentine's hand. The postmark stamp clearly said *Pondicherry* and was timed yesterday evening.

Amita busied herself clearing away Maliha's used sari, blouse and petticoat.

Maliha slid the letter opener into the top of the envelope and sliced it open with more force than was necessary. The paper, which was not of the best quality, came apart with a satisfying rasp. She dropped the letter opener on to the tiled floor, pulled out the letter and dropped the envelope on the other side.

Dear Miss Anderson

'Miss Anderson' is it? Clearly he was over his infatuation. Good.

As she scanned the rest of the letter written in his untidy hand and lacking proper punctuation and even grammar—so like him— she felt her anger boiling up. She climbed to her feet and stepped out of the bath, dripping, on to the floor.

"Amita."

Amita glanced round and seeing her standing there went for the towel.

"Leave that," growled Maliha. Amita paused and faced her with fear in her eyes. Maliha brandished the letter. "This is from Valentine."

Amita collapsed to the floor and prostrated herself, reaching out to touch Maliha's feet. "I'm so sorry, *sahiba*, I did not think you would want to know."

"He says you met with him," Maliha was helpless to control the anger that poured acid into her words.

"He found me. I was doing as you bid me."

"And he recognised you and he messed things up?"

"Yes. No. He did not know."

"He never does."

"I am so sorry, *sahiba*, I will pack my things."

"What?"

"I will leave your service, *sahiba*, I have betrayed you and failed you."

Maliha looked at the letter and then at Amita lying on the floor. "Get up, you're getting wet. Bring me my towel," she said. "And then you will tell me everything that happened."

Amita climbed slowly to her feet, taking great pains not to look at her mistress. "Yes, *sahiba*." She found the towel and offered it, looking no higher than Maliha's ankles.

Maliha took the towel, wrapped it around herself and re-read the letter. He was going at things with his usual lack of finesse. Honestly she was surprised he had not gone charging in himself and got himself shot for his trouble. Still she was glad he had not, otherwise she would be missing this piece of information.

She sent for some tea and sat in the window. She read the letter several more times. Then folded it up. *Dear Miss Anderson* indeed, and he had signed off with *Your servant, W A V Crier.* He never did like her using Valentine instead of Bill.

Amita served the tea, still acting as if she were about to be beaten.

"Sit down, Amita."

She promptly crossed her legs and sat on the floor. Maliha thought she would be glad when Amita got over this guilt.

"All right, tell me exactly what happened that night. Do not leave anything out."

Amita looked worried. "Everything?"

Maliha frowned. "Yes, of course, everything."

"Yes, *sahiba*. Everything." And still she hesitated. A worry grew inside Maliha; was it possible that she was completely wrong about Valentine's preferences? Did he prefer men the way the General had done? She prepared herself to hear it all.

"Begin."

* * *

"And he kissed you?"

"Yes, *sahiba*, I am sorry. Only on my cheek. I know he is yours and not mine. I should not have let him."

The sun had reached the horizon. Maliha had grown accustomed to the long twilights of England. The way the sun simply fell below the horizon near the equator was something to which she had not fully accustomed. She still expected the evening half-light to go on for hours.

When Amita had described the false love-making Maliha was almost unable to contain her laughter but she managed for Amita's sake. The poor thing was so embarrassed about having "taken" her man. And it was so like Valentine; he was like a puppy blundering into a table leg.

And he had kissed Amita. Maliha smiled to herself; that too was like him. The two of them had shared something so intimate and he had shown his gratitude in a way that meant something.

But she still did not forgive him for killing Guru Nadesh and stealing her prize.

She stood up and realised she was still only wrapped in her towel. Grandmother would be calling her down for an evening meal soon.

"Stand up, Amita."

She did so, again only staring at Maliha's feet.

"Look at me."

Amita failed to do so. Maliha took a step forward and into her line of sight. "Look at me."

Amita glanced at her face for a moment then looked away. "I am angry you did not tell me what happened but I understand why you did not. As it is, the outcome was satisfactory so we will not dwell on it."

"Yes, *sahiba*."

The gong for dinner rang out, but instead of simply ringing twice, it rang again and again like an alarm. Maliha looked down at her state of undress. "Go down and find out what's happening while I get dressed."

She opened the door to the dressing room, went through and pulled on the clothes that Amita had laid out for her. The sound of the gong continued for minutes. It was quite irritating, since everyone in the house would know by now.

Maliha threw the *pallu* over her shoulder, slipped on her sandals and headed downstairs; there was a crowd of servants around the gong and it was Maliha's grandmother striking it.

The wall of servants parted as Maliha reached the bottom. Her grandmother was hunched over the gong, the hammer in her hand, striking it again and again. Maliha reached out and took hold of her wrist. Her grandmother struggled against the resistance until she seemed to realise someone was holding her wrist. Silence fell.

"Grandmother?"

The old woman—and suddenly Maliha realised that she was old, as if she had never really seen her before—turned and looked at her.

She recognised Maliha and the deadness behind her eyes flamed into anger.

"It's your fault!" She pulled her hand free and tried to hit Maliha with the hammer. Amita's hand appeared and stopped the blow from landing. Amita snatched the hammer from the old woman's hand and released her. Her grandmother struck Maliha on the cheek.

"You did this!" Slap. "You, your shameful mother and that father of yours." Slap.

Then she broke down in tears. Maliha stepped forward and put her arm round the old woman and guided her into one of the reception rooms. And shut the door on the servants.

"What's happened, Grandmother?"

"You had to interfere; you had to make waves."

"Tell me what's happened? Is it Grandfather?"

"I'm sure you'd be happy if it was."

Maliha controlled her temper at the complete lack of logic. "Just tell me what's wrong, Grandmother."

"Savitha."

"What about Auntie?"

"She has been arrested!"

"What? Aunt Savitha?"

"Yes, *Aunt* Savitha. You disgusting chit, I am ashamed to have birthed the daughter that birthed you!"

"Grandmother, just tell me, why has Aunt Savitha been arrested?"

"She has killed her husband."

iv

Maliha engaged the brake and vented the excess pressure. Amita handed her down from the carriage. There was a crowd of people outside the gates of Aunt Savitha's house and the policeman on duty took some persuading to let her through.

Every window glowed with light, and lit the family and servants weeping outside the building, or standing with a look of horror etched into their faces.

Renuka ran up to Maliha and flung her arms around her. Maliha stroked her head. "I need to go inside. You must stay here and look after your sisters."

Her cousin clung for a moment then released her but stayed with Maliha as she walked up the steps into the building. Maliha paused at the top and Renuka grabbed Maliha's hand again; her eyes were red with weeping but her face was dry. Maliha hugged her. "Stay with your sisters."

She pulled herself away and went into the brightly lit foyer. She glanced around. It was empty, no police on duty. But Maliha knew where they were. She headed through the building towards the courtyard.

One of the French police stood next to an opening in the wall, where there had been no door before. He watched her as she crossed the courtyard to the holy plant, slipped off her shoes, and touched a leaf. There was a formless prayer in her mind. She would have to make it all come true herself anyway.

She put her sandals back on and went to the opening. The young policeman stretched out his arm to bar her way.

"You can't go in, *mam'selle*."

Amita loomed over her shoulder.

"I am Maliha Anderson, I am investigating the death of the girl at the wedding here last week. This is related, and your Inspector Abelard was quite clear that I could carry out my investigations."

She did not speak aggressively but with a firm tone that would brook no disagreement. "This is no place for a young woman, *Mam'selle* Anderson. There was been a murder."

"Which is precisely why I am here. Must I contact the commissioner?"

His control of the situation had been tenuous at best. He stepped back.

"Stay here, Amita."

Maliha stepped through into a short corridor. The walls were white-washed and there was a slight smell of carbolic acid. Almost clinical.

She turned back and examined the door. The locking mechanism was a simple bolt that pushed through into the solid wood of the door which had been faced with stone to match the exterior. The mechanism could be operated from the inside by a lever. There must be a similar one accessible from the outside.

It was only a few paces to the door at the other end. This one required a key but again was solid but not complex.

She took a deep breath and hesitated. It was not the thought of seeing her dead uncle that concerned her; she had seen enough dead bodies in the past, and even examined them. It was what else she would find. When she discussed "de Sade" in such casual tones with the French Doctor or with Françoise, she was hiding the horror she did not allow herself to feel.

She pushed open the door.

Everything here was also white. The light from the electric lamps shone with a bright sterility. It was all white except on the floor between the manacles where the dark stains of blood and other bodily secretions, from the years of torture, could not be washed away. She touched her hand to her neck as a wave of cold went through her.

There were manacles driven into the floor and matching ones that hung from the ceiling. On the wall was a cabinet carrying a range of canes, whips and even a cat-o'-nine-tails. On a fold-out section of the cabinet was a wooden block with a selection of knives, a cut-glass box containing needles three inches long, and a second block of thin metal skewers, one missing. In a corner there was a sink with a tap and cleaning materials.

It was easy to dismiss the activities of her uncle when you thought that it was hidden away, such care was taken to keep it clean, and it was not his particular desire to kill anyone: merely inflict some pain that could be easily forgotten. But Maliha could see the years of agony given both willingly and unwillingly.

But it was the armchair with a small table and selection of drinks, probably alcoholic, that made her skin crawl and the hate well up in her. It faced the manacles in the centre of the room, and she knew why it was there. So he could sit in comfort and inspect his handiwork while his wife, or his slave-gift, hung there, weeping from the pain while their blood stained the floor. Their skin pierced and flayed as their body's nerves screamed.

Even if his intention was not to kill, how close would he come to causing death to satisfy his desires? And there he now lay with his own blood staining the whitewashed floor.

She shivered and felt the bile rise in her throat.

There was a man in a suit standing beside the body, but he was staring at her. He was in his thirties.

"*Mam'selle?* Perhaps you should not be here?"

She took a deep breath and calmed herself. "How did he die?"

"And you are?"

"Maliha Anderson," she stepped across to her uncle's body. Uncle Pratap wore the Western suit he affected to give himself a better image and to separate himself from the common people. "Is there no doubt my aunt killed him?"

"*You* are Maliha Anderson?"

She looked him in the eye. "You were expecting someone older."

"Yes, I was. Not such an attractive and young woman."

"And my physical attributes are relevant to the case in what way? *Monsieur*..." she allowed her words to trail off expectantly.

He grinned in what she imagined he thought to be a winning way. "Detective Gerard Belleville." He put out his hand to shake hers, across the body. She looked down at her uncle. The blood seemed to be coming from his abdomen.

"You are not married, detective."

He withdrew his hand. "How did you know?"

"Woman's intuition." Along with the rank smell of sweat, his greasy and unkempt hair, the overall impression he gave was that he wanted to touch her, intimately. He was so despicable even Grandmother would have sent him on his way.

She squatted down to peer under the body. She lifted up his blood-soaked jacket. The blood furthest from him had dried, but under his body it was still sticky. News travelled fast; he was less than two hours dead.

"Is there a murder weapon?"

"I think he's lying on it."

She looked up at Belleville to see his eyes scanning her breasts. "And there's no question my aunt committed the murder?" She repeated.

He shrugged and dragged his gaze up to her face. "She confessed to it."

Maliha nodded and looked back at the body. "Are you going to turn him over?"

Belleville bent over and grabbed the jacket. He rolled the body away from her. Her uncle's shirt, tie and jacket were drenched in blood that made the cloth hang heavily—where it wasn't glued to his skin.

She pointed at the wooden handle that matched those of the skewers. It was buried to the hilt in his abdomen but tilted upward. In her mind's eye she followed the path of the metal through his stomach, diaphragm and into the heart. The shirt was pierced in many places, but the last thrust, where her aunt finally released her grip on the weapon, was probably the one that killed him. He had suffered for a while. Maliha felt a certain satisfaction in that knowledge.

"That would do it," said the detective and let the body drop back. "His very own torture chamber. Do you think he killed many people in here?"

"He didn't kill anyone," said Maliha. "He just destroyed their lives."

Maliha looked around the room again. She realised she was standing on the blood-stain. A shudder ran through her and she stepped back. She reached down and ran her fingers across it. The fact that there was no difference in texture between the stain and the rest disturbed her. She felt there should be some fundamental quality that could be sensed where someone's lifeblood had been spilt. She felt sick again as images of the two women pushed into her mind.

She suppressed the thoughts. She would betray Riette and Aunt Savitha if she did not think clearly. She did not imagine her uncle had allowed Riette to roam free in the room when he was absent. There was no cot or pallet but there was a pot for night-soil next to a single manacle set in the wall on the opposite side of the room to the tools of his sadistic hobby.

The manacles were unlocked and took a simple key. It would be easy to pick if one had the right equipment. Or the key. Somehow Riette had escaped the manacle, passed through the door lock and out into the courtyard at exactly the right moment to drink the same poison as had killed an Irish woman in Madras.

"Sick." The detective said. She glanced up to where he stood examining the whips. She watched him as he almost caressed the strips of the cat. He glanced over at her and grinned.

Rational thought was subsumed in a terror that leapt from her heart. She had barely sufficient control to walk from the room instead of flee. She maintained a semblance of poise until she reached the courtyard then ran from the house.

* * *

Maliha was not entirely sure how it happened but she dropped Amita off at her grandparents' house and now found herself parked outside Françoise's home, in the dark. Most of the lights in the house were off.

She told herself that she had not come here because her uncle's torture room had disturbed her, but she always knew when someone was lying. She imagined Riette strung between the manacles being lashed until she bled. And then her aunt hanging there, willingly, letting her husband kill her by stages. Learning to want the pain. Maliha shook her head. How could anyone want such a thing?

She realised she was crying. She needed someone to hold her. She was adrift while the only members of her family who cared for her were deep in their own grief. She wanted her mother, or her father, or Valentine. He was in the city somewhere, perhaps if she could find him—she pushed him from her mind.

Françoise was here, now.

Maliha almost tumbled from the carriage, and stumbled as she climbed the stairs. Her left thigh had the ache in it she had all but forgotten. She told herself she was just tired, and while that was true, it was not the whole truth.

Françoise opened the door. She saw the look on Maliha's face, took her by the hand and drew her inside. The French woman pushed the door closed and took Maliha's hands in hers.

"What's wrong?"

Maliha shook her head.

Françoise took Maliha's face in her hands and placed a gentle kiss on her lips. Her right hand snaked round Maliha's neck while the left slipped down, under her sari and round to press against her bare back, crushing the two of them together.

Maliha relaxed and allowed her arms to encircle Françoise's waist. She could feel her hips beneath the heavy fabric. Maliha's arms tightened as if trying to force the two of them closer. She felt rather than heard a gentle growling noise from Françoise that made Maliha's tongue tingle. She was desperate for the physical contact and to feel Françoise's skin against hers.

Françoise released her. Maliha felt adrift again but Françoise took her by the hand and drew her through the hall and up the sweeping marble staircase.

"The servants?" whispered Maliha.

"Nobody is here but us."

She led the way up to the first floor and along the polished wooden floor. The light from a bedroom flooded out into the dark hallway but Françoise extinguished it with a flick of the switch as they entered.

Maliha pushed the door shut, her eyes adjusting to the darkness. Françoise was in front of her again and kissed her lightly. Françoise pulled the sari's *pallu* from Maliha's shoulder then untucked the rest of the cloth from her waistband and let it fall to the floor.

Standing in the pool of silk Maliha felt more undressed than she did in front of Amita. Françoise kissed her neck, and then bit her, sending a spark of energy through her. Françoise's hands brushed along Maliha's arms, down her back, across her stomach. It seemed that Françoise was never still. Then the older woman stepped in close. Her arms embraced Maliha again and Maliha felt the warm lips pressed against hers again.

Maliha parted her lips and allowed the other woman's tongue to enter her mouth. She felt a pain, not physical, but as if her heart were breaking, as if she had lost everything, and Françoise was the only thing left in her life.

As Françoise stepped away again Maliha discovered her blouse was unhooked. She removed it and let it fall. Françoise placed a kiss on Maliha's lips and stood back. She took Maliha's hand and pulled her to the bed, gave her a gentle thrust against her collarbone and Maliha sat.

A little light filtered in from the outside. It highlighted the curves of Françoise's body in peaks and shadows. Françoise turned her back on Maliha.

"Unlace me."

Without thinking about what it meant Maliha pulled the bows and loosened the cords of the dress, then unhooked it. She helped Françoise lift the skirts up and over her head. The material brushed against her breasts, making her shiver. Françoise threw the dress to one side and now, also bare from the waist up, faced Maliha. Without any apparent sense of embarrassment, Françoise hooked her thumbs into her underskirt, slid it to her ankles and stepped out of it.

Maliha had seen naked girls before at school, and in better light than this. But here it was as if the air was filled with the electric, so unlike the way it had been with the Guru. With him it had been so planned. Here there was passion.

Françoise reached out her hands. Maliha stood, feeling curiously awkward as she was not yet naked. Françoise caught her hands and brought her close. She stroked Maliha's cheek, then her hair. They moved closer. Their bare skin touched. Maliha jumped. Françoise laughed. She crushed her body against Maliha's and nibbled her neck.

Françoise hands caressed Maliha's bare skin. They were always moving, tracing across her skin. Maliha's mind buzzed with feelings she had never before experienced. Françoise pulled away again, their skin separated reluctantly and Maliha realised they were both sweating.

Standing back from Maliha, Françoise regarded her. "Nakedness is truth. Shall I remove your petticoat?"

Maliha hesitated. Françoise smiled and fell to her knees. She grabbed handfuls of the petticoat on each side and yanked it down. Maliha looked down at the top of Françoise's head as she knelt before her.

"I promise I won't try to kill you," said Françoise. Maliha felt a moment's pain at her words. Then Françoise leaned forward and kissed her.

* * *

Maliha woke at the sound of a shutter banging somewhere in the house. She lay on her back listening to the wind in the trees and staring at indistinct shadows playing across the ceiling. Her hand prickled with pins and needles. As she attempted to lift her arm up to rub her fingers, she realised her arm was both numb and trapped. She turned and saw Françoise on her side, watching her.

"Can I have my arm back?"

Françoise pushed herself up on her elbow. She was naked and her curves were like the shadows and highlights of a charcoal drawing. Maliha awkwardly pulled her unresponsive arm out from underneath her.

"It's gone to sleep."

In an easy motion Françoise move into a kneeling position and gently took Maliha's arm.

"Here, let me," she said. Maliha did not protest and Françoise massaged from the fingertips along the forearm and back. The arm stung as sensation returned.

"Renuka said you came back to Pondicherry because of a man."

Maliha felt odd thinking about Valentine when she had been enjoying earthly pleasures with someone else. Françoise had taken her lack of response as an affirmative.

"What is his name?"

"Valentine."

"A good name for a lover."

"We weren't lovers. We barely even walked out together."

"And yet you came back. Did he hurt you?"

"No. Yes—" Maliha broke off in confusion. She gathered her thoughts. "No. He did not touch me."

"Did he torture your mind?"

"No. He is a decent man. A good man."

"And still you came home?"

Françoise stopped her massage and placed Maliha's arm so it encircled Françoise's back as she leaned forward so her face was directly above Maliha's.

"So it must be that you prefer women to men?"

Maliha did not reply but pulled Françoise down until their lips met.

v

The Sûreté in Pondicherry was another new building, perhaps only twenty years old. There were few old buildings in the city.

Maliha stopped her carriage just beyond the main entrance, beside a bicycle leaning against the wall. She was alone and wearing the same sari as she had yesterday. The night with Françoise had been…not what she was expecting. She smiled at the memories of physical pleasure that had purged the horrors of Pratap's torture room. Françoise had been surprisingly skilled and quite inventive.

Maliha climbed the stairs and pushed her way into the interior. The building lacked grandeur; it was utilitarian and small. There was a uniformed French policeman at a desk.

"Good afternoon, Miss, can I help you?"

"Maliha Anderson, to see Savitha Ganeshan please."

"Please wait." He indicated a line of chairs against the wall. She went and took a seat. The policeman disappeared into the back. He returned in a few moments, threw her a momentary smile that contained no emotion, and sat down to continue with whatever it was he was doing.

She waited. The place was quiet.

A door somewhere opened and closed; the sound echoed through the building. Footsteps. And Commissioner Abelard came out from a side corridor.

"*Mam'selle* Anderson." She stood up as he approached and he shook her hand. "Please, come."

She followed him back the way he had come and through a door into what she assumed must be his office. His desk was a pile of documents. "Please, sit."

She sat and he followed suit.

"A serious business."

"I find it hard to believe my aunt killed her husband."

He shrugged. "Yet it is so, she has admitted it. And explained why."

"She feared her husband would beat her daughters."

He gave a sad smile. "You already know. I thought you might." He leaned forward. "I believe I owe you an apology, *Mam'selle* Anderson."

"If it's that you thought I was incapable of successful investigation, you need not apologise. I am quite used to it."

"Even so, *mam'selle*, I am sorry for underestimating you."

"When can I see her?"

"Soon," he said and searched through the papers in front of him until he found a letter. "But there is something else. I have received a letter from the British Foreign Office. They would like our assistance in removing, as they put it—" he squinted at a place halfway down the letter, "—*removing a stain on the honour of France*."

"Smugglers and slavers."

"You know of this also?" he shook his head. "*Mam'selle* Anderson, I do not quite know whether to applaud you or exile you. We had a quiet city here until you arrived and now you turn it all upside down."

She frowned at him. "It was already upside down, Commissioner. I am turning it the right way up."

He paused as he absorbed her admonition then grunted in acknowledgement and stared at the letter again. "I will agree to their request, of course. What with our *Entente Cordiale* and the fact they have a much bigger army than my few officers, I can only agree. Still, they will be the ones getting their men killed. We will simply observe."

"I would like to be there."

He raised his eyebrows then shrugged again. "Very well."

"Can I see my aunt?"

He got to his feet. "This way please."

*　*　*

A prison cell is a prison cell. There are no pleasant ones. Aunt Savitha sat on her bed and stared at the wall.

Maliha sat beside her, not knowing what to say. Their last conversation kept replaying through her mind. The one where she had given her aunt no options.

"I have brought shame upon my family," said Aunt Savitha.

The words did not echo in the small room, but echoed in Maliha's mind. "I am at fault, Auntie."

"No, Maliha. You did the right thing."

"If I had given you another option…"

Aunt Savitha touched Maliha's hand, spreading out her fingers and intertwining them with her own. "Then I would have died and my daughters would have suffered his cruelty."

"And instead they will be shamed by a mother who killed their father," said Maliha. "They will hate you."

"Better that."

"And you will be dead."

"That will make it easier for me to bear the guilt."

Maliha heard the strained levity in her aunt's voice and sighed.

"Do not be sad, little Maliha. Think that perhaps I have rid the world of someone who brings pain to others. Just as you do."

Maliha smiled at her aunt. "You must tell me exactly what happened, every detail."

Savitha tensed and looked down but nodded. Maliha allowed her the time to gather the strength to speak.

"Over the years I have come to know when Pratap must relieve his…need. He angers more easily and strikes the children," said her aunt. "When he lashed out at Purvaji yesterday morning and lost his temper at the servants I knew the time had come again. I did not forget what you said, Maliha, but what choice did I have? I am his wife."

Though anger boiled inside her Maliha kept her thoughts to herself.

"In the years that I succumbed to his will, we made a private language that would tell him that I was ready for him. I said the words to him and he became himself again. Excited that once more he would have me as his offering."

"Offering?"

"My husband believed he had been cursed by the gods and only by giving the offering of pain and blood, from someone he cared for was better, only then could he prevent the curse from coming about."

"And you believed this?"

She nodded. "What if it were true, Maliha? How could I tempt the gods?"

But Maliha was barely listening. She recalled a time when she had visited with Aunt Savitha and Uncle Pratap. He had used a stick to punish Renuka and Maliha. He had whipped their hands until they were cut. Then hugged them and given them lime-flavoured water to drink and made them laugh with silly antics. Though she had been only eight she had thought it strange. And painful. She absently rubbed her hand.

"I'm sorry, Auntie, please continue."

"The girl, Riette, she did not love him of course. Nor did he care for her. So he beat her and cut her, so there was more pain and blood. I tried to comfort her as best I could, but it was my fault."

Maliha realised they had become side-tracked. There was little doubt her aunt would avoid speaking of what she had done. She must be redirected. "What happened yesterday?"

"I went to the room."

"I'm sorry, Auntie, I must ask: The room cannot be a secret to the servants?"

"The room is not a secret inside the house, but what happens there is a secret to most."

"Renuka?"

Aunt Savitha shook her head vehemently. "No, we have kept it from the children."

Maliha thought of Renuka's reaction at the *sangeet*. She knew.

"Please continue."

"When we got to the room, Pratap wanted to chain me as he had done to Riette, but always before I had simply accepted his beatings. I am his dutiful wife; I would not stop him doing what he must.

"But your words had made me strong. I said he need not bind me and that he must take care, otherwise he might kill me and then he would have no one to protect him from the curse."

Aunt Savitha tensed, and her voice hardened. "Then he laughed. He said that would be no problem. He knew I might die, so he had already discussed with Grandfather that he would have you, Maliha. He would marry you, by force if necessary, and the gods would be doubly pleased that a disobedient woman was brought to them and tamed."

She began to breathe hard. "And when he said so, I had such an anger in me that I have never felt before. You are my niece, you are strong and I would never let him touch you the way he touched me. So, while he laughed, I took up one of his blessed tools, and I looked him in the eye. Yes. I looked my husband in the eye and I saw fear in him. So I stabbed him. But he did not fall. So I stabbed again, and again, and again. And then he fell.

"And I had his blood on my hand."

The cell absorbed her panting breaths. She held her hand up as if she gripped the weapon and stared at the imaginary skewer. Then she returned to herself, dropped her hand and blinked. "I did it to save you, Maliha, because you are the avatar of vengeance."

Maliha tutted to herself and changed the subject.

"Was it you who let the girl out, the night before when I visited?"

Aunt Savitha looked at her and nodded. "We practised the plan."

"You said that you bought the girl, Riette."

"Though it is against the law to own another human being, yes, I bought her as if she were a goat and gave her to my husband to use."

"And she spoke English?"

"Only a few words. We made a language between us." A pained look came across her aunt's face. "But when she cried out, or cried afterwards, she spoke then. Her language was something I did not recognise."

"It was not French?"

"No. I do not think she understood French at all. Perhaps it was from her native Africa? What language do the black people speak?"

"They have as many languages as we do," said Maliha distractedly. She was thinking. There were Germans in Africa and also the Dutch. She could not speak Dutch but they had been taught German in school. *"Did the language she spoke sound like this?"*

Aunt Savitha looked up in surprise. "It was like that."

Maliha summoned the memory of the Dutch trade attaché she had met on various occasions a few months before. Including the time when he had planned to kill her and Valentine. She tried to speak German using his Dutch accent. *"Please stop, please don't hurt me anymore."*

Aunt Savitha nodded. "Yes, yes, that was it. Like that."

"She was from South Africa, somewhere occupied by the Afrikaans—they are Dutch in origin. Probably from the city otherwise she would speak her native African tongue, especially when in pain."

Her aunt winced at the mention of the torture the girl had undergone. Maliha knew what her aunt had done was wrong, but she had endured her uncle's mistreatment for fifteen or more years. Maliha might not understand why anyone would endure it without doing something about it, but she could understand wanting to save her own flesh and blood.

"People talk about the things you have done, Maliha," said Aunt Savitha. Maliha took a deep breath, suppressed the anger deep inside, where it always boiled, where she had always been able to keep it.

She turned to face her aunt, under control.

Her aunt prostrated herself and touched Maliha's feet. "You will avenge this girl's death, yes?" She emphasised the word avenge and did not move from her prone position.

Maliha felt awkward. It was wrong of an elder to behave this way towards her, as if she were a guru or, heaven forbid, a goddess—damn that foolish priest. But she knew what her aunt was waiting for. She had to give her blessing. If she did it then she accepted the honour her aunt had given her, but if she did not she would destroy what little remained of her aunt's self-respect.

She reached down and touched her aunt's head.

Her aunt got up from the ground but squatted to one side, as if she did not deserve to be on the same level as Maliha, or as if Maliha were a guru. She kept her gaze averted and awaited for Maliha to speak.

"Riette was well fed and her wounds tended."

Her aunt waved her hand in front of her as if warding away the guilt. "I did what I could."

"Did she repeat any words?"

"Many times after she was beaten, she would say *Ik bennit vammin moder*, and she would cry out to *Marten*."

The name *Marten* was clear enough, Maliha thought: someone she cared for, perhaps the father of the child. And the other phrase might be *I am not my mother*, which was interesting but dealt with matters before she had arrived in India, so not directly relevant to the case.

"When did Grandmother and Grandfather know of Pratap's vice?"

Aunt Savitha's hesitation told Maliha everything she needed to know.

"When we were first married, I asked my mother whether Grandfather beat her. That was when I learnt Pratap's needs were not like those of other men. I showed my mother what he had done and begged her to let me return home. She refused me."

Maliha stood up and faced the wall. She ground her fist against it. If Grandmother had been here now Maliha did not know what she would have done to her. Her heart felt like it would burst with the anger in her. Why did everybody lie? Didn't they know she could see through it?

She needed to see Françoise again. Right now.

vi

She drove back to Françoise's house at break-neck speed.

Anger fed her every action. She slammed the controls, swerved at high velocity past obstructions. More than once pedestrians had to leap from her path as she yanked on the steam whistle and ploughed through the crowds on the street.

It was barely mid-day and the sun's heat poured down, fuelling her temper.

Never had she felt such anger and she did not care. She thought about her grandmother and how much she would love to wring her neck like a chicken's. To condemn her own daughter to a lifetime of pain and misery, and then finally to force her into the position where all she could do was take the life of her husband.

She slammed on the brake lever and the wheels locked. The clutch mechanism barely engaged in time, threatening to shred the teeth from the cogwheels as the vehicle slid to a stop on the gravel before the quiet house.

The curtains were still drawn on all the windows. Not a servant moved, not a gardener, not a maid, no one.

Maliha stormed up the steps and slammed through the front door. It crashed back, echoing through the dark house.

"Françoise!" yelled Maliha. The woman emerged cautiously from the passage that led to the kitchens. She had a half-eaten baguette in her hand, and wore a silk dressing gown that did little to hide her shape.

"Maliha?" she said. "What…why are you here?"

Maliha stormed across the tiled floor and glanced through one of the open doors into a reception room where the furniture was covered with white sheets. She closed on Françoise—who looked like she was about to bolt.

Without a word she ripped the filled baguette from Françoise's hand and tossed it across the hall. She grabbed Françoise by the wrist and yanked her up the stairs, along the landing and into the bedroom. She pushed her on to the bed and slammed the door. She turned the key.

"Take off your clothes."

"Why should I?"

"Because, as you said, there is truth in nakedness."

"I will not."

Maliha stalked across the room like a thunderstorm. She grabbed Françoise by the hair and crushed their lips together, then pulled her head back and slapped her across the cheek. "Take them off or I will rip them from you."

"All right!"

She reached for the belt, keeping her eyes on Maliha. It was too slow. Maliha yanked Françoise to her feet, pulled the dressing gown off her shoulders and down to the ground taking the belt with it. She gave Françoise a violent shove so she fell backwards on to the bed. Maliha grabbed her bloomers and pulled them off her.

Françoise finally pulled herself together and retreated across the bed. She grabbed a pillow to cover herself. "What is wrong with you?"

Maliha threw off her sari and underclothes, then crawled on to the bed. She loomed over Françoise. She kissed her hard as if inflicting a wound.

"Now there will be no more lies."

"What lies?" Françoise's voice betrayed her uncertainty. "What's wrong with you?"

"Who are you?"

"What kind of a question is that?"

Maliha slapped her again, hard. "Do you know how much I am tired of lies?"

Françoise raised her hand to her cheek. "I am Françoise Greaux."

Maliha grabbed her by the hair again and pulled her head back. Maliha leaned over her. The pillow between them prevented their skin touching. "There is nobody living in this house. There are no servants; there is no cousin. Just you. So I ask you again. Who are you?"

"My name *is* Françoise Greaux," she hissed. "And this house belongs to my cousin."

"But he is not here."

"No."

"And the servants?"

"They do the minimum as the family is away."

"Why did you seduce me?"

"I recall that it was you that kissed *me* first, Maliha Anderson."

Maliha tightened her grip in Françoise's hair and pulled her head back further, exposing her neck. "And then you seduced me. When I was vulnerable and needed someone to be considerate, you brought me to this bed."

"I did not notice you protesting," said Françoise. "At *any* point during the night."

Maliha kissed her hard again. Pushed her tongue into the woman's mouth. Françoise accepted it and responded.

Maliha pulled away and sat back. She rested her hand on Françoise's thigh.

"Why are you here?"

"The same reason you are."

Maliha almost snarled. "I don't mean here in this bed."

Françoise pushed herself back, sliding her leg from under Maliha's hand. She sat up letting the cushion fall away. She leaned back against the pillows bunched up behind her. She scratched her shoulder. "Neither did I."

"What are you talking about?"

Françoise sniffed derisively. "You need me to explain it to your great intellect?"

Maliha frowned. She felt the urge to slap her again. She found it gave her pleasure and she thought of Pratap.

"You are running away, Maliha Anderson," said Françoise quickly, to forestall any further violence. "Just like me, only I'm not afraid to admit it."

"Really? And what am I running from?"

"The same thing as me, only for a different reason."

Maliha felt her blood run cold, and the anger within her turned to ice.

"I am not running away."

"Of course you are," said Françoise. "You're running from your Valentine."

All Maliha's senses seemed to cease their natural function. She felt as if she could not move. But Françoise continued.

"And I am running from a man as well."

"Why would you run from a man?"

Françoise looked away, slightly embarrassed. "I did lie to you about one thing."

Maliha felt a small spark of triumph, but it did not burn into a warming flame. She remained numb. "What did you lie about?"

"When you asked whether I had kissed another woman as a lover," Françoise said. "I said I had not but I have, of course."

"That explains…much."

Françoise laughed. "You British are so understating." She looked directly into Maliha's eyes. "Listen to me, Maliha Anderson. I am very experienced making love with women, I have had a great deal of practice, and I have been greatly admired for it."

"So when I spoke of kissing—"

"I really could not believe my luck." Françoise folded her legs under her and knelt forward beside and facing Maliha. She put her arms around her. "But I was disappointed to find that your heart was not to be mine."

"I am not running away from Valentine—"

Françoise silenced her with a kiss. "Stop lying to yourself, little Maliha. I am allowed to lie, that is my nature, but it is not right for one such as you." She ran her fingernails from Maliha's neck to the tip of her breast. Then withdrew her hand with a sigh. "Such a pity."

"A pity?"

"I rather liked this version of you. So firm, so angry, even the violence—" she touched her cheek again and smiled, "—quite stimulating. I am usually the one who leads. It made a most refreshing change."

Maliha found her anger had dissipated, leaving her empty, tired and sad. She reached out and put her arms around Françoise's waist, and rested her head against the woman's shoulder. She ran her hand along Françoise's arm just to experience the soft cool skin and the tiny hairs. She liked Françoise and was sorry she had hurt her. "I could stay this afternoon," she said, then wondered if she might be misunderstood. "With you. Together. In bed."

"I love your hair," said Françoise and ran her fingers through it. "I think perhaps I may be a little bit in love with you, Maliha Anderson. But you are not like me. You do not love women. And as much as I would enjoy dallying with you, I do not think it would be fair of me to take advantage of you."

Maliha smiled. "Again."

"Yes," said Françoise. "Unfair for me to take advantage of you, again."

Then she sighed. "You are the sweetest thing, *Mam'selle* Anderson, but you must go. Before I change my mind, tie you to the bed, and make love to you until you cry for mercy."

Maliha blinked; after the previous night she had some idea of what that might mean. She could almost imagine it.

Françoise laughed again. "You are incorrigible." She pushed Maliha hard so she tumbled to the edge of the bed and barely saved herself from crashing to the floor. "Put your clothes on and get out."

Maliha stood reluctantly, fished her petticoat from the floor and slid into it. She fastened her blouse then set about organising the sari. Françoise merely watched.

"You did not tell me who you were running from," said Maliha as she wrapped the sari around her waist and pleated the *pallu*.

"I am betrothed to a man," said Françoise indifferently. "I will not marry him, of course, but my family is quite insistent."

"Is he a good man?"

"Oh, I like him well enough." Françoise got off the bed and went to the window. She stretched and Maliha could see her muscles working under her soft curves. "But let us say he would curtail my activities. And I really am uncomfortable with men's—" she waved her hand "—things."

Maliha ensured the sari was tucked firmly into her waistband, located her sandals and slipped them on.

"Do you want to continue accompanying me on the investigation?" she asked.

Françoise turned round. She seemed so comfortable in her nakedness. "I would like to do that. If you do not object to my presence and if your Amita does not mind."

"I will explain the situation to Amita."

"Really? You would explain this," she pointed at the rumpled bed, "to your maid?"

Maliha was not about to reveal Amita's secret, so she just nodded. "Oh yes, it will be entirely appropriate."

"As you wish," Françoise shrugged. "When will we see one another again?"

"Would I be right in thinking you can drive a steam carriage?"

"Oh yes, my father owns one similar to yours."

"Then I will collect you at nine this evening, Miss Greaux," said Maliha with a hint of a smile in her voice. "But I suggest you wear durable clothes and the strongest shoes you possess."

"An adventure?"

"I imagine it will be."

CHAPTER 7

i

Valentine waited at the meeting point on the beach nine miles north of Pondicherry, in British-owned territory. He had managed to find some shade under a palm tree and dozed.

There were fishing boats out in the bay and men with rods on the beach. The ocean kept the whole coast provided with more than could be eaten, and yet a hundred miles inland one bad season would bring people to the point of starvation.

He was roused from his sleep by a drone that grew louder until it filled the air. A dark shape grew in the sky. The Royal Navy troop ship flew in across the ocean. The powerful down draughts from its eight gargantuan rotors stirred up the sea and drove the fishing ships across the water. He saw one of them capsize.

It was only a hundred feet up when it crossed to the beach, driving a sandstorm before it. Valentine turned away and covered his face. The sand stung his skin for a few seconds until the roaring vessel passed beyond the beach and came to a stop above the undergrowth and trees.

The ship descended light as a feather. If a feather possessed roaring rotors and pumped smoke and steam from its four funnels. Valentine had travelled to India aboard the *RMS Macedonia* sky-liner that carried five hundred passengers, yet this Royal Navy carrier was twice its bulk.

It sported artillery points along its sides, the portholes were armoured and its skin was riveted steel. From its top deck protruded the wings of other craft. It flew a Royal Ensign flag and the name *HMS Alexandria* was painted on the hull.

It touched down with barely a bump. Valentine could not approach as the down draught from the rotors was still overwhelming, but their whine was decreasing in pitch and volume. A hatch folded out and formed a ramp. Crew members, some armed, disembarked and set up a cordon.

Valentine approached ensuring that he kept his hands visible and open. It was obvious he was a white man but the enemy wasn't Indian, or even French; it was the Kaiser and his desire to build an empire as great as Britain's.

He stopped at a non-threatening distance and allowed the armed men to come to him. He answered their challenges appropriately and handed over his identification. One of them went back into the ship while two others kept their weapons at the ready, watching Valentine.

Two more hatches opened and steam artillery carriages drove out. Where there was just one of these armoured machines to guard the entirety of the Fortress, three crawled from the belly of the ship. The self-powered artillery possessed one main gun with a three-inch bore, four smaller guns and two machine guns mounted on the top.

Like everything, they were driven through steam, and utilised the Faraday effect to allow monstrous constructions; each required a crew of twenty to operate the power unit, drive, navigate and man the guns. It was known the Germans had mobile fortresses with crews of over one hundred.

There was no question that war was coming. It was only a matter of when.

Another vehicle descended from the ship. This one lacked any major armament but was long with many wheels: a troop carrier and support vehicle. Finally the whole squadron had disembarked and lined up on the ground.

The air-ship's rotors had slowed down to the point where the individual blades could be observed. Men were out on the stubby wings checking the control and drive systems. Valentine was so busy watching the activity he did not notice the group of officers walking towards him until they were almost on top of him.

He stood to attention but did not salute as he was not in uniform nor a soldier. The officer in front, a brigadier by his insignia, stuck out his hand. "Mr Crier, Brigadier Stewart. Your documents are all in order, and I'm pleased to make your acquaintance."

Valentine took his hand and shook it. "Thank you, sir. Glad I could be of some assistance."

"Well, we don't always agree with you Foreign Office types, too much diplomacy if you ask my opinion. But it's always important to give the boys some live fighting experience, so we're happy to help out when the steel fist is needed. Never know when it's going to come in handy, do we?"

"I think this might be overkill."

The brigadier shook his head. "Can tell you're not a military man, Crier. Overkill for them is underkill for us. If you see what I mean. If we have sufficient force to overwhelm them fast, it means fewer of my chaps are going to get hurt."

He paused as if he were allowing his wisdom to sink in and then continued. "Will we be taking the froggies along?"

"The French? No, sir, they'll make their own way in."

"As long as they don't get in the way."

"They'll stay clear until we're in control of the area."

"All right. You'll be riding in the Unicorn with me; you can advise our navigator as to the exact position of the target."

With that he turned and, flanked by his officers, headed towards the first of the wheeled vehicles. To the rear Valentine could see perhaps a hundred soldiers climbing into the personnel carrier.

* * *

Coming from the north, rather than the south as he had done on his first expedition, Valentine was not able to give them specific information as to the terrain, but their maps were good.

There was something about these self-powered artillery that he found quite terrifying. They seemed to be virtually unstoppable. They proceeded along the roads initially and made excellent time, as they had an impressive turn of speed.

There was no attempt at stealth. The speed of these vehicles far outstretched what any person on foot, or even on horseback, could achieve. Besides the slavers had managed to keep their location a secret from everyone, so nobody would be running to tell them of the approaching forces.

After a few miles, when they were almost within sight of Pondicherry, the command was given to head inland. Valentine almost failed to make it into his assigned seat in time and had to grab the chair straps to avoid being thrown across the cabin. Once off the road the machines bucked and dipped with every contour of the landscape—but barely slowed.

The crew seemed to take perverse pride in riding out the bumps at the highest possible velocity. Astonishingly, at least to Valentine, once in a while one of them would get up from their chair and walk across the tossing deck. Of course the reduced gravity meant that a fall would not be quite as damaging, and would occur at a slower rate giving time to compensate. However it was not an experience he was willing to try out.

As they approached the low hills in which the slavers' base was located a command was given of which Valentine could make neither head nor tail.

"Notify squadron. Damp furnaces, switch to Spanish."

He had been concerned that they were arriving much earlier than the planned time for the attack. They intended to go in at midnight, and it was only beginning to get dark.

Whatever the command meant, the captain received acknowledgement first from his own engine room and then from the signalman as the other machines reported their compliance.

They reduced speed to the point where Valentine dared unstrap himself.

"Want to go up top?" asked the brigadier.

"I wouldn't mind, sir."

"Heading up there myself, now we're being *stealthy*," he laughed loudly at his own humour.

He went to a door which a crewman undogged and held open for them. Beyond it was a ladder going up and down. The brigadier stepped across the open space and on to the ladder without hesitation. It was hard to fall when there was so little gravity.

Valentine followed him up and they emerged in a space fenced off by steel plating. There was room for about five people. There was a crewman on watch staring out into the dusk and scanning the horizon.

Directly behind them were the three other vehicles. Only the slightest wisps of smoke emerged from their stacks, almost invisible in the dark. The engines still continued to huff. Steam emerged from side vents and dissipated into the evening air.

Valentine was curious about the lack of smoke, obviously connected to the "Spanish" but idle curiosity was not appropriate to the situation.

He watched ahead as the machine crushed its way through the undergrowth and smaller trees without changing its course.

Another twenty minutes passed as the vehicles headed into the hills. There was a flashing behind him; the semaphore flags had been dismounted and replaced by signalling lamps.

The vehicle went quiet but they kept moving.

"Electric," said the brigadier. "Nice, eh?"

Valentine assented.

The vehicles continued to crash through the terrain but now they might as well have been nothing but a herd of elephants for all the noise they were making.

They came to a halt at the entrance to a valley which he and the navigator had decided was close to the one they wanted, which meant their target was most likely directly ahead, over the ridge. Now there were other matters to deal with.

There was little more than a rustling in the undergrowth as teams of infantry were deployed from the personnel carrier. Some set up station a few hundred yards from the vehicles while others, trained in sabotage operations, headed up to the ridge. They would remove any patrols when the time came to move in.

The Faraday device had been switched off to maintain battery reserves and Valentine climbed down the ladder and back into the main cabin carefully. There was nothing to do but wait. He would have enjoyed a few hands of cards but the rest of the crew had duties. He was the only one at a loose end.

The combat screens had been lowered over the windows so that the cabin could be illuminated without the light giving away their location.

He tried not to look at his watch but there was a clock located directly above the main window. It crawled as time passed. He took time over a toilet break outside but the crew were uncomfortable with him delaying and he soon had to go back inside.

The air inside remained very fresh, almost invigorating, which he found surprising but that too was something he was not about to question.

"Are you armed, Mr Crier?" asked the brigadier at about eleven o'clock.

"Yes, sir."

"Good," the brigadier gave him a wide grin. "Waiting's over. Time for the action."

"Yes, sir."

ii

The Faraday was engaged at exactly eleven-thirty. The interior lights were extinguished and the combat shields raised. As his vision adjusted to the dark Valentine realised they were already moving; he barely noticed it.

With only the slightest sound the vehicle crept forward on its electric motors. He assumed the others were following. The deck tilted as they climbed towards the ridge. Scouts had reported back and confirmed the exact course they needed to take, which was slightly to the north of what he and the navigator had thought.

Valentine sat back in his chair. All he could see was star-filled sky. The British had decided to move fast because this was the new moon, where otherwise they would have had to wait another month.

At a quarter to twelve the captain ordered the "Spanish" to be engaged. The steam engines began to pump and power surged through the vehicle and its climb rate increased.

The brigadier was not seated but hung by a strap set in the ceiling. He kept glancing at the clock but said nothing. His job was done. He would not direct the action as it happened; that was for the men on the ground.

They topped the ridge and the vehicle deck became horizontal.

"Strapped in, Mr Crier?" said the brigadier. "You had better be." There was the sound of sheer delight in his voice.

"Fire up main furnaces, decouple the Spanish."

There was a pause then the vehicle throbbed with noise and power.

At exactly eleven fifty-five: "Charge."

The engines roared like a bull elephant, the gears engaged and the vehicle cannoned forwards directly at the slope that fell away into the valley ahead.

"Tally-ho!" yelled the brigadier as they went over the edge. Valentine gripped the arms of his chair in terror. All the weight left him as the machine flew off the edge. His stomach felt as if it wanted to engage with his mouth. Then it crashed into his seat as the machine landed and tilted forward.

For a terrifying moment Valentine thought the whole vehicle would turn over as the rear bounced upward and all he could see was the ground. Then the front drive wheels bit hard and yanked the whole vehicle forwards, slamming the rear back down.

He could see the compound, as brightly lit as it had been only a couple of nights before. Though the big ship was not there, there was a smaller one.

This had been a question he had discussed. A full military assault would endanger the lives of the very innocents they wanted to protect. Contingencies had been set in place but the military objective had been given priority. Thankfully it looked as if there would be no slaves.

"Secondary turrets open fire."

Valentine could not imagine how the guns could possibly be accurate at this speed and across the rough terrain because the machine was bucking and dipping as it careened down the slope.

The flash from the shot burst across the landscape, closely followed by two more, one from each side. The shells arched down into the valley striking close to the fence. They were high explosive and erupted, shooting stone, soil and smoke into the air.

There were more shots, targeting the fence. It was brought down in several places.

"Cease firing."

They were halfway down the slope but below them Valentine saw soldiers breaching the fence through the holes that they had made. They moved, paused and fired, then moved again.

Men were coming out of the buildings firing off rounds. Valentine, with the full backing of the Foreign Office, had made it clear that they must, under no circumstances, destroy the buildings. It was vital they were kept in one piece to preserve potential evidence.

This was a concern because there was a good chance that any of the pirate leaders would try to destroy those very same records given half a chance.

They reached the bottom of the hill. The vehicle dug in and raced across the open space. It crashed through the nearest fence without a pause. There was the occasional sound of something metallic striking the vehicle and Valentine realised they were being shot at. There was little chance that small arms could do more than scratch the surface.

The machine he was in had been tasked with disabling any flyer that might be present. The one that was present was a small passenger air-craft of a standard British design, unlike the big one.

Disabling it was simple. They drove into the wing and crushed it.

"Your turn, Mr Crier," said the brigadier and indicated the exit hatch which was being undogged. Valentine put on his regulation cap so that he would be recognised and not shot at by some trigger-happy infantryman.

He jumped from the artillery engine. The change from reduced to normal gravity caught him by surprise as he hit the ground sooner than he expected. He ended up on his knees but was otherwise unhurt and got to his feet.

A glance around the compound showed him that the pirates were already on the run and attempting to hole up in one of the buildings. He joined some infantrymen racing across the compound attempting to get to the building before the slavers managed to set up any defences.

They reached the wall of the building. Valentine prepared his pistol and headed for the door but one of the infantrymen grabbed his arm. "Only if you're in a hurry to die, sir."

Then one of them pulled a cylindrical canister from his belt and pulled a pin out of the top. "These are a bit rubbish, sir, but if it works it'll help."

The first man ran to the door and fired through it; the second followed him and pushed the door open and threw the canister inside. Streamers flew out behind it as it went into the dark. There were shots from inside and the second soldier dived out of the way.

An explosion erupted from inside, blowing the door off its hinges, and showering Valentine with broken window glass.

"Follow us, sir."

They headed inside.

* * *

Within twenty minutes all firing had ceased; the slavers were either captured or dead. And the buildings were intact.

The lights around the compound were still lit. Valentine stepped from the door he'd entered the short time before and crunched down the steps covered in broken glass. The brigadier strode towards him, looking pristine.

"Excellent. Operation completed successfully."

"Thank you," Valentine started and then looked up. Two steam carriages were moving into the compound. The brigadier turned at the sound of the engines.

"Aha, your Frenchies. Can't stand the blighters."

He strode away, his officers in tow. Valentine walked slowly towards the cars as they approached and turned off to the side. A young man stepped down from the driving position of the first carriage and walked directly towards him. Valentine noted he looked surprisingly thin around the waist. He was fiddling with his driving hat and goggles. His face hidden from view.

As he got closer Valentine realised that the proportions could only be those of a woman, in men's clothing. She removed her helmet, and her hair cascaded across her face. She lifted her head and brushed back her hair.

"You are Valentine?" said the woman, with a French accent. She looked him up and down with disdain. "I suppose you might be considered handsome but I can't imagine why she would prefer you over me."

iii

Father Christophe pedalled his bicycle through the dark streets. The letter from the Anderson girl lay in the bag slung over his shoulder.

He swerved to avoid the barely seen cow standing in the street. There was no moon, just the stars, but light spilt from windows and doorways: Sometimes the muted glow of candles and oil lights, occasionally the harsh brightness of electric, but his attention was on the contents of her message.

She had not been explicit in her accusations but she had mentioned the midwife Mary O'Donnell so it was clear she knew something. Potentially it was something that could ruin his career in the Church.

And she had demanded he meet her in one of the worst districts of the city and so late at night. What choice did he have? He needed to find out what she knew, and deal with it in whatever way seemed the most appropriate.

He found the mosque she had referred to and dismounted. His bicycle would be safe enough and he thought his robes would protect him from all but the most fallen sinner.

He took the alleyway that led down the left side. With buildings closed in on each side it was almost impossible to see anything. His shoes and cassock would need a good clean when he returned. Perhaps he should get one of those hand-held electric lights in case he needed to travel in the dark again. Perhaps have them fitted to his bicycle.

He bumped into a wall. The unexpectedness of it jolted him. He let out an exclamation, and suppressed the sudden panic that engulfed him.

"This way, Father Christophe." He did not know her voice well enough to recognise it as Maliha Anderson, but there was an English accent in the otherwise excellent French. He looked to the left, the direction from which the sound had come.

She did not sound close by and in the distance he saw a rectangle of grey in the solid black that reached up until it blended with the sky, and against the grey, the dark silhouette of a woman in a sari.

"*Mam'selle* Anderson?"

"Of course."

He stumbled along the passage and emerged on to a narrow wharf with buildings on one side, and one of Pondicherry's wide estuaries stretching out before him, dotted with the dark shadows of boats. He looked around more carefully and a wave of recognition came over him. The woman was standing right on the edge, looking out. She must know. His stomach knotted up.

"It is beautiful, don't you think?" she said as he came up beside her.

The lights on the opposite bank reflected in the gently rippling surface. The stars too shone both above and below.

There was a flicker of light beside him and he glanced to the side. A small light shone on her uplifted wrist illuminating a small silver watch that was more like a bracelet. It also illuminated her bare midriff and the curve of her upper body, covered with a silk sari of blue and gold.

After all these years he was used to the way the Indian women displayed themselves so immodestly. It did not normally cause the stirrings it once had. But he did not normally stand close enough to smell their perfume. He would have to disclose his weakness at his next confession. The flesh was always so weak.

"Don't look at me," she said without accusation. "Do you see the hills beyond the city?"

He looked and marked the undulating line where the stars were cut-off by a raised horizon. "Yes."

"Keep watching."

They stood for minutes. At one point, with his attention fixed on the hills, his balance became uncertain and he stepped back from the edge to avoid tipping forwards into the water.

This meant that what he saw was not the bright light as it flashed in the hills but its reflection in the water. The brightness outlined the ridges of the hills and then was gone.

"What was that?" he said.

She turned away from the edge and took a few steps away from him along the wharf. "Battle."

"Battle? Between whom?" He followed her.

"What do you think of slavery, Father?"

"It is wrong for one man to own another."

"The Old Testament is full of slavery; it was perfectly normal behaviour."

"The teachings of Christ say something different. We have learned much."

"What about the Africans, Father?" she asked in the same relaxed and somehow disarming tone. "Do they even have souls? After all, if they do not then to own one is no different from owning a goat, or a china plate, or a wife."

"There is no official edict on the matter."

She faced him. "Do you need an edict to tell you whether someone has a soul? Someone who lives and breathes; who thinks, laughs and grieves; who feels pain, and love? For this, you need an edict?"

He did not reply. One part of him, the part that adhered to the rules, said she was a heathen woman sent to test his faith. The other part knew she was right. But if he cared only for his career there was only one viewpoint he could have.

She turned away from him, walked along the wharf and stopped beside a door.

"Why are we here, *mam'selle*?" he asked. "Do you wish to purchase a slave?"

"You have been here before."

"My ministry takes me to many places."

A light out on the river flashed for a moment and reflected in the whites of her eyes and highlighted the contours of her face. She was a beautiful woman, and unlike the others of her race, she had no difficulty looking him straight in the eye. But then she was half-English.

"How will your God feel when you have not confessed your sin or received absolution before you die?"

"You are the voice of Satan."

"If I am anything, Father Christophe, I am your saviour," she said. "By your actions you have brought about the deaths of three people."

He was not sure about three but he knew he had God on his side. "No Christians. And one of them an evil abuser who will suffer in the deepest circle of hell for all eternity."

"One of them an innocent child and," she paused, "you do not know? Mary O'Donnell herself. One of your own."

His legs felt weak, a vision of her face swam before him, her hair spread out on the grass, lying without shame beneath him, laughing. He reached out for the wall. "Mary's dead?"

It had been so many years since he had succumbed to her flesh. The joyful sinning. He told himself that it had been to the good, for he understood those who came to confession and told of their sins of lust and fornication. There were those of his order who listened with sinful lusts to such things, but he had experienced them all, and the pain of separation. The separation he had enforced himself though she cried for him to stay. She had even wanted him to leave the order. But it was his calling.

"You loved her." There was surprise in the young woman's voice. "I did not know."

"How did she die?"

"She was poisoned the same way as Riette."

"Riette?"

"The African girl," the sympathy in her voice was gone and the hardness was back. "She had a name, Father."

"Who poisoned my Mary?"

"I have not rejected you as a potential culprit."

"I loved her, why would I kill her?"

"Perhaps because she was going to reveal the fact you had falsified the birth records in the hospital."

It felt as if his heart had stopped. As if the whole world held its breath. He thought about denying it, holding on to the bravado.

"I was foolish," he said in the end. "I was in love."

"You were trying to protect her."

"Yes."

"Because Balaji and Renuka are brother and sister."

He felt the strength leave him finally; he was adrift but somehow relieved. It was the one sin he had never confessed.

"She told me that the two women were giving birth that night, one of them with twins. The woman with the single child had birthed a boy but he was dead. The woman with the twins had delivered both successfully. My Mary was a good woman in her heart, perhaps too good for this world."

"So she exchanged the dead boy for the live one."

"She confessed it to me and I gave her absolution. Then I went to the British records and rewrote history."

"You shouldn't have left them out of the records completely."

"No."

He jumped as the door in the wall opened. An old man stepped out; he looked at them suspiciously, slid by and headed down the alley.

"There are no slavers here tonight," Maliha said. "And they will not be trading from here any time in the near future."

"How do you know?"

"Because the light you saw in the hills? That was the British navy attacking their base."

In the half-light her face seemed calm, almost angelic. "Have you ever thought of converting to Catholicism?" he asked.

"No. At least in my religion a woman can also be a god."

He turned as if to go, then back. "Shall I accompany you back to more civilised parts?"

She laughed quietly. "I was never alone, Father." She looked over his shoulder and he turned. A large woman in a sari emerged from the shadows. "My maid is entirely sufficient for my protection." He looked at the imposing figure and judged she might well be.

"However," Maliha continued, "If you would indulge me for one question more. It was Françoise that told you about the impending marriage, was it not?"

"Françoise Greaux? Yes. She became part of the congregation when she came to Pondicherry. She has befriended many of the other ladies."

"I'm sure she has."

iv

She almost sounded like Maliha, the same mocking tone, except with a French accent. But she was completely different. She had wavy hair that was probably brown. And her skin was white, of course, and physically more rounded.

She thrust out her hand and he shook it. Her grip was firm, while her sardonic smile lacked any warmth. She was studying him.

"Françoise Greaux. You are Valentine Crier, *n'est pas?*"

"Yes, but my name is Bill," he said. "Miss Greaux?"

"Yes, she explained that. And I agree with her, *Valentine*—" she made the name roll around her mouth as she said it "—is a much more pleasant name than Bill. I will also call you that."

"As you wish, Miss Greaux," he said. He pursed his lips. "I cannot say I understand why you are here."

Behind her three men were disembarking from the carriage. Their bearing, annoyed mutterings and impressive moustaches suggested these were the French officials.

Françoise looked over her shoulder at them. "Well, somebody needed to drive them; they are very backward here. Maliha lent them her carriage."

"That's hers?"

"*Oui*, it is larger than the one I had at home but they are all the same once you know how to increase steam pressure and guide them." She stared at him again, as if she was tearing off his skin and looking underneath. It made him itch. Then she shrugged and, to his embarrassment, reached inside her décolletage to withdraw an envelope.

"She wrote this for you," she said. "And asked me to deliver it, which I thought was quite *présomptueux*. It would seem I am not a suitable replacement for you."

Valentine frowned; there was something about her remarks that made him uncomfortable but he could not put his finger on what they were. He took hold of the envelope, it was warm, but she did not let go.

"Valentine Crier. If you ever hurt my Maliha I will tear your heart from your chest and feed it to you. Do you understand?"

He nodded in astonishment and she released the envelope. He turned it in his hands; his name was written in Maliha's neat hand in the middle of the flat side. It was sealed shut. He looked up but the woman had wandered off to the group of French officials who were now in conversation with the brigadier. Valentine saw him look up as she approached and a broad grin crease his face. She lifted her hand; he took it and kissed it.

Valentine shook his head and returned his attention to the letter. He carefully tore it open and slipped the folded note from inside. It wasn't a letter. There was no greeting or signature, just an address and a time. He glanced at his watch, and then up at the group of soldiers, police and diplomats. The woman was looking over her shoulder at him.

What was it he had said to himself? If she wanted him back she would have to ask. He looked at the note. It was probably as close to asking as she would ever get. She wanted to meet him in an hour, somewhere in a city that he did not know. It could easily take him that long simply to get there. He would have cursed but she would not approve, and she had no doubt done it deliberately.

He looked at the address. She was testing him. How much did he want to see her? She had allowed herself to be touched by the guru and had been angry when Valentine had killed the man for doing it. She had driven him away and now she did this.

She was the most infuriating woman he had ever had the misfortune to know. But this was more than a test, he knew: It was an ultimatum. If he failed to arrive she would decide that he did not want her, that he had no interest in her. That he did not…

Did not what? Love her?

He screwed up the letter and tried to shake the thought from his mind. He looked up at the clouds of stars filling the sky.

"Oh Christ!" he yelled and ran for the steam carriage. The French officials and brigadier stared at him as he ran past. He yanked the driver's door and was surprised to find the seat inside filled.

"Other side, *Valentine*. You don't know where you're going." The Greaux woman must have gone aboard while he was troubling over the note. "*Très romantique*," she said, and slammed the door closed. He wasn't sure if she was being ironic.

He ran around the front of the vehicle and pulled open the door. The engine thumped hard and the machine began to roll as he clung to the handle. He clambered up, the transition from normal gravity to lightweight carried him through so he almost landed on Miss Greaux.

"Hold on tight, *Valentine*. It is going to be a bumpy ride."

With the vehicle's electric lights illuminating the ground ahead, she engaged the highest gear. The carriage tore across the open field and out on to the track. With Valentine hanging on for dear life.

"Of course," said Miss Greaux. "If I were to get you there late, I might have a chance with her *une autre fois*. But then, she tests me also."

Once again Valentine found he could not make head nor tail of the strange Frenchwoman but the drama of the ride soon occupied all of his attention.

* * *

The steam carriage rocketed down an empty street, juddering across the stones. There was a moment of terror as a cyclist appeared from nowhere. Miss Greaux responded smoothly and drove around him. Then proclaimed in surprise. "That was Father Christophe, I am certain."

The journey came to an abrupt stop in a dead-end. Grateful to be on solid ground, Valentine staggered away from the steam carriage into the shadowy heart of Pondicherry. He had never been here before. He looked at his watch but there were no lights and he could not see the time.

Miss Greaux had instructed him as to which way to go. He edged down an alley, took a left turn and exited on to a narrow wharf no more than a yard wide. Across the water he could see the hills from which he had just come outlined against the stars. Their apparent tranquillity was at odds with the state of his mind.

A muffled woman's voice penetrated the silence. "Your mission was successful then."

He jerked his head round to the right, where the voice had come from, but there was only darkness and an open door leading into the blackest shadows.

"Maliha?"

"In here, Valentine." She sounded distant.

He readied the gun, his electric torch, then moved towards the door. It was impossible to see into the interior. He slipped through the gap and stood to the side, out of the way of the small amount of light that filtered in.

There was insufficient light to see anything except the vague shapes of pillars. There was no option but to switch on his electric torch, though it would make him a target.

He pointed it at the ground, but continued to stare ahead, and clicked it on. Electric torches were not powerful but in this deep blackness the light was like a flare and lit up the space with reflected light.

He breathed in with a gasp. A cage filled the middle of the space, its black bars running from the floor up eight or ten feet, then across. Inside a woman stood with arms stretched upwards, chains attaching her wrists to the bars across the top.

He did not run to her. He stared around trying to see if her captors were in view.

"There are no enemies here, Valentine." Her voice sounded strained. "You can put up your gun, but leave your light on." There was a pause. "Please."

She never said *please*.

He hesitated but there was still no movement around them. He knew no force on earth could make her lie. If she said there was no one, then they were alone.

He uncocked the pistol and put it away. Keeping the torch pointing down to illuminate his steps, he walked towards her. He stopped at the bars, raised one hand and placed it on the cool metal. She hung from the manacles, arms at full extent, the folds of a sari looped across her shoulders and hanging down across her otherwise unclothed body.

He had seen her naked before but that had been through a haze of fury. She was naked beneath the cloth and the light showed the curves of her body. A wave of something like sorrow went through him; she was doing it to herself again.

"What is this, Maliha?"

"Experience." Again her voice caught in her throat. The way she was strung up meant she could not speak properly.

"*Why would you do this to yourself?*" He had not intended the words to come out like a pained hiss but it seemed he had no control of his own voice. He looked around and saw the entrance to the cage.

"I have to understand." Each of her words seemed to come out as a pant.

He pulled the metal gate open, its hinges grinding with rust. He slipped inside. Now his light penetrated the cloth and he could see her naked body beneath the folds.

"On the floor."

Did she want him on the floor? He looked down. No. There was a bamboo cane a metre long lying near her feet. The past months had taught him things about the world he wished he did not know, and he knew what this meant.

"No."

"Do it, Valentine."

"No."

"You *must*."

"No, Maliha. There is no must. I will not do it. I won't hurt you."

She tilted her head in his direction, the first time she had moved. It must have been an effort. "Won't hurt me *again*."

His anger flared. "I was protecting you. Why do you refuse to understand that?"

Her head sagged back and she looked down. "I do understand."

"I don't want to hurt you."

"I know." She seemed tired, almost broken.

He shook his head. "Can't somebody else?"

There was a long pause and she forced her head round again. "I trust only you, Bill."

He stared at her with her hair hanging forward and hiding her face. He reached down and placed the electric torch on the ground. Its beam cast a curve across the ground, and tiny stones threw long shadows. He picked up the cane. It was lighter than he expected. He grasped the other end and it flexed between his hands.

He moved around to her side, the shadows from the light curved around her. He could have counted the vertebrae of her back.

"Hurry up."

He almost smiled at the return of her waspish tone. He would have if numbness had not spread through his body.

"How…" his voice choked, he cleared his throat. "How many?"

"I'll tell you when to stop."

"Why me?" he almost shouted in desperation.

"Because—" her voice cracked, "—because I love you."

And he did not know what to say. He hesitated.

"Bill, *please.*"

Goaded by her plea, he drew back his arm, looked across the smooth undulations of her back, braced himself and struck.

She jerked, then shook her head. "No. Harder."

"For God's sake, Maliha."

"*Do it harder,*" she cried, then sobbed. "*Hurt me.*"

Without thinking, he lashed out. The cane buzzed through the air and snapped against her skin. Her choking cry jammed an icy knife between his ribs and into his heart. There was a movement outside the cage. Valentine snapped around and reached for his gun.

"No, Amita. I told you, I have to do this. He has to do this."

Valentine looked into the face of the maid through the bars, and saw enough anger and hate directed at him to fill a life of revenge. But she backed away into the shadows again.

"Again, Bill. Harder."

He took up a better stance. Now he had done it once it seemed easier to do it again. He weighed the cane in his hand and whipped it against the naked skin of her back. Her cry resolved into one word. "*Again.*"

He did not count. All he could think about was the cane, her back and each of her screams that cut him to the quick. He felt tears on his cheeks. He watched as the red lines multiplied and criss-crossed her back. A trickle of blood seeped from one wound, and her skin grew darker where it bruised.

If he hesitated too long she would hiss "*Again*". He struck and he struck. And she screamed.

When she finally uttered the words "*Oh god, stop, please stop now*" it was a reprieve from the gallows. He dropped the cane as if it were red hot and threw himself in front of her. He put his arms around her waist, careful to avoid the injuries. He lifted her to reduce the strain on her arms. She was so light. Amita untied the chains holding the manacles and Maliha fell limp across his shoulder, the chains rattled down beside them. He collapsed into a sitting position on the naked stone and cradled her.

She sobbed as Amita unlocked the manacles. Amita brought out some oils and lotions that she gently applied to Maliha's back and then her wrists. If Valentine had not known Maliha so well he would have been shocked at how well she had prepared.

Shadows moved beyond the cage. Valentine realised there was someone else there and looked round. It was the Greaux woman, her face streaked from weeping.

He was surprised at how he felt none of the usual embarrassment holding Maliha, naked, in his arms.

Amita touched his arm, and he looked up. She nodded and gestured to the door. With the maid's strong arms for assistance, he struggled to his feet still holding Maliha. She was not asleep, just looking into his face without a word.

The maid adjusted the cloth to ensure her body was covered and they made their way out. The French woman pulled back the door and he stepped through into the cool air.

They returned to the steam carriage.

*　*　*

The French woman drove carefully through the dark streets and they arrived at a house with a wide gravel driveway.

Valentine followed Miss Greaux to a room with covered furniture. She pulled the sheets off the double bed and Valentine laid Maliha down. She had gone to sleep on the journey and, though she now slept in a bed, he found himself unwilling to leave her.

There was a *chaise longue* under a sheet. He pulled the cloth back, lay down so that he could see Maliha, and pulled the sheet over himself. Amita bustled about for a short while and Valentine fell asleep.

v

A child cried somewhere nearby. It penetrated Valentine's sleep and brought him awake in a bright room with sunlight diffused by drawn curtains. Valentine was no expert but he thought it was quite a young baby. After a few moments the crying stopped.

He rubbed his eyes and sat up stretching his stiff limbs. He looked across at the woman lying in the double bed. Maliha. The night's events flooded back and he felt nothing but contempt for himself.

The door opened and Amita came in carrying a tray. She deposited a cup of tea and a plate of toast beside him without even acknowledging his presence. There was a second cup and plate on the tray, and a small pot of ointment.

Valentine stood up. He felt sweaty and the grime of being unwashed since before the battle last night. "Amita."

She turned back to him, her gaze downcast like a good Indian woman.

"Let me."

At which Amita looked into his eyes, almost as if she might defy him. She turned away, moved to the bed and placed the tray on the side table away from Maliha and stalked from the room.

Valentine went to the bed. He knelt on it and pulled back the counterpane. She was naked beneath it but all he could see were the red lines across her back. In places the skin was broken and had bled. There were dried streaks and scabs. The welts were red but her dark skin turned even darker and blue with bruising.

"Admiring your handiwork?" she said.

"I am so sorry."

"I did not give you a choice."

He hesitated. "There's always a choice."

"So why did you choose to do it?"

This time the words came easily but he held them back for a long time, until they would not be denied. "I didn't want to lose you again."

That seemed to satisfy her and she fell silent.

Valentine reached back, took the jar of ointment and unscrewed it. A refreshing scent of herbs emanated from it and it had a smooth consistency, even if it did look a dirty shade of green. He took some on his fingers and gingerly pasted it on one of the less inflamed marks. She shivered.

"That feels good," she said.

He continued to lave the mixture onto her skin, though she jumped when he covered the broken skin. They said nothing. He found that now he took the opportunity to look at her skin, the undamaged skin, it was a very attractive colour. She lay on her left side, her right leg forward so she was lying almost face down. He could see part of the old scar on her left thigh.

After a while she said. "Aren't you going to ask me why I made you do it?"

"No."

That answer satisfied her too and she fell silent again. He finished and screwed the lid on the pot.

"Thank you," she said. Moving with extreme care, she sat up in the bed with her back to him, making no attempt to cover herself. "Would you mind opening the curtains?"

He climbed off the bed. His legs were stiff from kneeling so long. He made his way across to the window and let in the sunlight. He turned to see Maliha walking towards him. She had wrapped some material around her waist but her entire upper body was exposed. He turned away quickly and looked out the window. It was all very well treating her lying down when she was unwell but to see her walking around unclothed was a different matter altogether.

She came up beside him. He glanced sidelong at her, surprised at how small she was. There was something about her presence that always made her seem taller. She took hold of his hand and lifted his arm. She ducked under it and laid it across her shoulders. She pressed herself against him, her arm around his waist.

"You're embarrassed," she said. "Don't be."

The baby cried again, the sound muffled by the closed door.

"I will try not to be." Although having Maliha so close this way was…difficult. He looked out of the window. Beyond a garden area there was a beach, and the sea.

"Where are we?"

"Françoise's cousin's house, apparently. Though I'm not entirely sure how much I can believe anything she says," she said. "But there's no one here that will cause us any problems. At least for the time being."

"Is the baby hers then?"

Maliha laughed. Valentine liked it when she laughed, it was so rare. "No, not hers. Definitely not hers." Her humour seemed to last as something went through her mind. "I suppose the baby's mine."

"Yours, but…?" he trailed off, this was getting into a dangerous subject area.

"No, there has not been *quite* enough time for me to have conceived and birthed a daughter." He frowned. That was the Maliha he knew, the one that took pleasure in making him feel awkward. He could almost forget the fact that if he glanced down he could see the beautiful curves of her body. "No, but I am the closest thing to a mother she has. And I haven't been a very good one. I shall have to do better."

He heard the door open and panicked. He seriously considered tearing down the curtain to cover Maliha's body.

"Oh, am I interrupting?" said Françoise. Valentine felt as if he was going to die of shame.

"No, Françoise, we're just talking." Maliha said, as if they were discussing the weather on the promenade.

"*You have no clothes on,*" hissed Valentine.

"I am not entirely naked," she said. "And, seriously, I could not wear anything above the waist at present. You were quite thorough. I need time to heal. Besides," she continued, "it's nothing Françoise hasn't already seen."

"I think I should not stay," said Françoise. "I do not think *Monsieur Valentine* is ready for a *ménage à trois.*" There was a throaty laugh followed by the door closing.

Valentine felt as if the world had collapsed on him. Too many thoughts; too many ideas; too much of everything.

Maliha extricated herself from his arm. "Do you want to sit down?" She pulled a sheet off a hard-backed chair next to the window and almost pushed him into it which put his gaze on the same level as her breasts. Thankfully she moved away and sat on the *chaise longue*, perched on the edge, with her legs crossed. She stretched then winced at the pain.

"What do you want to know?" she said.

"This Françoise…"

"What about her?"

Damn woman. She was deliberately making this as hard as possible. "You and her?"

Maliha sighed. "Yes. Just once. She seduced me—but I allowed it; I could have said no."

"But you didn't."

"I was upset. I needed someone," she paused and looked at him. "And you weren't here."

"You drove me away."

"I was wrong," she said.

Words he never expected to hear from her mouth. "Last night you said you loved me."

"Yes, I did."

"Was that just to make me do that—" he waved his hand at her, "—to you?"

"No."

He felt his heart crash. It must have been written on his face.

"I mean," she said. "I didn't say it just to make you do it."

"Which means what?"

She shook her head. "Are you completely lacking in any comprehension of logic? It means I love you, William Albert Valentine Crier. I love you."

There was a muffled cheer from just outside the room. It had a French accent.

She glanced at the door and smiled, then looked back at him. "Do you love me?"

The words fell from him without a moment's thought. "I think I've loved you from the first moment I saw you."

The smile that grew on her face was the most beautiful he had ever seen. "Will you forgive me?" she asked.

He stood up and crossed the room to where she sat. His stride so purposeful that a flicker of worry crossed her face. He took her hands and drew her to her feet.

He leaned down to her upturned face and kissed her.

She pressed her body against him. He placed a hand on her waist and the other on her shoulder to avoid her injuries. Her tongue pressed between his lips. He opened his mouth to her and closed his eyes.

vi

It had been a week since the attack on the base of operations of the slavers. Maliha's back had healed to the point where she could wear a sari blouse that Amita had modified to reduce the material at the back. But it still chafed and made her back itch. If she wore it too long the worst cuts became inflamed again.

She rested her hands on the stone balcony wall, where she had first seen Riette, and looked down into the courtyard. The guests were assembling below. One group consisted of her grandparents, whom she had not spoken to in nearly ten days, with Renuka.

The commissioner stood with Françoise and Valentine. She had offered to call him Bill, as an olive branch for all the pain she had caused him, but he said he preferred Valentine. He was lying, of course. But it was a way that he showed his forgiveness. There had been other ways too, and she smiled.

There was a commotion below and Aunt Savitha was brought in flanked by two policemen. Police always overreacted, she thought.

Her grandparents turned away but Renuka wept at her mother's condition.

Maliha looked at her watch; she would like to start soon but there were still two guests expected. Still, she should get down so that she was ready. There was a full length mirror in the *zenana*. She looked at herself. Amita waited in the background and would have corrected anything about her that was not perfect.

She knew some of the marks on her back were visible and there would be some permanent scars, but she was not ashamed of them. Valentine tended them every morning and evening. She smiled again at his gallantry. He slept on the *chaise longue* every night, and though he had become accustomed to her semi-nakedness he had not taken advantage. It was something she looked forward to.

With Amita in tow, Maliha headed out and downstairs. As she descended the final flight the front door opened to admit Father Christophe and Naimh O'Donnell. She was dressed in the same threadbare sari as before. But Maliha already knew what she was going to do about that.

She allowed the latecomers to go first, escorted by one of the staff, and paused for a suitably dramatic amount of time before heading through and out into the sun where the groups were now seated in a rough semi-circle.

They had decided that Maliha would speak in French while Françoise translated into English for Valentine and Naimh. That had been another revelation for Maliha; it seemed Françoise's concept of truth was very loose—it was whatever suited her at the time. And it had been convenient for her to pretend that she did not speak good English. Yet somehow Maliha could not bring herself to dislike the woman. Despite her many—very many—faults, she had a sense of justice, even if it was quite self-centred.

Her grandmother noticed Maliha enter. "*I might have died of shame for all you care,*" she said in Hindi.

Amita leaned towards Françoise and Valentine, translating the Hindi into English. A momentary smile crossed the commissioner's face, then he composed himself.

"We are speaking French, Grandmother."

"I do not even know why you have dragged your grandfather and me to this cursed place."

"French."

Her grandmother crossed her arms and ceased speaking.

Maliha took a deep breath. "Commissioner Abelard has been kind enough to allow me to bring you all together so that we can resolve the mystery of four deaths."

There was a stir. "Four?" asked the commissioner.

"Yes, sir, there are four deaths. The first was a tragedy that began this whole affair, two are murder and one, well, that is up to your discretion." She paused; she had their attention.

"The biggest difficulty in this case has been the question of why."

"Why the girl was killed?" asked the commissioner. "She was poisoned, was she not?"

"She drank poison, yes, but no, *monsieur.* Why did she do it during the wedding?"

"The girl, Riette, had been purchased to provide a body so that Uncle Pratap could satisfy his desires. His wife, Aunt Savitha, had suffered a permanent injury from his years of abuse and if she was beaten again she might die."

Grandmother got to her feet and made to leave. "I will not hear this." With all eyes on her she got as far as the door but the two officers did not let her pass. No one said anything. She returned to her seat. "I will stay for the moment."

"Because a replacement needed to be found Aunt Savitha bought a slave girl so that Pratap would not beat his daughters."

She glanced at Renuka who was staring at her mother. "It would have been all right mother, I am strong; you should have let him beat me."

"How could I? You knew nothing."

"Of course I knew, mother."

Maliha glanced at her grandmother who held her gaze for a moment then looked away. They all knew. Maliha turned to Savitha.

"But there was something else, wasn't there?"

Savitha looked down at the ground. One shackled hand gripped the other squeezing it tight, digging the nails in.

"You wanted it. Needed it."

"No!" shouted Grandmother. She was on her feet. "Tell them you did not *want* it, Savitha. Tell them!"

"But I did, mother. It was the only attention he ever gave to me. Those times alone together became precious to me."

Grandmother stood with her mouth open until her husband gently pulled her back into her seat.

Maliha stalked over to where her grandmother sat. The old woman deserved one more slap in the face. "How did Savitha know where to get a slave, Grandmother?"

Grandmother looked flustered. "How would I know?"

"You told her," said Maliha. "It was you that went to the *devadasi* and found out. Then, when the girl killed herself, you went back to bribe her to keep her mouth shut. Are you aware, Grandmother," said Maliha with a certain relish, "that suppressing evidence is a crime?"

Her grandmother's angry silence turned to fear and Maliha turned her back on the old woman.

"But still this does not answer your question, *Mam'selle* Anderson." The commissioner pointed out.

"Not yet. Remind me, Commissioner, the poison that Riette drank. What was it?"

"Cyanide."

"And in what form?"

"Green paint."

"Scheele's green. Renuka?"

The girl looked up in horror. "My green paint? I knew I had not used so much."

"You did not approve of the African slave, did you? You just said that you would have let your father beat you rather than have her there."

"I did not kill her."

Maliha faced her directly. "How long have you known what your father did in the secret room?"

"She has never known," shouted Savitha. "None of the children knew."

"Of course we knew, mother," said Renuka. "Do you think we have not eyes or ears?"

"And you knew about the girl?"

Renuka nodded while Savitha wiped away fresh tears.

"So," said Maliha. "You could have given her the poison and arranged for her to get out during the ceremony?"

"But why would I do that? Why would I stop my one way of escaping? I would go to my husband's family. I would be safe from my father."

"Because you would be able to take your mother's place and save her life. Would you not give up your life for your mother?"

"Of course, but—" Renuka looked around at the others pleading with them "—I did not do this."

Maliha said nothing. The commissioner looked pleased and seemed about to get to his feet.

"I did it," came Savitha's voice drifting quietly through the courtyard. "I gave Riette the poison to drink. I told you that."

Maliha looked at her. "Yes, you did. And you killed Mary O'Donnell the same way."

The commissioner looked confused. "Who is Mary O'Donnell?"

After Françoise had translated Naimh stood up. "Mary O'Donnell was my mother; she died three weeks ago."

"She was poisoned with cyanide," Maliha added. "During the last trip that Savitha and Renuka made to Madras to see Balaji's family before the wedding."

Renuka's had went to her mouth. "When she left me with Balaji's family."

"I know nothing of this murder," said the commissioner.

Maliha nodded for Naimh to sit. "She was murdered in Madras, but they are poor and outcasts, and there was no real reason to think it was murder so the death was not investigated. The murderer had been let in, poisoned her and cleaned up. There was no obvious sign of foul play. I found traces of the poison, and green colouration, in the floor."

"I am representing the British Crown in this matter," said Valentine. "But we will not interfere with French justice."

"We cannot try her for a murder in Madras," said the commissioner.

"No, but she killed her husband," Maliha said.

"It was a crime of passion and, it seems, entirely justified," said the commissioner. "She will not receive the death penalty for that."

"And Riette?"

The commissioner nodded. "It is possible that case might not succeed."

Valentine butted in. "In that event we would want to extradite her to stand trial for the murder on our territory."

Maliha frowned. This was getting out of hand and off the subject. "Gentlemen, are you not curious as to why my aunt chose to disrupt the wedding in such a dramatic way?"

They ceased their discussion. Valentine flashed a smile of apology.

Maliha turned to her aunt once more. "Renuka has a brother, does she not?"

Grandmother had apparently recovered. "Savitha has never been able to produce a male heir." Her tone was one of disgust and disappointment.

"That's not correct," said Maliha turning on her grandmother. "Renuka had a twin brother."

"He was weak. He died."

"No, he did not," said Maliha. "Mary O'Donnell was the midwife when Balaji's mother birthed a dead son, and Savitha had living twins. The woman realised she could swap the dead child for a living one and both families would be happy with a living child."

"What value is a daughter?" Grandmother only realised what she had said when Renuka stood up and moved away from her, taking up a position next to her disgraced mother. Maliha looked at her grandmother with a calm disgust.

"You are a daughter," she pointed out. Her grandmother settled back in her chair and studied the *tulsi*. Perhaps she might gain some enlightenment from it. "Besides, Mary O'Donnell was a Westerner, she did not understand."

"It was Françoise who had ingratiated herself into the family—" that earned her a swift frown from the French woman, "—and learnt of the impending marriage. She mentioned it to Father Christophe, who knew what had happened with the babies because he had received confession from Mary O'Donnell." Maliha took a deep breath and turned to her aunt. "And he told you, didn't he, Auntie?"

She nodded.

"So it is my fault?" said Françoise in horror.

"And if you had not done it Renuka would be married to her brother, and that would be very bad indeed, especially if they were found out."

The non-natives looked confused, while the Indians were horrified.

"Ritual suicide at best, stoning to death perhaps," said Maliha, she turned back to Savitha. "So you convinced Riette to kill herself during the wedding. You had access to the room and the shackles, so freed her before it started."

"Yes."

"Did you tell her the truth? Did she do it out of a sense of honour?"

Savitha shook her head. "I told her it would be the best way to revenge herself on Pratap."

The commissioner stood up. "I do not think you will be requiring an extradition, *Monsieur* Crier." He nodded to the uniformed officers and they came forward to collect Savitha. "The girl may have taken the poison voluntarily but she was tricked and that is murder in my book."

He walked over to Maliha and held out his hand. She took it and he bowed over it rather than shaking it.

Aunt Savitha was found lying on the floor of her cell one morning a few days later, barely conscious. She was brought to the infirmary but the doctors could do nothing to stop the internal bleeding.

The verdict was suicide. There was very little evidence, the commissioner had told Maliha when she enquired. But there had been considerable bruising on her arms, legs and abdomen, some several days old, that no one had noticed because no one cared. Though, when asked, the staff had said she had not eaten anything the previous day.

It appeared she had been throwing herself into the walls in an effort to reopen the internal wound her husband had given her. And had eventually succeeded.

Maliha wondered whether she had enjoyed that pain the way she had learnt to appreciate the beatings. Maliha understood how it could happen; her experience with Valentine had taught her that. There was a twisted love in the act of giving oneself to pain, at the hands of someone trusted, or loved.

She had thanked the commissioner and he had, again, given her his thanks in return. He even seemed to ascribe the destruction of the slavers base to her in some convoluted fashion. Though that was entirely Valentine's doing.

She climbed aboard her steam carriage with Amita huddled in the rear. Maliha chose to drive more slowly. They drove out towards the docks, across the bridge, past the lighthouse and along the coast to Françoise's cousin's house. It had been a pleasant week, just the six of them. A holiday. She had even spent time with the baby.

While not declaring it publicly, her grandparents had all but disowned her. She had taken a trip out to her parents' house to see how the rebuilding was going—it continued at a snail's pace—only to find that all her belongings from her grandparents' house had been packed up into tea chests and deposited at the site.

She had gone through the boxes with Amita to determine which items she needed and which could be stored. She was glad she had already removed the babe and her nurse; more than likely they would have been thrown on to the streets.

She would not be surprised if they burned the shed the baby had been in.

Maliha came to herself and realised that Amita was holding the vehicle door open for her. She removed the scarf and goggles, and dropped them into the seat as she squirmed out of the chair. A pain shot through her back. It was almost healed but, in spite of the regular application of Amita's unguents, there was scar tissue that did not stretch and every now and then it would pull and hurt.

She dropped to the ground. There was the sound of the baby crying in the house. She did not find it an unpleasant or irritating sound, more like a call. The baby sounded hungry. She smiled at herself, and at the curious knowledge that meant she understood what was wrong.

Maliha walked with her long purposeful strides towards the door. It swung open as she approached and Valentine stepped out. She thought he always looked a little worried. That was her fault: all the times she had snapped at him and criticised him. He was like a puppy that was beaten one moment and loved the next without any understanding as to why.

She lifted her head and smiled at him. She climbed the steps on to the verandah two at a time and threw herself at him. His arms enclosed her. She did not care that her grandparents had thrown her out. It was not as if they had ever given her anything but guilt and shame. Now they had more than enough for themselves.

She sagged in his arms.

"What's wrong?" he asked.

She hugged him tighter and pressed her cheek into his shoulder. Western men did sweat in the Indian heat, but she did not find his aroma unpleasant.

"You are not the cause of everything that makes me sad, Mr Crier," she said. "To think so is the height of arrogance."

"You are a cruel woman," he said and then fell silent at his own ill-chosen words. She could feel the tension rise in him. He had not forgiven himself for what he had done to her. And she did not know what she could do to help him leave it behind.

She did not want to let him go, but she stepped backwards slowly. She reached down and took his hands in hers. He hung his head like that naughty puppy. He needed something to keep him occupied. Too much idleness allowed the memories to come forward.

"First things first, Mr Crier."

He looked up and she kissed him on the lips. She opened her mouth and felt his tongue. She smiled.

"The entire world can see what you are doing, *mes amis*."

Maliha felt Valentine start to move away and cupped her hand behind his head. When she was satisfied she had made her point she released him. He was not smiling. He loosed his hands from hers, touched her cheek and pushed past Françoise into the house.

Françoise raised an eyebrow. "Are you certain you would not prefer my company, *chérie*?" she said. "I would not pull away from your kiss."

Maliha raised her hand to her neck, looking at the shadowy gap where Valentine had disappeared. She shook herself and looked at Françoise with her full attention and saw the folded letter in her hand.

"You have some news?"

Françoise glanced down at the letter. "*Oui, chérie.* It seems my cousin and his family are returning and while my presence may be acceptable to them, you and your *entourage* might be difficult to explain."

"I was planning to leave."

"Does *Valentine* know this?"

"I haven't had a chance to tell him."

Françoise closed the distance between them. Maliha thought for a moment she might be on the receiving end of another kiss, but although Françoise brought her face close to Maliha's they did not touch.

"It is strange I must advise you on men," she said in a voice that was barely above a whisper.

"What do you mean?"

"*Valentine* is not your maid."

"Of course not," said Maliha. "Explain your point?"

Françoise stepped back and took in a deep breath. "*Non, ma chérie.* I will not explain." She poked her finger at Maliha's chest. "You are very clever, *n'est pas?* That is what is said by everyone. You will work it out."

She turned and went back into the house.

* * *

Maliha found Valentine in the drawing room with an empty whiskey glass. He was standing by the empty fireplace staring at nothing. He did not acknowledge her presence.

She sat down, perched on the edge of a sofa.

"I would like to go to South Africa."

"Then go," he grunted.

She bit back a sharp retort. "Please come with me."

He shrugged. "You don't need me."

Her anger broke and she jumped to her feet. "No, Valentine, you are wrong. I do need you." She crossed the floor and stood directly in front of him. "But I am not sorry for anything I have ever done to you; I am not sorry for every mocking tone; every harsh word; every frown when I should have smiled; every joke you cracked that I did not laugh at."

"You're *not* sorry?"

"No! I am *not* sorry," she shouted. "And I am not sorry for driving you away when you killed Nadesh and stole my justice from me on behalf of all the women he had shamed."

"If that's how you feel," he said, and put the glass on the mantle. He turned to go but she grabbed his wrist.

"No, I am not sorry for any wrong I have done you, and yes, I have wronged you." She let his arm drop. "But that does not mean I do not need you, and believe me when I say that you had your revenge. Though I had to put the weapon in your hand and demand that you use it!"

"I did not want any revenge, especially not that!"

"So you are nothing but a woman in men's clothing?" she said. "Willing to suffer anything just to maintain the status quo. To take anything just to be near me? You are no better than Savitha. It should have been me with the whip and you hanging from the chains."

His expression was strangely neutral. "If you need me, and if you love me, then marry me."

She closed her eyes and opened them again. It was still Valentine standing there. "What did you say?"

"Marry me."

"I don't understand."

His eyebrow rose in scornful derision. "It is not a difficult concept."

"But why?"

"I would have thought that was obvious to someone as clever as you."

Maliha hesitated. She had lost the thread. He had gone off at this tangent and she was left flailing, bereft of argument. She shook her head.

"I won't marry you…Bill."

"You think that using the name I prefer will make any difference? Do you think it somehow affects me more deeply? Should I call you Alice then?" He took her by the hand and went down on one knee.

Her eyes widened and she felt something akin to panic. He would not do it, surely.

"Alice Maliha Anderson—"

"Stop."

"Will you consent—"

"Bill—Valentine, stop, don't do this. A joke is a joke."

"To be my wife?"

Her voice evaporated. He reached into his pocket and pulled out a ring. He had a ring. On his person. She found her voice.

"When did you get that?"

He looked at it. It was a simple gold band with a small diamond in a basket setting.

"The day after we disembarked from the *Macedonia*."

"No," she breathed. Almost a year ago, when they barely knew one another.

He shrugged. "Yes. Though I have thought of selling it on a couple of occasions since then."

She said nothing, just looked at him.

"Well?"

She knelt down in front of him. With her free hand she caressed his cheek. "You know what my life is like. I am neither Indian nor

British. Neither trusts me. Neither accepts me, and I have just lost what little family I had left."

"Your family is here," he said. "And we won't send any of our children away to school."

"I don't fit in anywhere."

"We fit well enough with one another."

She hesitated. "You would not want to marry me, if you knew everything."

"I do not believe there is anything you could tell me that would stop me from loving you."

"Amita is a man in women's clothing," she said. "My maid is a man."

He smiled with slight embarrassment. Only smiled. "I know," he said.

She was taken aback. "You do?"

"How stupid do you actually think I am, Miss Anderson?"

"And you don't mind?"

"I wouldn't say that exactly," he said. "But you never do things the normal way. Though if we do marry, there will have to be changes."

Maliha held his gaze for a moment then nodded. "When did you realise?"

"Most women don't have bristles when you kiss them."

"Oh," she said. "Then."

"Yes," he said. "Then."

They knelt there in silence for a while, Maliha contemplating the "then" and what it must have been like for him.

Valentine squeezed her hand. "Have you run out of reasons for not marrying me?"

"It will confirm what my grandmother has always suspected."

"Which is?"

"That I am worthless."

"Do you think I am worthless?" he asked.

She took his face in her hands, rubbing her thumbs across his cheeks. She smiled. "No, dearest Valentine. You are far from worthless."

"If I am not worthless, and I choose you, then clearly you are not worthless either."

She looked at him askance. "Does that make sense?"

"I saw something like it in a book; I thought I'd give it a try."

"I think you got it wrong."

He shrugged. "So your final excuse is that it would confirm your grandmother's opinion of you?"

She nodded.

"When did you start caring about other people's opinions?"

"When I realised I was lonely, Valentine," she said. "I am tired of being lonely."

"Then you need to marry me."

She was silent for a long time and her thigh began to ache as she knelt there before him. She leaned forward and rested her head on his shoulder. He swayed as she unbalanced him.

She contemplated the ring he held in his hand between them. She leaned back, looked him in the eye and stretched out her left hand. He took her fingers gently in his and slipped the ring onto her third finger. It was loose and the weight of the diamond kept making it hang crookedly. She made a fist to hold it in place. He kissed her knuckles.

When he looked up his face had a look of such happiness she felt like crying again, or was it the happiness that threatened to burst out of her?

"Now," she said, "when can we leave for South Africa?"

~ end ~

Read **THUNDER OVER THE GRASS**
The next incredible book in the **Maliha Anderson** series.

Steve Turnbull was born in the heart of London to book-loving working-class parents in 1958. He lived with his parents and two older sisters in two rooms with gas lighting and no hot water. In his fifth year, a change in his father's fortunes took them out to a detached house in the suburbs. That was the year *Dr Who* first aired on British TV, and Steve watched it avidly from behind the sofa. It was the beginning of his love of science fiction.

Academically Steve always went for the science side, but he also had his imagination—and that took him everywhere. He read through his local library's entire science fiction and fantasy selection, plus his father's 1950s *Astounding Science Fiction* magazines. As he got older he also ate his way through TV SF like *Star Trek*, *Dr Who* and *Blake's 7*.

However, it was when he was 15 he discovered something new. Bored with a maths lesson, he noticed a book from the school library: *Cider with Rosie* by Laurie Lee. From the first page he was captivated by the beauty of the language. As a result he wrote a story longhand and then spent evenings at home on his father's electric typewriter pounding out a second draft, expanding it. Then he wrote a second book. After that he switched to poetry and turned out dozens, mostly not involving teenage angst.

After receiving excellent science and maths results, he went on to study computer science. There he teamed up with another student and they wrote songs for their band, with Steve writing the lyrics. However, they admit their best song was the other way around, with Steve writing the music.

After graduation Steve moved into contract programming but was snapped up a couple of years later by a computer magazine looking for someone with technical knowledge. It was in the magazine industry that Steve learned how to write to length, to deadline, and to style. Within a couple of years he was editor and stayed there for many years.

During that time he married Pam (who also became a magazine editor), whom he'd met at a student party.

Though he continued to write poetry, all prose work stopped. He created his own magazine publishing company which at one point produced the subscription magazine for the *Robot Wars* TV show. The company evolved into a design agency, but after six years of working very hard and not seeing his family—now including a daughter and son—he gave it all up.

He spent a year working on miscellaneous projects including writing 300 pages for a website until he started back where he had begun, contract programming.

With security and success on the job front, the writing began again. This time it was scriptwriting: features scripts, TV scripts and radio scripts. During this time he met a director, Chris Payne, who wanted to create steampunk stories, and between them they created the Voidships universe, a place very similar to ours but with specific scientific changes.

With a whole universe to play with, Steve wrote a web series, a feature film, and then books all in the same Steampunk world and, behind the scenes, all connected.

Join the mailing list at http://bit.ly/voidships